OTHER BOOKS BY JAMES RADA, JR.

Fiction

Between Rail and River

Canawlers

October Mourning

The Rain Man

Non-Fiction

Battlefield Angels: The Daughters of Charity Work as Civil War Nurses

Beyond the Battlefield: Stories from Gettysburg's Rich History

Echoes of War Drums: The Civil War in Mountain Maryland

Looking Back: True Stories of Mountain Maryland

Looking Back II: More True Stories of Mountain Maryland

No North, No South…: The Grand Reunion at the 50th Anniversary of the Battle of Gettysburg

Saving Shallmar: Christmas Spirit in a Coal Town

For Amy,
who has made the journey with me for 24 years now.

LOCK READY

A Canawlers Novel

by
James Rada, Jr.

LEGACY
PUBLISHING

A division of AIM Publishing Group

LOCK READY

This is a work of fiction. All the characters and events portrayed in this book are either fictitious or used fictitiously.

Published by Legacy Publishing, a division of AIM Publishing Group.
Gettysburg, Pennsylvania.

Printed in the United States of America.
First printing: May 2014.

Cover photo courtesy of the National Park Service.
Cover design by Stephanie E. J. Long

315 Oak Lane • Gettysburg, Pennsylvania 17325

CONTENTS

1. Decisions, December 1863 1
2. School Days, December 1863 11
3. Starting Anew, December 1863 20
4. Meetings by Chance, January 1864 33
5. Woman's Work, January 1864 43
6. Mother?, January 1864 55
7. Labor Troubles, February 1864 66
8. Mother and Son, February 1864 72
9. For the Cause, February 1864 79
10. Winter Work, February 1864 84
11. Idle Boats, March 1864 90
12. Murder in Shanty Town, March 1864 100
13. The Season Begins, April 1864 105
14. Eyes Open, Heart Closed, April 1864 119
15. Mudslide, April 1864 129
16. The War Ends for One, May 1864 137
17. Family Reunion, May 1864 148
18. Investigations, May 1864 159
19. Unfair Fights, June 1864 172
20. Betrayal of Duty, June 1864 180
21. Life After Becky, July 1864 195
22. Making Amends, July 1864 201
23. Closure, July 1864 209
24. Attack, August 1864 217
25. Bad Dreams, August 1864 230
26. Going Home, August 1864 237
27. A New Life, March 1865 246

CRITICAL ACCLAIM FOR THE WORKS OF JAMES RADA, JR.

Saving Shallmar

"But Saving Shallmar's Christmas story is a tale of compassion and charity, and the will to help fellow human beings not only survive, but also be ready to spring into action when a new opportunity presents itself. Bittersweet yet heartwarming, Saving Shallmar is a wonderful Christmas season story for readers of all ages and backgrounds, highly recommended."

- *Small Press Bookwatch*

Battlefield Angels

"Rada describes women religious who selflessly performed life-saving work in often miserable conditions and thereby gained the admiration and respect of countless contemporaries. In so doing, Rada offers an appealing narrative and an entry point into the wealth of sources kept by the sisters."

- *Catholic News Service*

Canawlers

"A powerful, thoughtful and fascinating historical novel, Canawlers documents author James Rada, Jr. as a writer of considerable and deftly expressed storytelling talent."

- *Midwest Book Review*

Between Rail and River

"The book is an enjoyable, clean family read, with characters young and old for a broad-based appeal to both teens and adults. Between Rail and River also provides a unique, regional appeal, as it teaches about a particular group of people, ordinary working 'canawlers' in a story that goes beyond the usual coverage of life during the Civil War."

- *Historical Fiction Review*

Canawlers

"James Rada, of Cumberland, has written a historical novel for high-schoolers and adults, which relates the adventures, hardships and ultimate tragedy of a family of boaters on the C&O Canal. … The tale moves quickly and should hold the attention of readers looking for an imaginative adventure set on the canal at a critical time in history."

- *Along the Towpath*

1

DECISIONS

DECEMBER 1863

David Windover had told himself that he would stay outside in the freezing cold until he reached a decision. Now that a chilling wind was slicing through the heavy fabric of his peacoat, he doubted the wisdom of his commitment. Freezing cold temperatures had come to Western Maryland two weeks ago leaving a thin, translucent crust of ice on the water along the edges of the canal each morning. It always melted away by midday and was never thick enough that the Canal Company sent out its ice breakers. It was just a matter of time, though. It was only getting colder.

Canallers had started taking bets on when the C&O Canal would shut down for the winter and were rushing to make one more delivery of coal or grain to Georgetown before it happened.

The Canal Company had sent out word two days ago that the stop locks would be opened this week to start draining the canal. Until the weather warmed up again, crews would work in the empty canal making repairs to the canal prism, locks and aqueducts. Much of the damage had come from Southern sabotage, heavy foot traffic from soldiers on the towpath and normal wear and tear from a busy season.

Since the news of the closing had been released, the canal boat captains had been rushing to either get back to their hometowns along the canal or to the basins at Williamsport and Cumberland in the hopes of getting a good position to take on a load of coal when the canal reopened next year. The *Freeman* was tied up at Snyder's Wharf in the Cumberland basin between the Potomac River and the downtown area of Cumberland. This is where the boat would stay until spring returned.

David had hoped that the cold night air would clarify his thoughts. Having paced outside for an hour, he now hoped that the cold would cause him to make his decision quicker so that he would be able to go back into the warmth of the hay house. So far, the only decision he'd reached was that his fingers were numb but not frostbitten. He slowly flexed them inside of the woolen mittens that Alice Fitzgerald had knitted for him last year.

He stood on the race plank—the narrow walkway that ran along both sides of the canal boat—and pulled his peacoat tighter around him. Not that it did any good. The coat felt useless against the wind and the cold he felt wouldn't be warmed away by keeping in body heat. He sighed and his breath turned to vapor for a few moments and disappeared. If only he could get rid of the problem that caused the sigh as easily.

A few days ago, the *Freeman* would have floated barely above the water of the Potomac River. That was when the cargo holds were full of bituminous coal and the canal boat had wallowed in the water like a pig in mud. Now that 120 tons of coal from the Appalachian Mountains filled the holds of the steam ship *Newcastle* and were bound somewhere north of Georgetown to keep New Englanders warm this winter or power steam ships in the War Between the States. And the *Freeman* sat lighter and higher in the water.

The canal boat was ninety-two feet long and made of Georgia pine milled back when Georgia still considered itself part of the Union. Hugh Fitzgerald, Alice's dead husband, had named the boat as a way to remember what his Irish ancestors had done so that Hugh could live in America as a free man. It seemed even more appropriate when he remembered that the Fitzgerald had sometimes hidden escaped slaves under the *Freeman's* deck.

David shook his head. He had never met Hugh Fitzgerald. By all accounts he was a good man, but he had been murdered in Shanty Town two years ago. Still, his ghost was always present when a person was on his boat. It was why David had to leave.

Water lapped against the side of the boat. Each gentle wave seemed to carry away a little of his stress and exhaustion. The sound wasn't something he heard often, which is odd, considering he worked on the water, but he boated on the Chesapeake and Ohio Canal not the Potomac River. The river was unnavigable with rapids around Harper's Ferry and the Great Falls outside of Washington. At times during the summer, sections of the river were too shallow to float barges with heavy loads like the canal boats carried. On the canal, the idea was for the water to be calm and at a consistent depth so that the boats could be pulled east or west by mules.

What caused the lapping water now was that the Canal Company was draining the 184.5-mile-long canal. The inlet locks had been closed. With no water entering the canal, the existing water would run into the Potomac River at the tidal lock at Georgetown and river locks near the dams. The company had opened the stop locks earlier than expected. David wondered how many canallers had lost money on that bet.

The company officials expected some limited boating to continue from Williamsport to Georgetown, but Cumberland was in the mountains and more than 620 feet higher than Georgetown. The air was colder here and the ice came quicker.

The Canal Company sometimes used ice breakers—boats with heavy wedges on their prows—but eventually either the ice grew too thick or there were too many loose chunks floating in the canal for safe navigation. Since the canal needed repairs, the company wasn't going to use the ice breakers this year, but rather work on the repairs and get them completed as soon as possible.

David stared into the water, looking at the wavering reflection that looked back at him. He could barely see it in the dim light from his lantern. His blurred reflection showed how he felt. He couldn't figure out who he was or where he belonged. Was he a Northerner or a Southerner? Did he belong here? Not just on the *Freeman* but with the Fitzgeralds? He couldn't be honest around Alice Fitzgerald or she might realize how he felt about her. He couldn't be honest around anyone outside of the Fitzgerald family or they might realize that he was a former Confederate soldier. He couldn't be honest with himself or he might ask questions that he didn't want to hear answered.

"You know you can't really see the water level drop."

David turned around and saw ten-year-old Thomas Fitzgerald coming out of the mule shed. He was bundled in George's hand-me-down wool coat and he had a stocking cap Alice had knitted pulled low so that it covered his ears.

The mule shed was the twelve-foot by twelve-foot cabin at the opposite end of the canal boat from the family cabin. During the day, the pair of mules not pulling the canal boat would rest inside until their turn in the harness came. At night, all four of the mules were picketed on the towpath so they didn't have to be crowded into the small shed. They could roll around to their hearts' content or just relax without having to pull the boat. The Fitzgeralds owned four mules that had been purchased on a farm in Kentucky. Though some captains used horses to pull canal boats, pound for pound, mules were stronger and they lasted longer, particularly if they were well cared for, which Thomas made sure of.

"I know. That's not why I was looking at it. I was just thinking," David said. He bounced up and down on his toes to try and warm up a bit. If the canal hadn't been being drained, it would be frozen in the morning.

Thomas climbed up onto the curved hatch covers that arched across most of the length of the *Freeman*. He walked over to stand near David and look over his shoulder. From his position on the hatch cover, Thomas could see over David's shoulder into the water.

"I set up a net to catch some fish as the water drains out. When the canal's empty, I'll check the net to see if I caught anything. I could wind up with a barrel of fish," Thomas said excitedly.

Add fish to his pet collections, David thought.

The young boy collected anything and everything that caught his attention, but he particularly liked animals. It wasn't unusual to find a rabbit, bird, possum or even a fox caged up in the mule shed. He had once caught a bear cub until the she bear scared him off.

"That's sounds like a good idea, Thomas. We'll have plenty of fish for frying and stews this winter," David told him.

"You're not thinking about dinner, though."

David shook his head. "No, I'm not."

He glanced toward the family cabin at the other end of the barge. The shutters were closed to keep out the cold night air, but David could still see some light from around the edges of the windows. It glowed as two pale, parallel lines three feet apart. He could hear Alice moving around inside the cabin and mumbling about something. It wasn't a happy mumble either like when she sang to herself when doing the laundry on the roof of the family cabin during a warm, sunny day.

"Actually, what I'm thinking about makes me lose my appetite," David said.

Thomas frowned. "Then you must be thinking about girls or school. They're the only things that make me feel like that."

David rocked his head side to side. "You might be right about that."

He patted Thomas on the shoulder and turned away. He walked along the race plank to the rear of the canal boat where the family cabin sat on top of the holds. He trudged down the three stairs and stepped inside the twelve-foot by twelve-foot room.

A quarter of the space in one corner had been sectioned off for the captain's cabin. The rest of the room was an economy of space. Bunk beds were mounted on one wall while doors that opened into the pantry and additional storage space under the quarterdeck took up another wall.

Alice Fitzgerald was sitting at the table under the window at the opposite side of the room. Her ledger book was open and she was writing some figures on the page. David watched her quietly. He stared at her slender fingers as they held the pen and her other hand brushed a stray wisp of red hair from her face. He had imagined that hair falling across his chest and shoulders as he held her. She finished writing and set the pen aside. She puckered her lips and gently blew on the page to dry the ink. David stared, longing to kiss those lips.

David's resolve almost left him. He took a deep breath and let it out slowly. No more living in dreams. It was time for him to live in the real world.

"Alice," he said. He had meant to sound firm, but what came out had been barely more than a whisper.

"Hmmm?" she said without looking up.

She picked up the pen, dipped it in the ink well and scratched out something she had written and started over. The cuff of her blue wool dress was darkened with ink smudges.

"I need to talk to you about something."

For a moment, David thought he could still back out of this conversation. Alice was so focused on her ledger that she might not have the time to talk. She hated working with numbers, but she felt it was part of her responsibility as the owner of a canal boat.

Alice shut the book, laid the pen down and rubbed her eyes. Her green eyes were a bit red from straining as she read over the ledger by lantern light. "I needed a break anyway. Why do we always seem to only just get by?"

"That's kind of what I wanted to talk to you about." David stopped unsure of where to go now. Finally, he just took a deep breath and started, "With George back with the family and Tony and Thomas a little older, you've got quite the crew."

"And don't forget you," Alice added and smiled at him. How he loved the way that smile lit up her face. It stripped the years and stress from her face and made her look so vibrant. He wished that he had met her years ago before she had met and married Hugh Fitzgerald. Even though Hugh was dead, he was still the ghost between them.

David nodded. "I'm not forgetting, but I've come to realize that providing for your family should be your priority. If you didn't have me around, you might not be just getting by. I'm just a burden to you now. I'm an extra hand you don't need and an extra mouth to feed."

Alice stood up. "David, that's not what I meant when I said that. You're not a burden. You're part of the family."

"No, I'm not. George and Thomas are your sons and since you faced down Sheriff Whittaker about Tony, he is too. Me, I'm just someone who helped out when you were short-handed," David said.

He really couldn't bring himself to say the real reason why he wanted to leave. It would embarrass both of them and put a taller wall between them that he didn't want, even if he was going to leave. But, really, how could he stay aboard the *Freeman* and be in love with her, knowing that she still loved her dead husband? He felt guilty for feeling jealous of a dead man, but Hugh Fitzgerald was dead. David didn't want Alice to forget her years with her husband, but he wanted her to be able to move on. That wasn't happening.

It hadn't been David whom she had called for when she was delirious with fever in August. It had been Hugh Fitzgerald whom she had wanted to hold her and comfort her. David had been wrestling with what he should do since then and now with the boating season over for 1863, it was time to make his decision.

Alice walked around the table and grabbed David's arm. Her touch made his skin tingle even through his shirt and coat sleeves. "David, don't do this. You would break everyone's hearts if you left."

Not everyone, David thought, *and that's why I've got to leave.*

"I've already thought this over and over again." He looked away unable to meet her stare. "It's what I need to do. I'll pack up and move out in the morning."

Alice took a step back. "What will you do?"

"I'll work in Cumberland for a while and save some money. I can't go home, not after what my father wrote." He had written his father to try and explain why he had abandoned the Confederate Army and decided to stay in Maryland. His father had sent him a letter from the family plantation in Virginia disowning David because he was a traitor to his country. A part of David had expected that response, but another part of him had hoped his father would say that he understood even if he didn't agree with David's decisions. "Tony talked once about going out west and getting his new start. Maybe that's what I'll do."

Alice looked at the floor. "David, you said you'd be there for me always."

David closed his eyes and sighed. "Alice, you know it's not proper for me to stay here. People are saying things about you that aren't true." He wondered if he would feel differently about leaving if the rumors had been true.

"What people are saying hasn't really bothered you the past two years," Alice said.

That's because back then they hadn't seemed like rumors to him. Their whispers behind his back had been well wishes. Now they were barbs or taunts.

"I don't want to hurt your reputation," David said, realizing that it was a weak reply.

Alice snorted. "It's my reputation and if it's been hurt, that has already happened. It makes no difference now."

"I'll still be there for you. You can write or telegraph me and I'll come."

Alice's eyebrows rose. "From two thousand miles away?"

David looked away. "It can't be helped."

He turned to leave, knowing that he might never be able to get her acceptance of his decision. Did that mean she loved him even if she wouldn't admit it? *No.* No, he needed to leave before he said or did something that would make her force him to leave.

"I'm not going to see you again, am I?" Alice asked suddenly.

David stopped at the door, but he didn't turn around. He didn't want Alice to see the tears in his eyes. "I don't know," he said.

He walked out of the family cabin and along the narrow race plank. He went into the hay house, the smaller cabin in the middle of the boat. It was used to store hay for the mules but David and George also slept on the hay piles in the cabin because there was no room in the family cabin for them.

David pulled open the wooden hatch that covered the opening on the side of the hay house. He stepped inside onto the hay that formed the mattress of his bed. The cabin had very little room to move around in because it was mainly used to store hay, but then, he and George only slept here.

He pulled his knapsack—the very one he had used as a Confederate soldier—from off the hook on the wall and began filling it. Not surprisingly, it only took a minute. David had accumulated very little in his time with the Fitzgeralds. He'd bought a book by Edgar Allan Poe in Georgetown and had a couple of notes from Alice saved in its pages. The notes said nothing personal. It was just his way to remember her. Maybe, in the back of his mind he had always known that he would eventually be leaving. Other than that, he had his civilian clothes, a Bible and his army pistol.

As David stood looking at all he had in the world, the hatch on the other side of the hay house opened. George Fitzgerald, Alice's oldest child, stood in the opening looking in at him. He was a slim young man with light brown hair. He was frowning, which was a mirror image of Alice's frown, but unlike his mother, George rarely smiled since returning from the war.

"So it is true then," George said. "You're leaving."

"This makes you the man in charge," David said. George had recently turned nineteen years old, though he seemed older now. It was more than simply him living additional year. George had seen things and experienced things that a nineteen-year-old man should not have to see and experience. The sparkle of life that Thomas still had in his eyes was missing in George's. David hoped that the young man would find a way to get it back, but then David had never been able to after what he had seen during the war.

"I suppose it does," George said flatly.

The two men looked at each other without saying anything. They had both fought in the war, though on different sides. David had never gone back to the fighting after being wounded while George had lost his arm and couldn't return. It always seemed to David that George had lost something more than his arm in the war. He had lost the ability to be happy.

"Mama's in her cabin crying," George said finally.

David closed his eyes and took a deep breath. What did she expect him to do? He couldn't stay, not with the way things were between then.

"She'll get over it," David said.

"Maybe." He didn't sound so certain.

"I'm just a hand around here, George. You know that. You're the one who's told me it enough times."

George snorted. "Since when did you listen to me? If you think that you're just a hand, then maybe you should leave."

David slapped the wall with the flat of his hand and then bowed his head.

"What? You want me to stay?"

"It's not my decision, but I would think that after all my family has risked for you, you would want to stay," George told him.

The Fitzgeralds could be arrested for hiding a former Confederate spy. When David had been arrested two years ago, they had risked their own freedom to free him from the Union soldiers who had arrested him.

David drew himself up straighter. "I risked my life for your family, too."

George nodded slowly. "I guess you have me at that." He was quiet. David thought George had said all he meant to say, but then he added, "You're doing this because of a woman. I know that, but I'll tell you something. If you do something for the wrong reason, you will regret it. It cost me my arm."

George had run off to join the army about a year and half ago because he thought it would impress a girl he was sweet on. He wound up losing his arm and returning home to find out he really didn't care what the girl thought about him anymore.

David glanced at his pack. He was ready to go. Not much need to stay around anymore. He'd said his goodbye. Anything more would just give people a reason to cry and try to convince him otherwise. He was afraid they might succeed.

David grabbed the pack and pushed open the hatch above his bed.

"So you're just going to leave things like this?" George said.

David didn't reply. He just walked away.

It was time to leave.

2

SCHOOL DAYS

DECEMBER 1863

Tony rolled off of the bottom bunk in the family cabin before the dawn and stoked the fire in the small pot-belly stove. It was difficult to cook a family meal on its flat top, but space was at a premium in the cabin and a full-size stove would have put out too much heat in the small room. Tony had to admit, though, on cold nights, this stove didn't put out enough heat to keep his toes and nose from freezing while he slept.

He stepped quietly past the door to Mrs. Fitzgerald's cabin. It wasn't really a door, but a curtain made of a piece of blue fabric with white stripes. He didn't hear her moving around on the other side. Hopefully, she was asleep. She had been crying late into the night and he had had to pretend that he hadn't been able to hear her.

Tony could feel the cold of the floor boards through his thick socks. He only wore his socks when he slept specifically so he wouldn't have to worry about his feet freezing on the floor in the winter.

Lucky for everyone Tony needed to make water. They would get to wake up in a warm cabin because Tony had decided to drink a cup of water before going to bed. He wrapped his wool blanket around himself and crept outside to empty his bladder into the empty canal basin. As he did, he wondered how many canallers would have to be doing the same thing at the same time to fill up the canal and float the hundreds of boats now stranded along its length. Just thinking about it made him feel like he had more water in him to get rid of.

By the time Tony went back inside, Mrs. Fitzgerald had come out of her small cabin. It was really just a smaller room partitioned off from the family cabin and just barely large enough for a small bed. Even Tony and his birth mother had never stayed in a room that small no matter how little money they had had. At least the partition gave the captain some privacy. She and Mr. Fitzgerald had shared the cabin before he had been killed in Shanty Town. Then she and Elizabeth had shared it until Elizabeth had decided to stay in Washington to learn how to act like a lady. Now Mrs. Fitzgerald slept in there alone.

It struck Tony as sad. He wasn't sure why. She certainly had more room now that she wasn't sharing the same small bed with someone.

Mrs. Fitzgerald began pulling out breakfast ingredients from the pantry tucked away under the *Freeman's* quarterdeck…canned fruit, flour, eggs. It was a storage area that you could enter through doors in one wall of the cabin. Though the pantry was nearly as large as the family cabin, it was only half as tall since it was under the quarterdeck. Some larger canalling families used it as another cabin. Tony had discovered that the Fitzgeralds had used it not only as a pantry but also as a place to hide slaves they had helped on their way to freedom along the Underground Railroad.

"Good morning, Tony," Mrs. Fitzgerald said. She sounded too happy in the mornings, especially a morning after she had been crying half of the night.

"Good morning," he mumbled. He, on the other hand, was still half asleep and wishing he was fully asleep.

"I thought I would make pancakes for breakfast."

"Thomas's favorite." Tony liked them, too, but doughnuts were his favorite breakfast.

Mrs. Fitzgerald grinned. "It will probably be the only way to get him up this morning. On cold mornings, it's like he's frozen to the bed."

"I'll throw a coal from the fire in bed with him if you want," Tony said with mock seriousness. "That ought to thaw him out and get him up pretty quick."

Mrs. Fitzgerald rubbed her chin as if she were considering the idea. "I think the pancakes will work fine. If I'm wrong, we can try your idea." Then she grinned at Tony.

As she poured batter into the frying pan a few minutes later, the small cabin quickly filled with the scent of pancakes frying. Sure enough, Thomas began stirring in his bunk. He sat up and rubbed his eyes. Then he took a deep breath and smiled.

"You two need to feed the mules," Alice said. "By the time you finish, breakfast should be ready. Oh, and make sure that George and Da…" She stopped and the smile slipped from her face. "Make sure George is awake when you come back."

"Flapjacks, yea!" Thomas said.

"Then you can get ready for school," Mrs. Fitzgerald said.

"School, no!" Thomas said and he flopped back in his bunk and pulled the blanket over his head.

Because canallers boated nine months or more out of the years, canal children didn't get much time in school. The kids didn't mind, but it made it harder for them to find work outside of the canal if they couldn't read or do math. Most of the children worked with their families on the boats. David and Alice used to try and teach the boys their lessons during boating season, but George had taken over doing it most of the time. He seemed to like it and he usually knew how to get his younger brothers to listen to him.

With the canal drained for a couple of months, the two boys would be expected to start attending school in Cumberland again. Tony sometimes thought that adjusting to a winter schedule was harder on him and Thomas than the adults. Thomas and Tony always started the school year later than everyone else, which tended to put them behind their classmates in learning their lessons. So they spent months trying to catch up to everyone else and just when they did, the boating season started again and they had to leave school. It left even the smartest children of canallers feeling stupid.

Tony walked over and yanked the blanket off of his brother and was rewarded with a scream from Thomas. He sat up hugging himself while Tony chuckled.

"Give me the blanket! It's cold!" Thomas yelled.

"Then you had better get washed so you can get dressed and be warm again," Tony told him as he tossed the blanket onto his bunk.

Thomas jumped out of the bunk and scurried off grumbling that he would get even with Tony.

For some reason, Tony found that he was looking forward to going back to school if only for a short time. Thomas would never like school. He liked being outdoors too much. Even in the cold, Thomas was able to find animals to feed, chase and collect.

Tony thought he was just looking forward to being around more people and different ones for that matter. He had lived in Cumberland, roaming the streets for most of his short life. He could walk along Baltimore Street and see hundreds of people from all walks of life—soldiers, bankers, laborers, railroaders, businessmen—intermingling as they moved back and forth. He had only worked on the canal for two seasons. He was still used to the noisy and rowdy life in Shanty Town.

That's not to say that he didn't like living on the canal. It had lots of benefits, not the least of which was the Fitzgeralds, but the canal life took a bit of getting used to. The *Freeman* was where he worked, but it was also where he lived. He was never far from either one. And though he walked from Cumberland to Georgetown many times each canal season, the canal boat was always nearby.

But during the winter, the canal boat didn't move. It sat in the basin between Cumberland and Shanty Town. Tony could roam the city once again, watching the people interact with one another. He learned a lot from watching people. He learned how to read facial expressions and how people acted different coming out of a saloon versus how they acted going in.

After breakfast, Thomas and Tony grabbed their books and headed for the school on Virginia Avenue in South Cumberland. Cumberland lies in the valley between Wills Mountain and Knobley Mountain in Western Maryland. The National Road had started here, which is one of the reasons that it had been a destination for both the canal and railroad when construction had started on both in 1828.

The school was a two-room, wooden clapboard building. The younger kids met in the front room and the older kids met in the rear room. Each room had its own pot-belly stove that kept the small building nice and warm.

As the boys walked out of Little Egypt where the *Freeman* sat in the empty canal basin and up the hill toward South Cumberland, Tony noticed a few other people out on the streets. The adults tended to be on a horse or driving a buggy or wagon this far outside of downtown Cumberland. The people who were walking were usually other kids on their way to school.

"Why do you want to go back to school anyway? Did you like getting picked on last year?" Thomas asked him.

"That ended after I fought Andy Cardeson."

Thomas's expression said that he doubted his brother, but Tony really wasn't afraid. His fear last year had been about being beaten up in a fight. Now that he had fought, it held no fear for him. Plus, he was bigger and stronger now. He would be able to hold his own.

"For last year, yes. He's had another year to get bigger and mean-er. If he thinks he can take you, he'll start up again," Thomas added.

Tony shrugged. "Then I'll fight him again."

Thomas rolled his eyes and shook his head. "He'll fight you just because he knows that even if he loses again, you won't be here long enough to make the other kids realize that he's just a bully."

"So what should I do?"

"Let me put a copperhead in his lunch pail. Then when he reaches in for his sandwich, POP! No more Andy. He's copperhead candy." Thomas laughed at his rhyme.

Tony stopped and looked at his younger brother. Thomas smiled unconcerned.

"You'd actually to that?" Tony asked him.

"Well, I have to do something with the copperhead I caught last month. He keeps wanting to bite me every time I feed him. I figured if I let him bite a boy and see how bad we taste, he won't want to do it again."

Tony was about to say something, but he stopped when he saw a girl walking toward him. She wasn't just any girl, either. She was pretty!

She had shiny blond hair tied in two ponytails with red ribbons. She wore a neat calico dress with white fringe that hugged her body and showed something Tony hadn't thought much about since he had seen what his mother—his real mother, not Mrs. Fitzgerald—did with men.

Thomas noticed his brother's reaction and punched him in the arm.

"Ow!" Tony said, grabbing his left arm.

The girl looked over and Tony felt himself blush. She waved at Tony and he stopped walking just to stare at her open mouthed.

Thomas rolled his eyes again and shook his head. Then he ran off to pet an old brown-and-white cat that was sniffing around a nearby garbage pile.

"Hello, Tony," the girl said. "I was wondering if you'd be coming back to school when the canal closed down."

Tony strained his memory, trying to remember the faces of the other kids in his class. He just couldn't place the girl's face. He was surprised because he thought he would remember her forever now that he had seen her.

"I'm sorry. I don't remember you and I'm not sure how I could forget you," Tony said.

The girl glanced at the ground for a moment and Tony thought he had insulted her. When she looked back up, she said, "I sat two rows behind you in class last year so you didn't have a lot of opportunity to see me, plus, my hair has turned lighter."

Tony still couldn't remember her.

"What is your name?" he asked, embarrassed.

"Jenny McCagh."

Tony nodded as if he remembered her, but he still couldn't place her. He had been so smitten with Laura Anderson last year that he apparently hadn't noticed any other girls in his class. He wondered if Jenny's parents would be angry because she was walking with a canal boy like Laura's parents had been. Canallers weren't high on the social ladder in Cumberland.

"Hey, Tony, look what I found!" Thomas called.

Tony turned and saw his brother holding a mangy gray cat that looked like it hadn't eaten in days. Its fur was matted in many spots and it was missing part of one ear. Thomas cradled the bony cat in his arms like it was a baby and it didn't seem to mind. Either that or it was as dead as it looked.

"Thomas, put that thing down. You'll get fleas."

"No more than I get from you."

Tony felt himself flush. "You can't keep it. We're going to school."

"I'll put it in a barrel until after school is finished," Thomas said. "Then I'll take him back to the boat."

"Mama won't let you keep it. Besides, I don't think the cat will like you as much if you pen it up in a barrel."

Thomas frowned, "Mama will let me keep it. He can hunt mice on the *Freeman.*"

Tony rolled his eyes. "And how many mice have you seen on a coal boat? Besides, the cat won't like being on the canal with water all around it. It will run the first chance it gets."

"Not if I put a leash on it."

"Then it couldn't roam to catch the mice."

Now it was Thomas's turn to roll his eyes. "Well, you just said there aren't mice on the boat."

Tony sighed and turned back to Jenny. "Let's go before I strangle him."

Jenny giggled and Tony smiled at the sweet sound. How come Elizabeth and Mrs. Fitzgerald never sounded like that when they laughed?

Still carrying the cat, Thomas fell into step beside them. "So are you sweet on Tony?" he asked Jenny.

"Thomas!" Tony yelled as he blushed.

"I'm just trying to find out if I need to tell her the kind of person you really are. I think she ought to know," Thomas said.

"Thomas, I'm going to pound you!"

His younger brother laughed as he ran off. His day would come, though, and on that day, Thomas would find his pants down around his ankles while he was talking to a girl.

"It's all right," Jenny said. "I have two little brothers and they do the same things to me."

"Yea, well this little brother is going to find himself stuck in the empty coal holds of the *Freeman.*"

"I like to substitute salt for sugar and make cookies for my brothers," Jenny said.

As they drew closer to the school, Tony saw some of children were still playing outside jumping rope and running. Even though Tony's breath was making a light fog, playing in the cold was better than doing your numbers next to a warm stove.

The other children stopped to stare at Tony and Jenny. Tony wondered if he was going to have more problems this year because the other boys didn't really like canallers. He flexed his fists. Well, he was ready if need be.

No one bothered him, though. When Jenny, Tony and Thomas got to the Virginia Avenue School, half a dozen other students were playing in the yard enjoying their last few free minutes before the bell rang to signal the beginning of class for the day. Not only didn't they yell at or berate Tony and Thomas, they waved at the two boys.

Thomas quickly ran off to show off his cat to one of the boys playing outside.

Tony and Jenny walked into the school. It had one large room with two large windows on the side walls and a blackboard that dominated the front wall where the teacher's desk sat. The teacher was standing at the blackboard writing the lessons for the day.

"That's Miss Conner," Jenny said.

Tony nodded. "I remember her."

Jenny turned to face him with her hands on her hips and a frown on her lips. "Oh, you remember her but not me?"

Tony scrambled for something to say. "Well, you sat behind me. Miss Conner stood in front of me," he said quickly.

Jenny just laughed.

She stood behind one of the desks in the middle of the back row. There were thirty-six desks in the school in six rows with an aisle up the middle.

"This is where I sit now," Jenny said as she sat her book on the wooden desktop.

"I like it because it's close to the door. You can be the first one out at the end of the day, but it's a bit far away from the stove." He pointed to the pot-belly stove in the middle of the room.

Jenny giggled. Tony sure liked the way it sounded.

"Hello, Tony. Your mother said you and your brother would start coming back to school today."

Tony turned around and saw that Miss Conner had stopped writing on the blackboard and was looking at him and Jenny. She was a youngish woman, Tony thought. Older than Elizabeth but younger than Mrs. Fitzgerald. Her dark hair was tied up in a tight bun on the back of her head, which made her look a little older. She had a friendly smile, though.

"Yes, ma'am. Thomas is outside with the other kids," Tony told her.

"Well, I won't be able to go back to the beginning of the school year for you two, but we'll see how well you can keep up with what we're already doing. If you can, that's great. If you have a problem, let me know at the end of the day and we'll find a way to address the areas where you need some extra help."

"That's fine with me, Miss Conner. My mama tried to keep me and Thomas doing lessons on the canal, but we really weren't much help to her in that regard," Tony said.

Miss Conner arched an eyebrow and gave a half smile. "I doubt that many young boys would be," she said. "I know I won't have the both of you for too long so I'll try and do what I can."

Tony smiled and nodded.

"Jenny, why don't you ring the bell to call everyone in," Miss Conner said.

Jenny walked over to the hanging bell rope and began pulling on it. Tony looked around and took a seat next to Jenny. Maybe school wouldn't be so bad this time around.

3

STARTING ANEW

DECEMBER 1863

David stepped into the large warehouse at the southern end of the canal basin in Cumberland. The bay doors had been swung open to allow sunlight to shine on the work going on inside. However, it also meant that the warehouse stayed cold inside. It was nothing more than a very long barn. The difference was that this barn housed canal boats not livestock. The Lewis Boatworks was one of a handful of boat yards in Cumberland that built and repaired canal boats for canallers.

During the summer, some work could be done outdoors if the warehouse had a large enough yard, but there was a greater risk of sabotage from Confederate sympathizers, railroaders or simply hooligans against the exposed canal boats. Confederate raiders or sympathizers had burned the bridge from Cumberland to Ridgeley, West Virginia, and torn up the B&O Railroad track outside of Cumberland early in the war. Because of that, Amos Lewis preferred to construct his boats indoors and then roll them on logs out the warehouse doors that opened onto the Cumberland Basin.

David saw three men hammering boards that would become the roof of the family cabin onto the cabin frame. The boats on the C&O Canal were all roughly the same shape and length in order to fit into the seventy-four lift locks along the canal. The boats were each ninety-two feet long. Most were made of Georgia pine, though new boats being built were understandably made of trees harvested in the north. The largest area on a canal boat was the cargo holds, which made up about eighty percent of the space on a boat. The remaining space was taken up by three cabins; a family cabin and a mule shed sat on opposite ends of the canal boat, and a hay house was located in the middle of the boat.

David could smell creosote and wood and hear men talking and laughing as they worked on the canal boat. He had once been surprised that Cumberland, which was a city in the mountains, had a reputation for shipbuilding, but after working on the canal, he knew it was deserved. From here, the canal boats could be ordered by individual captains or the Consolidated Coal Company and launched at the canal basin to be filled with coal.

Cumberland was an important shipbuilding city because the C&O Canal was the lifeline for getting coal from the mountains of Western Maryland to Washington City. Access to coal was one of the reasons that the first destination for both the C&O Canal and the Baltimore and Ohio Railroad had been to reach Cumberland.

The C&O Canal and the B&O Railroad both began construction on July 4, 1828; the canal from Washington and the railroad from Baltimore. In the following years, the canal was delayed by an extended legal battle at Point of Rocks, fighting for the right of way and by Mother Nature near Paw Paw, Virginia, to dig the Paw Paw Tunnel. By the time the canal reached Cumberland in 1850, the railroad had already been there and operating for eight years.

The need for coal had allowed both businesses to survive and grow. It was particularly important now because portions of the Baltimore and Ohio Railroad kept changing hands between the Confederacy and the Union. Part of the railroad's right-of-way ran through West Virginia, which still had strong Southern sympathies despite the fact the Unionists had gathered enough support to break West Virginia off from Virginia to form a new Union state. The C&O Canal had proven to be fairly reliable in getting much-needed coal to the capital city, despite the Confederacy's efforts to stop boating on the canal.

The Western Maryland coal mines produced bituminous coal. It was a soft coal that was of lower quality than the coal mined in the Pennsylvania coal mines to the north. However, bituminous coal was more affordable, especially since the cost of Pennsylvania anthracite coal was climbing due to war pricing. Western Maryland's coal was high-quality bituminous, which made it nearly as good as the coal coming from the Pennsylvania mines.

David smelled the odor of smoke from Amos Lewis's cigar before he saw the man. Amos had thinning, blond hair that he had to frequently brush out of his eyes. He kept his hair combed back to try and keep from looking bald. His wide shoulders and large frame could hold a lot of weight without looking fat, but he still appeared very heavy.

"David!" Amos called out as he blew out a huge ring of smoke.

David turned from watching the construction of the canal boat. He saw Amos coming at him with his arms outstretched.

"I can guess why you're here," Amos said with a smile.

David had worked for Amos last winter while the canal was drained. He had come to truly like the man. He considered him a friend.

"Can you use me?" David asked.

Amos raised an eyebrow. "Are you going to run off to go canalling in a couple months just when I get used to having you around?"

David shook his head. "No, I quit the *Freeman*. I'm looking for year-round work now."

Amos stared at David for a moment. "You quit?" David nodded. "And just walked away from Mrs. Fitzgerald? I didn't think that you were an idiot, David." Amos snorted and shook his head.

"You said it yourself, Amos. She's a missus," David said.

Amos put a hand on David's shoulder. "Just because she's a missus doesn't mean that she's not looking for a different mister. She wouldn't be the first wife looking to stay warm in the winter with her husband away."

David stiffened. This was the reason that he had left the Fitzgeralds. "Amos, I like you, but..."

Amos pressed down on David's shoulder. "Calm down. I'm not saying Mrs. Fitzgerald is that type of woman. She's not from all that I know about her, but she is a widow. There's a difference. She could be Mrs. Windover."

David shook his head. That dream had gone. "No. That's not how things are between us. She'll always be no more than Mrs. Fitzgerald."

Amos frowned and said, "And General Lee is sitting in my office in a drunken stupor."

"What?"

Amos feigned innocence. "Oh, I thought we'd moved on to telling tales."

"What are you talking about?" David asked. "Maybe you're the one in a drunken stupor."

Amos shook his head. "Not me. I never touch the stuff."

"Uh huh," David said skeptically.

"But just because you or I say something doesn't make it fact."

"I'm not lying to you."

Amos chewed on the end of the cigar for a moment and then said, "That's what you say. Maybe you even believe it."

David gave his head a slight shake. "So can you use someone to help around here who's familiar with your operation?" David asked to change the subject.

Amos nodded. "The books need work. When people fall behind in their payments, things go crazy in the books, too. And a lot of people have been falling behind."

"Why's that?"

"Do you have to ask? First, our own government confiscated our boats to sink them or use them for bridges so troops can cross the James River. Then the Johnny Rebs take after the boats and burn them or blow up one of the aqueducts so the canal drains. It can be hard to make a living as a canaller right now. War is not good for business."

David shifted uncomfortably under Amos's stare. Two years ago, David had been one of those Johnny Rebs. He wasn't about to tell Amos that, though. If word got out that he had been a Confederate soldier, they'd run him out of town or worse. Cumberland was an occupied town with probably nearly as many soldiers as citizens. They protected the railroad and the canal. The city also had a lot of temporary hospitals for the soldiers who had been loaded onto trains near a battle site and brought to Cumberland to be treated.

"So do you want me to look at the books now?" David asked.

Amos shook his head. "No. Why don't you supervise these boys? I'll get a space cleared for you and gather up the books and receipts that you'll need." Amos shook David's hand and clapped him on the shoulder. "Glad to have you back, David."

Then Amos turned and called out, "Harris, Josh, I'm going into the office. I'm leaving David in charge. He decided to settle on dry land. If you have questions, ask him."

Amos chuckled as he walked away, blowing out smoke rings from his cigar.

David turned and faced the men on the boat shell. He knew Harris Mueller and Josh Conlon from his time working for Amos last winter. He liked them both. They worked hard and were skilled with their tools.

Harris was nineteen years old. He was in good physical shape, but he wore glasses. He was not a likely candidate to be a soldier and the draft hadn't picked him either.

Josh Conlon was older, probably twenty-three, though he looked younger than Mueller. He was twig as far as size went, but he had large forearms that came from working with hand tools all day.

Harris waved. "Ho, David. I didn't think you'd be coming back here."

"I changed my mind about the place," David told him. "I guess I missed your smiling face."

Harris grinned. "Then you must be drunk."

When Amos came back about a half an hour later, he glanced over the ship with a knowing eye. Then he waved for David to follow him. They walked into the back room and David saw the familiar ledger books piled on the desk. Amos was more than a canal boat builder. He owned fourteen boats that captains were still paying for and he operated five of his own boats. He collected monthly payments from captains, but he also paid the captains he employed to transport coal.

While it had taken David weeks to get the company's books in order last winter, he didn't expect it to take nearly as long this time around. How much of a mess could Amos have made in less than a year?

"Do you have a place to stay, David, since you've left the *Freeman*?" Amos asked.

David turned from the desk. "I haven't figured that out yet. I don't have any money saved because I didn't work for wages on the *Freeman*." And what money he did have was in a bank in Virginia, but he couldn't tell Amos that.

Amos nodded as if he had expected as much. "I'll tell you what. I've got a spare room for you that was planned as another office here. No one's using it and it just stores odds and ends. You can turn it into a room if you want."

"Really?"

Amos pointed his cigar at him. "In exchange, you need to watch the warehouse at night. Things are getting a little tense around town of late. Sympathizers are causing problems here and there. They're afraid to do anything bold because of the soldiers, but there's always a chance they might try and do some damage here."

Confederate sympathizers had burned the bridge across the Potomac River. Angry Union supporters had destroyed the printing press and type for the *Alleganian*, a Cumberland newspaper with Confederate leanings. Even the C&O Canal President Alfred Spates had been arrested multiple times on suspicion of treason because of his Confederate sympathies.

"I appreciate the offer, Amos. Where's the room?"

Amos walked David over to another room at the other end of the warehouse. It was dark inside, but there was a window. It just happened to be so dirty that he couldn't see through it. The room must have been closed up for a long time because it smelled musty. A stove stood in one corner and some boxes were piled haphazardly against the wall. It was just about as big as a family cabin on a canal boat, only David wouldn't be sharing this one with five other people.

"This will suit me just fine," David said, smiling.

Amos clapped David on the shoulder. "Good. Why don't you get yourself settled in here and you can start work tonight. I'll leave the keys with you."

Amos left and David walked over to the stove. The first thing he needed to do was get a fire going to take off the chill in the room. The warehouse itself was perpetually cold because it was too large to heat, but the offices were kept toasty with coal in the cast-iron stoves.

The boxes were filled with old books and newspapers that apparently Amos couldn't bring himself to throw away. He saw copies of the *Alleganian,* the *Hagerstown Mail* and *Washington Intelligencer.* The most-recent date that he noticed was five years old. Among the books he saw *Great Expectations* by Charles Dickens, *An Essay on Man* by Alexander Pope and *Moby Dick* by Herman Melville.

David pulled the books out of the boxes and set them aside. He counted more than two dozen in all. He planned on looking at them more closely later. He recognized many of the titles from his father's library in Virginia. If they were intact, he would keep them to read.

His tried to picture the family plantation, *Grand Vista*, in his mind. It covered 400 acres west of Charlottesville. The house had been beautiful with its oak floors and high ceilings. It gleamed white against green fields in the summer. Many of the rooms inside held happy memories of his childhood for him.

Paintings hung from the walls showing his relatives back to the time they first set foot in America. His great-grandfather had fought with George Washington at Concord. His grandfather had fought to help defend Washington during the War of 1812. His father hadn't fought in any wars, but he had insisted that David enlist in the army and fight for Virginia when the War Between the States started.

He told David he would no longer pay the bills for him to attend the University of Virginia and that he should enlist. It was the expectation of each Southern family to send at least one person to join the army or to pay someone to take his place.

Just David, of course. David was the disposable son. He had been the one sent to war while David's older brother, Peter, was heir, and Peter was still safe in the main house at *Grand Vista.*

And David was here in a room with a dirt floor and low ceiling. Nothing grand and with the window coated in grime, no vista either, but it was his home for now.

It took David about an hour to move the boxes out of the room. He stacked them in a corner of the warehouse. By then, with the help of some of the old newspapers, he started a fire in the stove. Once the flames were going, he added some wood scraps to keep the fire going and the room warmed up until it was nice and toasty.

David threw his bedroll on the floor. It would have to do for his bed until he decided about where he wanted to go and what he wanted to do. He might stay in Cumberland, but he was considering Tony's old idea of heading west. It wouldn't matter so much whether he was Union or Confederate in California. He tossed his rucksack in a corner of his new room and looked around. His presence barely made a difference in this room. His life could be wrapped up in a rucksack and bedroll.

When David stepped out of the room into the warehouse, he was surprised to see that it was getting dark outside. The days were definitely shorter now. He would have to clean the window in his room so he could see out. He found Amos in his office going over quotes for lumber. By the way he was mumbling to himself, David guessed that Amos wasn't happy with the numbers he was seeing.

"Are you moved in?" Amos asked.

David nodded. "When you don't have much, it doesn't take long."

Amos shrugged. "You are the one who wanted to make a fresh start."

David nodded, realizing that was exactly what he was doing. It was the second time in two years. The first time had been when he had deserted the Confederate Army and stayed with the Fitzgeralds on the *Freeman*.

Amos frowned at something he was reading and shook his head. "I need to price this project. I have a contract to build one of the new ice breakers that the Canal Company wants. I'm also working with a new supplier for lumber. Since the war has cut off our lumber shipments from the south, I've been trying different mills in Pennsylvania and Ohio for a dependable place that can supply me with the hardwoods I need."

"I'm feeling a little bit hungry so I'm going to go into town and get something to eat and a few groceries to keep in my room. When I get back, I'll be in for the night."

"Good, good." Amos reached into his pocket and pulled out a $5 note and handed it to David. "Here, take a few dollars for the food and anything else you might need to get settled in. I'd suggest a thick blanket. It gets cold in here at night."

"You don't need to do that, Amos. I haven't even done any work for you yet," David told him.

"You're going to save me the cost of hiring a night watchman. I'll give you the keys when you get back and go over a few things with you." He sounded tired.

"Do you want to go over them now?" David offered.

Amos shook his head. "No, I want to finish this estimate. Besides, hungry men don't pay attention." He waved David away. "Go, stuff your belly. I'm used to this. It's how I make my living."

David waved to his boss and walked away. He left the warehouse and headed away from the basin, which was the wide area at the end of the canal where the boats could turn around and take on loads of coal. Most of the restaurants in town could be found on Baltimore Street or one of its cross streets so that is where he headed. It was relatively close to Amos's warehouse. He knew of a couple places where he had gotten good meals before so he would see if any of them had anything interesting on the menu for tonight. He would pick up his groceries afterwards so he wouldn't have to carry them into the restaurant. He'd get some fruit and vegetables only since he'd eat them fairly quickly.

The sun was beginning to set as David walked along Mechanic Street over to Baltimore Street and headed east. He walked quickly because he wanted to eat and do his shopping and get back to the warehouse before it got too late.

The crowds on the streets had thinned out and groups of soldiers were starting to light small fires around the area where they could warm up while they served a watch shift during the night. Cumberland was under military law and that meant guard patrols roamed throughout the city. David didn't want to give any of the army patrols a chance to stop and question him because he was on the street at night.

As he walked past the Donnelly Pharmacy and Kurtz and Johnson Jewelers, he saw a woman walking toward him struggling to manage two large baskets filled with food and other items. The baskets were hanging awkwardly on her arms and at least one basket looked like it might tip over and spill its contents onto the ground at any moment. David saw a man walking in the opposite direction pass the woman and only stare at her with open hostility. The man was well dressed, too. David would have expected better manners from him.

Then one of the woman's baskets did spill and cans of vegetables and three loaves of bread dropped to the hard-packed dirt of the street. The woman stopped and started looking around for a place to put her other basket so she could wipe off the loaves of bread that were lying on the ground. He blue shawl tangled around her arms hindering her movements.

The man who was closest to the woman still did nothing to help her. David watched the man pause to look at the woman and he grinned!

David broke into a trot. He reached the woman while she was looking around for anything still laying on the ground. David took one of the baskets from her arms and set it on the ground.

"You look like you're struggling a bit there, ma'am. Can I help you?" he said.

The woman looked slightly surprised to hear someone talking to her. Her blue eyes darted around, almost as if she was wondering if someone was watching her.

"My name is David Windover. I work at the Lewis Boatworks," David said as an introduction.

He bent down and picked up a can of tomatoes that had rolled away. It looked like she had had the same idea as David to do some grocery shopping.

"My name is Ruth Abercrombie," the woman said. "Thank you for your help. I wasn't sure what I was going to do. I bought too much on this trip to the store."

She was a woman in her mid-twenties, though something about her eyes make David think she was older. Her brown hair was tied in a bun up under her cap, but two locks had pulled loose and peeked out underneath the calico fabric of her cap.

"It's not a problem, ma'am. I'm only happy to help." Then David saw the man who had ignored Ruth's dilemma watching the two of them. "You should be ashamed of yourself for not helping a lady," David called to him.

The man snorted. "She's no lady."

David rose to his feet, his hands clenched at his sides. He wasn't going to let that insinuation stand. Ruth put a hand on his arm.

"Please don't do anything," she said.

"He's being deliberately insulting," David said loud enough so that the man heard him.

"But he's right."

David turned to look at her. A well-dressed woman stood before him who had enough sense not to want to be the cause of a street fight. She was a woman who held herself with a high degree of grace. She was a lady or he didn't know what one was.

"He's wrong," David said, shaking his head. "You've done me no wrong and I doubt that you've done him any."

"I haven't," Ruth agreed.

David grinned. "Then there you have it. You're a lady unless I see something that would tell me otherwise and I haven't seen that."

Ruth smiled and then looked at the ground. "You must be new in town." Her wide smile showed off her teeth.

David shrugged. "Not really. I was working on a canal boat until they drained the canal. Now I'm working at the boatworks like I said."

Ruth bent down to pick up her baskets. She was still having trouble holding both of them as overbalanced as they were. David picked up the baskets and held them.

"Well, thank you for your kindness, but that man is right. If you want to stay around Cumberland, you probably don't want to be seen with me," she said.

"Why are you so certain about that? You don't seem like a desperado to me. Maybe it's you who shouldn't be seen with me."

David could guarantee that if the truth about him ever came out. If she knew he was a former Confederate soldier, she would probably run away screaming for help from a Union soldier. Then Ruth said something that surprised him.

"I support the South."

She stared at David waiting for a reaction from him.

David paused, probably for too long, but her comment had surprised him. Finally, he said, "Is that all?"

Her eyebrows lifted. "It's enough in a town occupied by the Union Army. I'm watched all of the time because people know where my sympathies lie. The only reason the army or townspeople haven't run me off is because I'm a woman and my family has lived in Cumberland since soon after it was founded."

"Is your entire family in support of the South?"

Ruth shook her head and her blond curls bounced around. "Just me. They're ashamed of me, but not enough to turn me out."

David knew that feeling and worse because his father had been willing to turn his back on David when he decided he could no longer fight in this war. David had been proud to serve Virginia at first. He had seen it as a way to prove himself to his father and perhaps find his place in the world.

But battle hadn't been like David had imagined it would be. Even winning at Manassas hadn't been without its costs. Men had died on both sides of the battle and they always would. David's best friend, Ben Kyle, had been ripped apart by an artillery shell that nearly landed on top of him. All David had found of his friend afterwards had been Ben's right arm, shoulder, and head. The rest of him had been unidentifiable.

Then David had been asked to spy on the North along with two other miserable representatives of Southern life. One had been killed trying to sabotage the canal and David had killed the other when he had tried to rape Elizabeth Fitzgerald. That was the final straw that had led to him abandoning the army.

His father hadn't understood that. How could he? His father had never fought a battle. He had only grown up on the exploits of his father and grandfather, two men who had served with honor unlike David.

"I married a soldier who was killed at Gettysburg last summer. I had a brother who was killed there, too. Sometimes, I feel like my parents think I killed my brother. They don't seem to remember that the same battle that cost them a son cost me my husband," she said with a bit too much anger in her voice.

David was struck by a sense of guilt. He had given up everything to stay with the Fitzgeralds. His country and his family. True, he didn't have much of a choice at first because he had been wounded at the time, but that had been two years ago. Since then, he had had plenty of opportunities to return. He hadn't, though; because he had believed that the Fitzgeralds needed his help and that he might have a future with Alice.

He wasn't with the Fitzgeralds now, though. He could return to Virginia if he wanted to, but the truth was he didn't want to. He had abandoned his duty while men with Ruth Abercrombie's husband and brother had fought and died to do theirs.

"I'm sorry," David replied.

Ruth took a deep breath and gave David a small smile. "I am, too. We had only been married a few years. My family doesn't like my decision to support the South, but they already lost one child and they don't want to lose another one. So they tolerate their *Southern* daughter," Ruth explained.

"You can't be too horrible then if they still love you," David suggested.

"Well, they're the only ones who do love me."

David didn't know how to respond to that so he said, "Can I carry these baskets for you to wherever you're going?"

Ruth stared at him for a few moments. "You don't have to prove that you're a gentleman to me."

"I'm not trying to prove anything. I'm just trying to be of assistance."

"Well then, thank you, as you can see I need the help."

"It's my pleasure, Mrs. Abercrombie. I'm always happy to help a lady."

She smiled at the compliment, which made David smile in return as they started to walk down Baltimore Street.

4

MEETINGS BY CHANCE

JANUARY 1864

The *Freeman* sat on the dry canal prism in the Cumberland Basin and would until the weather warmed up. Alice had used a ladder to climb down to the muddy prism and walk around the squarish hull yesterday. She had inspected the wood to see if any boards would need to be replaced before spring. The gaps in the wood would need to be caulked with hemp and tar before the canal reopened, but the wood would have to dry out first.

Although the Fitzgeralds weren't traveling on the canal this winter, the boat would still serve as their home. Their home in Sharpsburg had burned down a year and a half ago during the Battle of Antietam and the *Freeman* was all they had left.

Alice draped a pair of George's long underwear on the rope line strung above the roof of the family cabin on the *Freeman*. The sun shone outside and the temperature was above freezing so the clothes would dry rather than freeze. Besides it was either this or crowd the family cabin with lines of laundry and it was cramped enough in there already.

She had started taking in laundry from other canallers and families who lived near the canal basin to earn extra money this winter.

The pay wasn't spectacular, but it would get the family through the winter. George had hired himself out as a clerk at a hardware store on Mechanic Street, which would also help. It wouldn't be easy, though. Last winter, they had had five mouths to feed but three of them had been working. This winter, though, there was one less person to feed but also one less person was working. David's wages had really helped out.

Working on the canal had never shown itself as an effective way to get rich. Not that that was the reason the Fitzgeralds worked on the canal. Canalling was what they knew. It was in the Fitzgeralds' life blood.

Hugh had grown up either canalling or watching his relatives dig the long ditch. His Uncle John had died of the cholera epidemic that swept through the canal diggers in 1832. His Uncle Dermot had lost an arm digging out the Paw Paw Tunnel when some black powder exploded while he was tamping it down. His father had had multiple scars, not only from fights with railroaders but from fights with Irish Prods and Germans. He also had cousins who had died or been hurt in those skirmishes.

Alice had known what she was getting into when she married Hugh. She had also come from a canalling family. Her father had run Lock 75 near Cumberland. One of her brothers ran the Indian Head Lock on the canal spur in Washington. Her other brother was a canal boat captain and she had been a canaller's wife and now she was a canal boat captain.

The Fitzgeralds made about twenty-five dollars for each trip between Cumberland and Georgetown. Although that was the amount after the tolls were paid, other expenses like hay for the mules had to be paid from that total, too. The war definitely made even getting by harder because of the frequent damage that Confederates did to the canal, which drained water and stopped the boat traffic. That meant canallers were making fewer trips each season and earning less money to carry them through the winter.

Somehow, their family always managed to get by, but then that was when Hugh had been alive. Of course, there hadn't been a war going on, either.

"Mrs. Fitzgerald?"

Alice stopped what she was doing and looked around the side of a blue dress with white polka dots that belonged to a woman much larger than Alice.

Harlan Armentrout was standing on the shore of the basin, shuffling his feet and looking around nervously. His hair was gray at the temples now. She was surprised that it hadn't turned gray years earlier living with a woman like Minerva Armentrout. Alice silently scolded herself for thinking such an un-Christian thought—though true—about the woman.

"Harlan, what are you doing here?" Alice asked.

"I was hoping that I could impose on you for a small amount of your time." He looked at the windows of the family cabin as if he expected to see someone staring back at him. He was probably hoping that no one would see him and recognize him since the canal was not a place for someone who was part of Cumberland society.

"I'm the only one here right now." Alice didn't want anyone drawing the wrong conclusion from seeing them together alone. David had left because of such rumors. Best not to start new ones.

Harlan nodded quickly. "I understand. I can come back at a later time."

Alice waved the man aboard. "No, that's all right. We can sit on the hatch covers and talk if that's all right with you."

Harlan's head bobbed. "That will be fine."

He was a heavy man, but he stepped across the gap from the shore to the canal boat with surprising ease. He held out his hand and gently shook Alice's. She pointed to the hatch covers and sat down facing the shore. Harlan sat down near her, but he left sufficient room so that no one would mistake his intentions.

"What can I do for you, Harlan? Is this about transporting slaves?" she said in a low tone. On occasion, the Fitzgeralds helped slaves escape to freedom along the Underground Railroad. They hid the slaves in the alcove behind the pantry in the family cabin and transported them to a safe place on the canal where a Quaker family would help the slave continue their journey north.

Harlan Armentrout closed his eyes and slowly shook his head. "No, I came today on a personal matter," Harlan said. "I was wondering if you knew where Michael was."

Alice stiffened. "Why would I know? My family hasn't had anything to do with your son since you forbid him to see Elizabeth and fired us from your employ."

That had been nearly a year ago in February of last year.

Harlan blushed and looked away. "Well, that wasn't my idea, you know. It was my wife's." Minerva Armentrout had thought her son too good for Elizabeth and had taken steps to end the blossoming romance, which left Elizabeth with a broken heart. Alice suspected that it had been one of the reasons why her daughter had decided to leave the canal and stay in Washington for a time.

"You could have stepped in and stopped your wife."

"Yes, I could have," Harlan admitted, not looking her in the eye.

"But you felt the same way she did."

"No, that's not it at all," Harlan said, shaking his head quickly. "But…well, you've met Minerva. You know how she can be." His shoulders slumped in resignation.

Alice knew. She knew all too well, having worked for the woman. It had not been a pleasant experience. She actually felt sorry for Harlan. When she had first met him, Alice had thought Harlan had been a different sort of man. She had seen him as stalwart in his abolitionist beliefs, so much so that he had risked arrest to help free slaves. Now that she knew him better, she wondered if his actions were him acting out. He couldn't free himself from the life that he had created for himself so instead, he freed slaves from their imprisonment.

"I am here because we still have not been able to find Michael and convince him to come home," Harlan said. "We have heard some reports that people have seen him working on the canal, but no one can tell me which boat."

"I wouldn't expect them to tell you even if they knew. Canawlers gossip amongst ourselves, but it stays among us. It's one of the reasons Hugh and I were able to help you with runaway slaves. Even if someone on the canal knew about what we were doing, they might argue with us about it but they wouldn't report it," Alice told him.

"I realize that, but I thought that maybe you would help me."

"I hope you don't think I know where he is. I haven't seen him in months, and quite frankly, even if I did know where he was, I'm not sure I would tell you."

Harlan's eyebrows rose in surprise. "Why not? He's my son."

Alice saw a flicker of anger across his features, but it quickly disappeared.

"But look at how you and your wife are trying to control his life. He didn't leave because he wanted to leave his nice home and work on the canal. He left because you and your wife drove him away. He's on his own now. He is going to be forced to become the man that he will be."

"But we can help him with that. We're his parents," Harlan pleaded.

"Yes, you could have helped him with that, but your wife's idea of help is to treat him like a servant."

Alice had no inclination to coddle the man. Either he knew what his wife had been doing and was too weak to stand up to her or he had agreed with her. Either way, Michael was probably better off on his own. He needed to grow into the man that he would be. He appeared to be stronger than his father since he'd been able to leave when his father couldn't.

"She did no such thing!" Harlan insisted.

Alice wasn't going to take this from him anymore. He was no longer her employer. He was someone who refused to see the truth of the matter.

"Oh, really?" Alice snapped. "She tells him to do something and she expects it to be done whether he likes it or not. She wanted to manage his life like she manages her servants' days. The only difference is that the servants can leave at night and be free of her for a few hours. Well, Michael finally had enough and he left, Harlan."

Harlan sighed and shook his head. "You paint us to be horrible people like Southern slave masters. We aren't."

Alice hadn't meant to sound quite so harsh, but she hadn't been sleeping well since David had left. She missed him and she worried that, in her own way, she had done to David what Minerva had done to Michael. She had driven him away.

"Then let him have his freedom, Harlan. Let Michael find out who he is. When he is ready, he will come home if only to show you who he becomes. If you're lucky, he'll come back because he misses you."

"What if he gets hurt or killed? What then?"

"We're in the middle of a war, Harlan. People are getting hurt and killed all of the time. Many times they don't deserve it. My husband was killed for doing nothing more than fetching George from a saloon. George lost his arm in the war. If something bad is destined to happen to Michael, it will. You can't stop it. You can only deal with it."

Harlan stood up and looked around.

"I refuse to believe there's nothing I can do," he said.

Alice said nothing. What could she say? Harlan wanted to take action and find his son. She would probably do the same thing in his place. She had done the same thing when George had run off. In Michael's case, though, she couldn't help but think that he was better off being away from his mother.

Harlan sighed and said, "I thank you for your time, Mrs. Fitzgerald. If you do see Michael, tell him to write to me, please, even if he won't come home."

Alice nodded. "I will do that."

Harlan's shoulders slumped as he turned and stepped ashore from the race plank. Alice watched him walk away and then turned back to her work. Once she had hung up the rest of the wet laundry, she separated the loads of clothes that she had finished yesterday to take into Cumberland to deliver to their owners.

David had the day off from work, not that he needed it. Amos insisted his employees take time off two days a week so that they could remain fresh at their work. That was fine for workers who had families that they could spend time with, but David was alone and he didn't have anything particularly pressing that he needed time off work to take care of.

And so, he found himself walking along Harrison Street in Cumberland between the three-story brick-and-stone buildings. The streets were crowded and noisy today. He could hear people talking and shouting to each other, horses' hooves clopping and the clink of glass and metal. The air was still cool and he could smell the wood and coal smoke from dozens of burning fires and stoves.

Among the hundreds of people on the street, David saw a lot of blue wool coats. The soldiers were very apparent at nearly every corner and walking along the streets. They seemed relaxed, but they all walked with weapons on their hips or shoulders.

David avoided the soldiers as much as possible not wanting to have to talk to them and have his accent raise suspicions about his past. David wondered if he should find a saloon to step into for a drink or get himself some lunch at a diner. His stomach won out over his mouth and he headed for the small inn that Alice had once taken him to on Centre Street.

He turned the corner onto the street and nearly ran into Ruth Abercrombie. He pulled up short as she gave a startled jump.

"Mr. Windover!"

"I'm sorry," David said, blushing slightly. "I was letting my mind wander and not paying as much attention as I should have been."

Ruth collected herself and smoothed out her dress. "Well, no harm done. I'm still standing."

David grinned. "Always the survivor. It is nice to see you again, Mrs. Abercrombie. How are you doing?"

She started walking along beside David. He felt slightly uncomfortable having her so close at his side.

"I'm doing fine. I had a meeting in town that just finished up. I was going to get a newspaper before I headed home."

"Meeting? That's nice. I got the impression the last time that we met that you considered yourself somewhat of a pariah in town."

Ruth nodded. "Oh, I am. Half of the people in the city right now are soldiers. When your husband was someone who might have shot at them, then you have half of the town against you plus those in the general population who are strongly Union."

David noticed that Ruth seemed to continually look around as if she expected someone to arrest her at any moment. David recognized it as something he had done for months after he had decided to stay with the Fitzgeralds on the canal. Ruth also probably gave the soldiers as wide a berth as he did.

"I know how that can feel. It's as if you always have a secret to hide," he told her.

Ruth nodded vigorously. "Yes, that is exactly how it feels. How did you know?"

"I'll let you in on my secret, Mrs. Abercrombie. My family lives in the South and is strongly Confederate in their loyalties."

Ruth's eyes widened slightly. She leaned in closer and said, "And you?"

While David liked Ruth Abercrombie, he didn't know her well. He wasn't willing to share that much about himself. Besides, you never knew who might be listening in an occupied town. He had to live here now. He didn't want someone identifying him as a sympathizer to the army, especially since he wasn't one.

"I have to keep some secrets about myself, Mrs. Abercrombie. However, I can tell you this; my father could care less about me since I chose to stay north of the Potomac. I believe he has probably disowned me by now. That does not mean that I would not like to see my home in Virginia. I would also like to see my mother again. I do not think she would reject me as my father had."

"I believe that your father would be willing to see you. You haven't rejected his beliefs. You've only chosen to continue your life here. It does not mean you don't support the Confederacy just as it doesn't mean we can't support the South and live in Cumberland," Ruth said.

She spoke with such earnestness that David felt two inches tall for having to lie to her. It was necessary, though. He had to keep telling himself that. He didn't want to wind up in a Union prison camp.

"I realize that, but how do I find out how she feels?" David asked.

He had to be careful. He had ventured from lying to telling the truth. He did wish he could speak to his mother and enfold her in his arms. He wanted to hear her sing while she sewed a dress or smile dreamily as she sat in a chair amid her flower garden.

He wanted to see her again and not only for his own sake. When George had been away in the army, David had seen how heavily the weight of not knowing what had happened to him weighed on Alice's shoulders. It pained him to think that his own mother was experiencing that.

"You could write to your mother," Ruth suggested.

David stared at her. "How? I thought that with the dominance of the Union Army in this area that the mail had stopped getting through."

Ruth grinned and patted his arm. "Maybe through the official channels. There's the Union post office here and the Confederate post offices in the South, but there's also an underground post office here in Cumberland. It's how we still communicate with our friends and relatives in the South."

"Really?"

Ruth laid her hand on his arm. David felt his skin tingle. "I'll let you in on a little secret of my own, David. There are a lot more people in town who sympathize with the Confederate cause than you might think given the number of military men in town."

David wasn't surprised. It was probably one of the reasons for the military presence in Cumberland. The residents needed to be constantly reminded which side of the border they lived on.

"Maybe it's because of all the military in town," he said. "People certainly can't enjoy feeling like they're being watched all the time. It might make some of the Union supporters waver a bit in their support."

"Perhaps, but more, like my husband, believe that the Constitution left certain things up to the states to decide and the federal government is ignoring that. It is the Confederate States that are truly the inheritors of the Constitution and the dreams of our fathers and grandfathers."

David had felt the same way at one time. Now he realized that this was more than a war about state's rights. It was a war about human rights.

"So how do you know about this hidden group of people with Southern sympathies if they keep to themselves for their own protection?" David asked.

Ruth grinned like a little girl. "Like you, Mr. Windover, I have to keep some secrets. I will tell you this, though, while some of these secret Confederates want simply to make it through the war without being arrested, others are actively involved in supporting the Confederate cause."

David nodded. "People help as they are able."

"Hello, David," a voice said from behind him.

David turned and saw Alice standing there holding a large basket full of laundry wrapped with strings. Her face was a bit flushed, which must have come from the effort of carrying the basket through town. Alice must have decided to earn extra money taking in laundry work. David should have been there to help here, but he had abandoned her just like he had turned his back on his family in Virginia.

She looked beautiful. The sun shone behind her streaming through her reddish hair. She smiled momentarily at him, but then it disappeared when she noticed Ruth.

"Alice!" he said, slightly startled.

"How are you doing?"

David glanced around nervously. "I'm fine. I'm working with Amos again and he's letting me a room in the warehouse. It suits me."

"I'm glad to hear that things are going well for you." Now that David was over his initial shock of seeing her he thought that her voice sounded a little strained.

David turned to Ruth. "Ruth Abercrombie, this is Alice Fitzgerald. Alice, this is Ruth. I used to work for Alice on her canal boat. She taught me to love the canal and helped me when I really needed it."

"I would say it was more than just hiring you as a hand. You were like one of the family," Alice said.

If so, it wasn't the family member he had wanted to be. He was a brother not a husband. He was a friend not a lover.

"Ruth lives here in town with her parents," David said. "She's a war widow."

"I'm sorry to hear that. I am a widow, too, though my husband wasn't a soldier," Alice said.

"I'm sorry for your loss, Mrs. Fitzgerald," Ruth said.

"How did you and David meet?" Alice asked.

David shifted uncomfortably from foot to foot. He wasn't sure he wanted to be here between these two women. He felt like he was being disloyal to Alice, though he couldn't say why.

"He helped me when I was in need of assistance and we started talking," Ruth said.

Alice smiled, but it wasn't her typical smile. She showed no teeth and her lips were pressed in a tight line. "That's nice. David can be very helpful like that, but sometimes when you need him, you'll find him nowhere around."

David's eyes widened. Where did that comment come from? It sounded almost jealous. But Alice had no right to be jealous. She didn't love him.

"It was nice to meet you, Mrs. Abercrombie," Alice said. "I've got to be going. I need to deliver these laundry orders."

She walked away along Centre Street and both Ruth and David watched her go.

"Are you sure she was only your boss?" Ruth asked.

"Yes, why?"

"Then you either made her very mad or you broke her heart."

5

WOMAN'S WORK

JANUARY 1864

Elizabeth Fitzgerald heard hoof beats outside of the church. It wasn't the heavy near-constant thudding of lots of horses pulling ambulances filled with wounded soldiers or the casual clip-clopping of someone casually riding a horse down the cobblestone street. It was a single rider moving quickly in the direction of the church that suddenly stopped. Someone in a hurry to get to a hospital was never good news.

The church had once been the First United Methodist Episcopal just four blocks from the Congressman Eli Sampson's home in Washington City. Hopefully, it would one day be so again, but for now it was a war hospital treating wounded soldiers who had survived a battle sometimes a day or more away from the Capitol City. A wooden plank floor had been nailed onto the tops of the pews in the chapel. This allowed the hospital to have a large open ward with plenty of room for beds. The basement had been converted into a lab, kitchen and storage area for items removed from the chapel.

Chesapeake rushed into the chapel, his black face covered with sweat despite the cold. Though he was a free man, he volunteered his time at the hospital just like everyone else there. "We've got wounded coming, Mrs. Carlyle. They are a few minutes behind me."

"How many?" asked Margaret Carlyle, the head nurse of the war hospital. Her husband was fighting in the war and Mrs. Carlyle had decided to do her part by volunteering to help in a hospital.

"I counted ten ambulances, but there could be more by now. They should be here in about fifteen minutes."

Mrs. Carlyle turned around and called out, "I need bandages and clean water out front. Set up the extra cots in here. We'll have wounded soon."

Elizabeth quickly calculated that ten ambulances could mean around forty men heading toward the hospital. That number of men would fill the open beds in the hospital and then some. One of the nurses had already started setting up cots in between the beds to increase the number of soldiers that could stay in the hospital. Hopefully, Chess was wrong about more wounded coming. If he wasn't, they would have to scramble to find additional bed space in nearby buildings.

The hospital became a rush of activity as Dr. Lyman Harris hurried to set up examination tables outside. Though it was cold out, the sun shone brightly. It would provide plenty of light for their initial examinations of the wounded before deciding whether to have an orderly re-bandage a wound and admit the wounded soldier or carry him into one of the back rooms of the chapel to be operated on. By performing the examinations and operations outside, it wouldn't take up needed room inside the church that was needed for beds.

Elizabeth shrugged on her peacoat. It had been the coat of a soldier who had died last month. His personal effects had been sent to his parents, but for some reason, his coat had been left behind. Elizabeth had discovered it while changing the straw in the bed mattresses and she had started using it when she was at the hospital. It was big on her, but it would both keep her warm and free of much of the blood that would come with the patients. She already had her auburn hair held back with a large bandanna.

She had been volunteering at the hospital for four months now. She had gotten used to some of the routines and the work that she performed to help the soldiers. So much of what she did was cooking and cleaning that it was like having to help care for ten brothers who were generally easier to deal with than Thomas had been. What she just couldn't get used to was the suffering faces she saw every time a new batch of wounded were brought from the battlefield. It made her chest tighten whenever she saw one of their bodies being covered and carried out behind the church. She couldn't help but wonder if her brother and Abel Sampson had looked the same when they had been injured, and in Abel's case, killed, in the war.

It amazed Elizabeth how little thought had been given to treating the wounded soldiers before the Union and Confederacy went to war, but then neither side had expected the fighting to go on for so long. For all of the hundreds of thousands of men fighting, there had probably been less than a thousand medical men to treat all of them.

Within a few weeks of the war starting, women had begun stepping in to do their part. Aid societies formed. The Daughters of Charity and the Sisters of Charity had shifted much of their civilian nursing to helping soldiers.

This was despite the fact that nursing at the beginning of the war was generally done by male soldiers and other patients. Many believed that women wouldn't be able to handle the sight of the blood and gore or that seeing men exposed was improper for women. However, neither government was in a position to turn away help when it was so badly needed.

Recognizing the need to coordinate the efforts of the aid societies and manage the women volunteering to be nurses, U.S. Secretary of War Simon Cameron appointed Dorothea L. Dix, a Boston schoolteacher, as the superintendent of the U.S. Army nurses. Though Elizabeth hadn't met the woman, she had heard stories about her from Mrs. Carlyle. Dix was an elderly spinster who had earned a national reputation for two years of working to improve the conditions of the mentally ill. Though not an army officer, Elizabeth had heard some of the surgeons at the hospital say that Dix acted like a general. She had no trouble ordering soldiers and doctors around.

She was also harsh with her nurses, insisting that they be older, plain-looking women. Elizabeth certainly didn't fit that bill with her emerald eyes, a head of strawberry blonde hair and only seventeen years of age. These were just a few of the reasons that Elizabeth hadn't met Dix. Whenever Dix was around, Mrs. Carlyle made sure that Elizabeth wasn't. Dix wanted all of her nurses to be at least thirty years old. Despite her restrictions with her nurses, Dix was generous with the wounded. She did a good job of making sure that the hospitals had the supplies that they needed.

As Elizabeth passed by Chesapeake who was looking anxiously out the door watching for the ambulances. She asked, "Are you staying to help, Chess?"

The black man nodded. "Mrs. Sampson said I could stay if I wanted to and I do. She's on her way, too, and should be here shortly." Chess was the butler for the Sampsons, friends of Elizabeth's mother who were helping Elizabeth learn to become a lady in Washington society.

Elizabeth liked Grace Sampson, but she reminded Elizabeth of her mother, which only made Elizabeth miss her family. Right now, she needed to be here away from Michael and his family. She needed to feel useful and wanted, neither of which she felt when she had worked for the Armentrouts.

By the time Elizabeth got outside of the church, the ambulances were rolling to a stop on the street in front of the church. They were wagons set up to carry two or four wounded soldiers on stretchers supported on frames in the wagon beds.

Elizabeth could hear the moans and cries of the wounded above the shouts of the orderlies and doctors as they climbed into the ambulances. The orderlies lifted the wounded soldiers out of the ambulances on their stretchers and passed them down to nurses and orderlies on the ground where they were carried to operating tables.

The walking wounded staggered off the ambulances and were helped to some place where they could sit down. Those with minor wounds were immediately allowed to enter the hospital where a nurse took their name and company. Once inside, another nurse would find a place for them to lie down. If the wounded soldier had a more-serious wound, the doctor pulled him off to the side to look at it. Sometimes, he would order an assistant to clean or close a wound until it could be looked at in more detail. Other times, the patient was carried into a tent, away from the stares of his companions, where he could be operated on. The tent did nothing to silence the screams of the soldiers. That came from ether, but the tent hid the bloody operations from the eyes of other wounded men. One doctor always remained outside the tent to evaluate the wounded and a line of soldiers soon began forming at the operating tent.

It took about an hour to process all of the wounded. At some point, Elizabeth had taken off her peacoat and draped it over a wounded soldier who had been shivering in the cold. Not all of the wounded had been taken inside after an hour, but they had been seen by Dr. Harris. Elizabeth went inside the church to help the wounded inside settle onto their cots. Her work was just beginning.

She and the other nurses began removing the dirty clothing from the soldiers and taking it outside to be washed. Other nurses washed the soldiers while still others began preparing a hot meal in the basement. This job took hours and left little time for the nurses to talk with the wounded soldiers and bring them comfort in that way.

Mrs. Carlyle's voice carried through the hospital as she directed the nursing staff to wash patients, dress wounds and get hot soup ready. She also made sure that each of the soldiers coming in from surgery had a bed close to the stoves where they could stay warm in the January air.

Despite their pain, Elizabeth heard some of the soldiers complain about the smell in the hospital. Elizabeth knew why they complained. The smell of human waste and rotting flesh dominated the scents inside the hospital. On warm days, the church windows were kept open for maximum ventilation, but in the winter, they were only opened occasionally. Elizabeth tried to spray lavender water around the soldiers to try and ward off the smell. It was only effective if it was close to your nose, though.

Elizabeth sat next to a young soldier who wouldn't meet her gaze. He looked young enough to be George's age, though she suspected he was older.

"How are you?" Elizabeth asked.

The young man didn't reply. He glanced at her and then looked away. Elizabeth wasn't offended. She was used to seeing shell-shocked soldiers. The problem would be if he remained that way.

She set down a clean uniform on the edge of the bed and gently pulled back the blanket. The soldier didn't resist.

"We need to get you out of those filthy clothes and dress you in some clean ones. You'll feel a lot better once we get all of that dirt off of you." The nurses had all learned to carry on a one-sided conversation with the soldiers. Hearing a woman's voice had proven to be soothing to the wounded soldiers. It reminded them of home and their wives and mothers. It encouraged pleasant memories and helped keep their minds off the horror they had endured.

As Elizabeth began undressing the young soldier, he grabbed her hand. She looked at him but didn't say anything. His eyes were wide with fear. She gently pried his hand off of hers. He didn't resist her.

"It's all right. It's going to be a little embarrassing for both of us, but probably you more than me. I've been trained to do this. You need to be clean. It will help you get better," she said softly.

Elizabeth had probably been more scared than this soldier when she undressed her first wounded man. She wasn't sure how she would react. Would she gag at the man's wounds or stare at his private parts? Her hands had shaken throughout that first washing and she had done her best to allow the man his dignity by focusing her attention on his face. Luckily for her, the man had been unconscious. Those were the only men Mrs. Carlyle had let her clean at first. That had been four months and a couple hundred soldiers ago.

Elizabeth slowly pulled the soldier's uniform off. It was still caked with blood and dirt. It had quickly become obvious that the soldiers who were kept clean after an operation tended to survive better. Elizabeth would rather be embarrassed than see a soldier die so she let her face turn red but washed until the soldiers' skins were clean of dirt and blood. She paid particular attention to cleaning any festering sores and burns.

She was particularly careful not to cause the young soldier any additional physical pain by irritating an unseen wound. It was best to try and salvage the uniform so it could be washed and given to another soldier, but sometimes that was impossible. Shrapnel and simple wear and tear turned a uniform into threads. Elizabeth tossed the man's shirt and jacket into a pile on the floor. They could both be re-used once they had been washed a few times. They just might not be reused by the original owner. When soldiers left the hospital, they were given a uniform that fit, not necessarily the uniform that they had come into the hospital wearing.

Next, she started wiping off the man's legs. He had taken shrapnel in both of his legs, which had also ripped up his pants. The cloth was so dirty that he could barely tell that it had been blue. The legs had been bandaged. Maybe he would be able to keep his legs since the doctors hadn't amputated them. If there was any doubt, the doctors usually amputated the limb. She would have to watch him closely for any signs of gangrene.

While his legs might have been saved, his pants were a loss. Elizabeth cut them off of him with a pair of scissors so she wouldn't have to move him around.

She used a cloth dipped in warm water to wash the soldier as he stared at the ceiling. She could feel his muscles twitching nervously as she slid the cloth from his chest to his stomach. Elizabeth kept the man's private parts under the sheet and did her work as quickly as she could. She talked to him about things happening in Washington and her family as she worked. It helped keep both their minds off of what she was doing.

When she finished, she dressed the man in a clean uniform and changed the sheets on his bed so they would be dry and clean.

"There that wasn't so bad, was it?" Elizabeth said as she stood up to go.

The soldier grabbed her arm again. He didn't squeeze it. He simply clamped onto her wrist.

Elizabeth smiled at him and patted his hand. "I wish I could stay longer, but I've got to help with all of the other wounded. I'll be around, though. I promise I'll come back and visit. After all, I want to see you walk out of here on your own."

The soldier let his arm drop down to the bed. Elizabeth turned and walked away.

Grace Sampson was standing a short distance from the foot of the bed. Her black hair was tied up under a white scarf and her large full-length apron was bloodstained. Her shoulders sagged from exhaustion, but she was smiling.

"Hi, Mrs. Sampson, I didn't see you come in," Elizabeth said.

"That's because I was downstairs helping with the cooking. I swear that Chess is a magician when it comes to food. He and I can use the same ingredients in the same amounts and his meals always taste better."

Elizabeth smiled. Chess was a great cook. She had enjoyed many a meal that he prepared at the house. Here, though, his meals weren't nearly as extravagant. It was hard to be fancy when you were cooking fifty or more meals at a time. However, he always managed to create delicious foods that didn't cause soldiers who had been living on camp rations to take sick.

"You handled that soldier with a lot of grace and kindness," Grace said.

"He's scared and he's in pain," Elizabeth said. "What else could I do?"

Grace nodded. "You're learning more about being a lady here than I could ever teach you."

One of the reasons that Elizabeth had chosen to stay in Washington City was to learn from Grace how to be a lady. Elizabeth had always admired the congressman's wife during their family visits to the Sampsons' house. She always seemed so elegant and well-mannered. Plus, if Elizabeth could learn to be a Washington lady that would certainly trump being a Cumberland lady like Minerva Armentrout.

"The only reason I'm here learning these lessons is because I followed your example," Elizabeth told her mentor.

Grace patted Elizabeth's arm and laughed. "Well, if you don't become a lady, you can always become a politician." Her husband, Eli, was a congressman from Pennsylvania.

"Mrs. Sampson, can I ask you something?"

"Certainly. Besides, I doubt that I could stop you."

"Why? Why do you keep doing this?" Elizabeth asked. "It's got to remind you of what happened to Abel."

Elizabeth and Abel Sampson had just started to express their interest in each other when he had been killed. The Sampsons' son and only child had been eighteen years old and stationed on the Alexandria Aqueduct. The aqueduct was a half-mile long spur of the C&O Canal that ran from Georgetown to Rosslyn, Virginia. It was the only connection between the Maryland and Virginia shores, and as such, it was a likely crossover point for an invading army. At the beginning of the war, the aqueduct had been closed off and drained and protected. It was supposed to be a relatively safe duty, but a Rebel sniper had shot and killed him more than a year ago. He had been brought to this hospital and he had died here.

Grace frowned and for a moment, Elizabeth thought that she would cry. "It's because of Abel that I do this."

"But you can't help him."

"True, but I can help these boys. Maybe because of my help some of them will live who wouldn't have lived otherwise. I do it because I hope there are other mothers who won't have to feel like I did when Abel died."

Eli Sampson hadn't wanted his son to join the army, but Abel had been insistent. Eli relented, but he arranged for his son to be stationed at the aqueduct. It should have been a safe assignment, but it hadn't turned out that way.

"I'm sure they are grateful," Grace said.

Elizabeth moved off to tend to some of the other soldiers in the church. Some of the soldiers who were able to move around wrapped a blanket around themselves and shambled over to sit close to a stove. The soldiers who could get around on their own were also asked to bathe and change themselves to help the overworked nurses in the church. There were only three ward nurses to care for the wounded during the days and another one at night.

The nurses who were working concentrated their efforts on caring for the soldiers in the beds. They had survived both the battle and the jarring ambulance ride to Washington City and now they would have to recover from the wounds.

As the sun set, the soldiers began perking up when hot soup and fresh bread was brought up and served to the men. As the smell of the bread reached them, they stirred in their cots and inhaled deeply. Those that could, sat up and looked around for the source of the smell. Elizabeth was always amazed at how hungry the soldiers were. They devoured the food no matter how ill they were. Many of them asked for more and if they were healthy enough. If there was extra, the nurses would provide an additional serving.

A tired and disheveled looking Dr. Harris made his final rounds of the day to check on patients before they headed home for the night after a stressful day. The day nurses checked on the patients one more time to make sure they were comfortable for the night. Elizabeth's young wounded soldier was asleep when she checked on him.

She patted his hand. "Good night. Have peaceful dreams," she whispered.

She hoped it was true, but she knew many of these men would suffer nightmares for weeks if not years because of what they had seen and been through.

Finally, when all was in order, the night nurse took over and Elizabeth and Grace left the hospital together. Chess was waiting outside for them with a carriage to take them home.

The Sampsons lived in a three-story brick home on Union Street. The white-shuttered windows were open to allow in some fresh air and light before they would need to be closed for the night. Elizabeth longed for the spring when flowers would be blooming in the flower boxes under the windows.

That was months away, though. Right now, she just longed for sleep. She walked in the front door and paused for a moment in the foyer. Large paintings created by Eli decorated the walls of the house. He was actually quite an excellent painter of country scenes. The broad front staircase ran upward and curved to the second floor where Elizabeth's room was located at the front of the house.

When Grace came downstairs for breakfast in the morning, Grace and Eli were eating eggs and toast. The dining table was made of cherry wood with a white lace tablecloth on it. Six of the wall sconces around the room gave the room plenty of light in the evening, but they weren't needed in the morning when morning light poured in through the window.

"It smells wonderful," Elizabeth said. "Why didn't someone wake me?"

"You had a long day yesterday," Grace said. "We decided to let you sleep as long as you needed."

Always the gentleman, Eli stood up and held out a chair for Elizabeth. She sat down and Chess brought out a plate with two fried eggs and toast on it. Elizabeth inhaled deeply. She was surprised to hear her stomach rumble.

Elizabeth buttered the toast and then took a bite. As she chewed, she watched Eli and Grace exchange an odd glance.

"What?" Elizabeth asked. "Do I have crumbs on my chin?" She reached up and brushed her hand across her chin.

"No, dear. Nothing like that. I was just talking with Eli about hosting a dinner party this Friday," Grace said.

"Really?"

"Yes, things are fairly quiet now that it's winter and I think a dinner party would be just the thing to bolster everyone's spirits. After all, we are having not only to deal with the realities of war but also the winter blahs."

"It sounds lovely," Elizabeth said.

"Besides, part of the reason that you are staying with us is because you wanted me to show you how to be a lady," Grace added.

Eli snorted. "Imagine trying to find a lady in Washington."

Grace slapped him lightly on his arm. "That's not nice, Eli."

Eli Sampson was a congressman from Pennsylvania. Though he lived in Georgetown when Congress was in session, he preferred his home in Lancaster. He did not think much of the Washington lifestyle.

"I thought we could invite the Harmons, the McKennas and the Franklins," Grace said. "With the three of us, that would make twelve…a full table."

"Do we have to invite another political family?" Eli asked. "I don't want to talk politics all night, trying to second guess the president and his generals."

"You're a congressman, Eli," Grace reminded him. "Most of the people we know are in the government."

"What about Mrs. Carlyle from the hospital?" Eli asked.

"I like Mrs. Carlyle," Elizabeth said. "She's tough at the hospital, but she's fair and kind to the soldiers."

Grace shook her head. "No, that won't do. She's a widow and doesn't have a son."

"Why is that important?" Elizabeth asked.

"Because I am also inviting families who have a teenage son," Grace explained. "I wanted to introduce you to some young men from good families."

Elizabeth stopped chewing on her bite of egg and stared at Grace. She put her fork down.

"What?"

"You've been working so hard since you've been staying with us. I thought this would be a good way for you to relax and meet some eligible young men," Grace said.

Elizabeth shook her head. "No, please. Don't do that."

"I thought that you would be excited. We could go shopping and buy you a new dress for the party and then curl your hair the night of the party."

"But…" Elizabeth looked down and shook her head.

"What's the matter, Elizabeth?" Eli asked. He folded his newspaper and lay it on the table.

"What about Abel?"

Eli frowned. "Abel? What's he got to do with this?"

"Don't you feel that having me meet other young men is...? What if I meet someone I like?"

"That would be wonderful!" Grace said.

Elizabeth shook her head and wiped away a tear. "No, it wouldn't. Don't you feel like it would be like I was betraying Abel?"

Grace started to say something. Then she stood up, walked around the table and hugged Elizabeth.

"Elizabeth, no it wouldn't be like that. Just because you might meet someone new doesn't mean that you feel anything less for Abel."

"But it feels that way."

Grace reached across the table and laid a hand on Elizabeth's arm.

"Elizabeth, if your mother meets someone, will you think that's she betraying your father? Someday she might want to get remarried?"

Elizabeth's brow furrowed as she thought. "No. I know she loved my father. I would be happy for her. I know she's been lonely since my father was killed. I want her to be happy."

Grace nodded. "And that's how I feel about you and Abel." She stroked the back of Elizabeth's head. "As for me, I've made my peace about Abel's death at the hospital, but it's not going to be where you find your peace."

"No?"

Grace shook her head. "No, dear. What you do at the hospital is needed and it means the world to the soldiers, but you've got your whole life in front of you still. You can't continue to live regretting your short past. It doesn't balance."

Elizabeth nodded slowly. Then she gave Grace a faint smile.

"So when are we going shopping for a new dress?" Elizabeth asked.

6

MOTHER?

JANUARY 1864

Tony sat at his school desk, rocking back and forth slightly on the hard wooden bench, which he shared with four other students. His eyes stared at the words in his history primer, barely paying attention to the story of General Washington and his men nearly freezing to death during the winter they were camped at Valley Forge. Tony was having trouble feeling the effects of a freezing winter at the moment. He felt flush.

He glanced sideways at Jenny McCagh who sat next to him on the back row of the classroom. He felt his cheeks redden even more.

"Are you all right, Tony?" Miss Conner asked.

Tony looked up from his book. His teacher had stopped writing on the blackboard at the front of the room and was staring at him with her intense green eyes.

"Yes, ma'am. I'm fine," Tony said.

He risked another glance at Jenny. She was staring at him, but then, so was just about everyone in the class.

"You look feverish. Are you sitting too close to the stove because I can move you?" Miss Conner asked.

"No, ma'am," Tony said quickly, shaking his head. "I mean I'm fine. Really, I am."

His teacher's gaze focused on him, but she didn't say anything for a few moments. *Please don't let her move me*, Tony wished to himself.

"Fine, but let me know if you start to feel bad," she said.

"Yes, ma'am."

Tony lowered his head and tried to concentrate on his history lesson. He focused his attention on the words on the page. He read them, though he wasn't sure how much he would remember.

A short time later, Miss Conner said, "Students, put your books away. I've written your homework assignments on the board. Once you've written them down, you can pack up your books and head home for the day."

The assignments were written in chalk on the blackboard and grouped by grade level. Thomas scribbled the pages he needed to read on the edge of a piece of paper so that he wouldn't forget them.

"Is anything wrong?" Jenny asked.

Tony shook his head. "No."

"You did look red."

"I guess I was embarrassed."

"About what?"

"Something I was thinking about." He felt his cheeks started to redden again and he looked away. "Do you want to walk into town with me for some candy? I've got three cents." That would be enough for three peppermint sticks. He could get one himself, Jenny and even Thomas to keep him quiet for a while.

Jenny frowned. "I can't, Tony. It sounds like fun, but I've got to watch my brothers this afternoon. Today is my mother's shopping day. She doesn't like to take the boys with her. She says that she can get shopping done quicker if she doesn't have to watch them to make sure that they don't steal anything. Can we go tomorrow?"

Tony's head bobbed up and down quickly. "Sure, I'd like that."

Jenny smiled at him. Tony's vision filled with her smile.

"I would, too," she said.

"Can I walk you home?" Tony asked.

"What about your brother?"

Tony looked around the classroom. Thomas was already outside playing. Tony picked up Jenny's three books and stacked them on his own pile.

"He can follow us if he wants or he can go back to the *Freeman* on his own," Tony said. "It's not like he doesn't know the way."

Tony hoped that his little brother went back to the *Freeman* because Tony would rather spend time alone with Jenny and not have Thomas trying to embarrass him.

They walked outside and the cold slapped them in their faces. Some of the students had stayed around the schoolyard to play and talk before heading home. Small groups were gathered talking. Others were playing on the swings, jumping rope or playing hopscotch. It might be cold out, but that wasn't going to stop them from having fun.

Thomas was digging worms out of the ground and putting them in his water cup. He would probably use them later to go fishing.

Andy Cardeson and two of his friends were standing under a tree and talking. Andy and his friends never included Tony in their group, but then, they didn't try to bother him either. Tony considered it better than a fair trade.

Laura Anderson jumped rope as two of her friends held the ends and rotated it around her. Laura hadn't talked to Tony since he had returned to school. She had seemed to really like him last year, but that had changed quickly enough after her parents had objected to her friendship with Andy.

Would Jenny ignore him next year? Tony wasn't sure, but he would definitely remember her name next year.

Tony walked over to his brother. "I'm going to walk Jenny home and then I'm going into town."

Thomas stood up and dusted the dirt off his knees.

"I don't want to walk a girl home," Thomas said.

"I'm not inviting you."

"How come you're not walking Laura home?"

"If you haven't noticed, she hasn't talked to me since we've been back in school," Tony told him.

"Oh." Thomas around his brother over at Laura and her friends. When he looked at Tony again, Thomas said, "I want to go into town, too."

That was not what Tony wanted to hear.

"I'll tell you what. I'll come back for you after I see Jenny home.

You can stay here and play until then."

Thomas smiled. "I like that!"

Tony walked back to where Jenny waited and they started walking down the street talking about their day in school. Suddenly, Tony heard a girl's scream. He spun around and looked back at the school yard.

Thomas was running toward him. He had apparently dropped one or more of his worms down the back of Laura Anderson's dress. She was dancing around in circles, shaking her dress to try and get the worms to drop to the ground.

"I think I'll tag along behind you," Thomas said.

Tony had hoped to be walking through Cumberland today with Jenny not Thomas.

Oh, well.

Jenny hadn't been lying about her mother's shopping. Mrs. McCagh had been anxious to leave for South Cumberland. She shot out the door almost as soon as Jenny walked into the house.

Tony had said goodbye to Jenny and walked back along Virginia Avenue toward downtown Cumberland, avoiding the area around the school in case Laura Anderson and her friends were lying in wait for Thomas.

When they reached Baltimore Street, Tony and Thomas walked south until they reached Centre Street, which ran north and south through Cumberland. Tony bought a loaf of bread with money that Mrs. Fitzgerald had given him for the errand. Then he walked along the street watching the crowds with a skill developed from living most of his young life on the streets of the city. He could still quickly pick out from whom he would beg, from whom he would steal and who he would avoid at all costs.

The woman with two children who kept tugging at her skirt was a likely target for thieves. The well-off young man in the neat suit who was walking with his doe-eyed sweetheart would want to impress her so he would be someone likely to respond to a plea from a pitiful child. The old man puffing on a cigar with tight features and squinty eyes was someone whom Tony would have avoided during his street urchin days.

While they walked, Thomas occasionally tossed small rocks at the brick walls of stores. Some store keepers eyed them suspiciously, thinking their store windows might be next, but since the boys kept moving, the shopkeepers didn't say anything. It always surprised Tony that one young kid looked the same as another to shopkeepers and all of them looked like potential vandals.

The boys stopped at the intersection with Baltimore Street. Tony set his bread loaf down and unbuttoned his heavy winter coat. It was warm out for a January day and he was perspiring in his sweater and coat that Mrs. Fitzgerald had bundled him into that morning.

Thomas pulled a dried apple out of his pocket and cut it in half with a small knife that he carried with him. He handed Tony one half.

"What do you want to do when we get back?" Thomas asked.

"Mama's going to want us to read and try and catch up with the rest of the kids in school," Tony said.

He didn't really mind being behind in his studies. He could read so why did he have to keep doing it? The same was true with his math. He could add, subtract, divide and multiply. What more could he learn that was worth going to school for so much of the day? Working on the canal, he was learning a trade and skills that would help him when he was older.

"I don't know. If we're quick, we might be able to get away before she thinks of something else for us to do," Thomas said.

"Uh huh," Tony mumbled as he chewed on the apple.

"We could go see David. He's helping build canal boats again this winter. He might let us help out with something."

Tony was about to agree with Thomas when he saw a face in the crowd walking along the street. It was his mother, his birth mother not Mrs. Fitzgerald. He hadn't seen her in almost a year. Her name was Carol, but Tony didn't know her last name. She changed it often. Tony had grown up not even knowing his own last name. He went by Tony Fitzgerald now.

Carol's dark-brown hair hung down straight. She only did it up when she went out looking for men. Her face looked even older or maybe it was simply because she wasn't wearing as much make-up as she wore at nights. She had hard lines in her face and looked thinner. Tony wondered how long it had been since she had eaten a hearty meal like the ones Mrs. Fitzgerald fixed each night.

The last time he had seen her was the time on the *Freeman* when she and Sheriff Whittaker had tried to get him away from the Fitzgeralds. It had been a spiteful plan that the sheriff had come up with to hurt Tony and Mrs. Fitzgerald because she had embarrassed the sheriff publicly. He hadn't liked that at all and he held a grudge.

Tony watched his mother walk down the street. She wasn't carrying anything in her arms and he wondered why she had come into town. She usually stayed in Shanty Town either drinking or "entertaining" men in her room as she called it.

"Tony?"

Tony looked around and saw Thomas staring at him. "What are you looking at?" Thomas asked.

Tony pointed. "That's my mother."

Thomas looked where Tony was pointing. "Did she see you?" Then he, too, ducked down.

Tony wondered if his mother would even recognize him if she did see him. She had changed little over the past year, but Tony was gaining some height and muscle. The height was simply from the fact that he was getting older and the muscle came from helping the Fitzgeralds haul coal along the C&O Canal. He walked miles each day and also spent time coiling the heavy ropes on the canal boat.

"No. She didn't look over this way," Tony said after a moment.

"That's probably a good thing." Thomas paused, and then added, "She looks a little bit like you, you know."

"Well, she is my mother."

"I know, but you're…you," Thomas said, waving his hands at Tony. "When I look at your mother, at first I see a lady, and then I start to see you in her face. It's weird."

"Why?"

"Because I don't think you make that pretty a woman."

Tony punched Thomas in the arm as the younger boy laughed.

"I want to see where she's going," Tony said suddenly. He wasn't even sure why he said it. He didn't want to talk to his mother or have anything to do with her so why should he follow her?

"Why remind her that you're in town?" Thomas asked. "She might try to get you back again."

That had been a nasty fight last year that Sheriff Whittaker had encouraged. He hated Tony for all of the trouble Tony used to cause stealing in town. He hated Mrs. Fitzgerald because she stood up for

Tony and against the sheriff.

Tony picked up his bundle of cloth and started walking down Baltimore Street after his mother. She turned onto Liberty Street, heading toward the city hall. She walked past city hall to the red brick building where the jail was housed.

Now why would she go in there? His mother was a prostitute. She should want to stay as far away from the jail as possible. Then again, she had worked with Sheriff Whittaker before to try and do something underhanded. His mother might have something on the sheriff.

"Can we go now?" Thomas asked. "If we take too long, Mama's going to pepper us with questions and then make us do lessons when we get back."

Tony waved him away. "You go ahead back and tell your mama that I just wanted to look around town some more. Tell her I'm not getting into any trouble and I'll be back soon."

Thomas looked doubtful. "Are you sure? Why are you doing this? You don't even like your mother."

Tony shook his head. "I don't know why. I'll be all right. I'm not going to talk to her or anything."

Thomas raised an eyebrow. "You're acting strange, Tony."

"I know, but it's not a bad strange. It's just a weird strange like the way you act all of the time."

Thomas picked up Tony's bag and headed back toward the canal basin with his arms full. It was probably a good thing. It would keep him out of trouble. Tony watched him go and then turned back to watch the jail.

Here he was still waiting for his mother. Thomas thought he had escaped her two years ago, but here he was again. He might not be hiding under her bed anymore, but he was still waiting for her to finish with a man.

As he sat against the city hall building and waited, he watched couples walk by him on the street. Did they do with each other what his mother did with men in her room? These couples on the street didn't seem to hate each other like his mother hated men, though. Why was that? Tony knew what his mother did with men was somehow wrong and not just because it had been his job to rob the men while his mother kept them distracted on the bed.

There was a lot that Tony didn't understand about women and he wondered how he would ever learn. Thomas didn't know any more than Tony. George just turned red when Tony brought up the topic and David wasn't around anymore to talk to about things like that.

His mother finally came out of the jail building alone and started walking down the street back toward the canal basin. Tony followed a ways behind so that she wouldn't notice him. He also kept his cap pulled down low so his face wasn't as visible. He was just another kid in Cumberland and below most people's line of sight.

His mother walked straight back to Shanty Town on the south side of Cumberland. Shanty Town wasn't a town. It was the waterfront area around the loading basin. Stores along Wineow Street and a few side streets sold food and dry goods, but the more-popular businesses were the taverns and red-light district. It was a place known for its rowdiness because so many of the canawlers spent their free time getting drunk in the taverns since the sale of alcohol was forbidden along the canal. Fights were a greeting in Shanty Town, at least among the men. The women had another way to greet the canawlers.

He was surprised to see that the Queen's Crown had been rebuilt. Tony had set fire to it after railroaders had stabbed Mr. Fitzgerald in it two years ago. The fire had killed four men, four railroaders, before it was put out. They had deserved it and Tony didn't regret his actions, though he had told no one that he was the person who had started the fire. The men in the saloon had either killed Mr. Fitzgerald or laughed as he had died in front of them. Then they had thrown his body out into the street like a bag of trash.

Carol went to the Potomac Saloon on Wineow Street, which was the only street in Shanty Town. Most of the businesses that lined the street were saloons. Most of the rest of the businesses were stores selling dry goods and groceries to canallers and railroaders. What Shanty Town didn't have was houses. Anyone who lived in Shanty Town stayed in rooms above the businesses.

Instead of going inside of a saloon, she walked around the side of the wooden-frame building and climbed the stairs to the second floor.

She must have a room above the saloon. She had lived over a different saloon when Thomas had been with her, but even then, it seemed like they had moved every few months. Each place was a small room, barely big enough for a bed and dresser. Occasionally, they would return to a room they had previously lived in because there were only so many rooms to let in Shanty Town, and it was doubtful that she could afford a room elsewhere.

Tony looked at the staircase. He had no desire to climb up the stairs to see her room. He was done with his mother. She didn't love him. Mrs. Fitzgerald did. She was his mother now.

Tony walked back to the canal basin, watching the railroaders and canallers along the dirt street. Men were walking along the boardwalk laughing and drinking. They jostled each other and spit tobacco into the street where most of the men tried to avoid walking. How many of them would be going to see a woman and do with her what men did with his mother?

Thomas had told him the basics of things by pointing out two dogs that were doing, according to Thomas, what men did with his mother. Tony hadn't even known that much since he had spent all his time under his mother's bed and not watching her.

There was more to it, though, at least for people. Otherwise, why would they do it in private and not anywhere it suited them like the dogs?

Tony was still wrestling with all of the implications of sex when he reached the *Freeman*. It was tied up at one of the wharf along the basin. It wasn't nearly as expensive to tie up at one of the Cumberland wharves as it was in Georgetown, but it still cost money even if a boat was wintering at the basin. The wharves offered boats a prime location to get a load of coal and be on their way. So it was either pay the wharf fees or tie up somewhere along the canal and be at the back of the line to take on a load of coal.

Tony saw George brushing the mules with a stiff brush—Jigger, Ocean, Seamus and King Edward, which he had staked out next to the canal boat on the shore. They were all Kentucky mules bought before the war when they were less than three years old. They had been trained to pull the canal boat by being hitched to logs and dragging them.

Tony stared at George for a moment and then took a deep breath.

"George, can I…can I ask you something?" Tony asked. He felt his face turning red and he couldn't bring himself to look George in the eyes.

George didn't stop his work. "I guess. Depends on what you ask."

"You know about men and women, don't you?"

George stopped and leaned across King George's back. "There's a lot to know about men and women. Some I know. Some I don't and some I doubt that I'll ever know."

Tony looked around nervously. "You know about what they do in…private."

George started to grin and then forced a neutral expression on his face. "You mean use the privy?"

Tony shook his head. "No, not that. I know about that. I mean what they do in the bedroom," Tony whispered.

"Sleep?" George asked with a barely suppressed grin.

"No, no, no." Tony paused and took a deep breath. "Other stuff they do in the bedroom …together."

"Aren't you a little young to be worried about that?" George asked.

"Thomas knows about it."

George snorted and moved around to the other side of Jigger and began brushing his flank. "Thomas knows about what animals do, but I'm not sure if he understands that it happens with people, too."

"He knows, but he doesn't understand it. That's why I'm talking to you."

George walked around from behind the mules. He turned a bucket over and sat down it. He grabbed one of Seamus' hoofs and laid it across his thighs so he could use his only hand and a hoof pick to clean dirt from the hoof.

"Why the interest?"

Tony shrugged. "I saw my mother—my real mother, not Mrs. Fitzgerald—in town today and started wondering about what she did for money. Then I started wondering if girls expected me to act like men act around my mother."

George shook his head. "Doubtful. Girls want to be courted, Tony. All that other stuff can come after you're married and it had better unless you want Mama to get after you. Also, don't let her hear you say she's not your real mother or she might get after you for that."

"Really?"

"She loves you, Tony. You're her son just like Thomas and me."

"I love her, too." He thought for a moment and then said, "You said all that other stuff could wait until I'm married. The men my mother sees aren't married to her."

"No, they're not, but you have to know the way your mother does things isn't right," George reminded him.

Tony nodded. "So you court a girl, marry her and then do the stuff in the bedroom. That's simple."

"If it was, I wouldn't be missing my arm." George held up his stump of a left arm and wiggled it.

"That happened in the war."

"It happened because I wanted to impress a girl so I ran off and joined the army," he said sharply.

He pointed his stump toward Tony and the young boy took a step back.

George had been wounded in Virginia and had his arm amputated on the battlefield. He'd been in the hospital for weeks before he recovered enough and the army discharged him because he could no longer handle a rifle.

"So was the girl impressed?"

George shrugged. "I don't know. I haven't seen her since I've come back. I haven't really wanted to. I stay in the family cabin whenever we go through the lock her father runs."

Tony chewed on his lower lip and stared at George. George let him work through his own thoughts.

"So what are you telling me? It doesn't sound like I should ever be able to understand a girl," Tony said finally.

George slapped his thigh with his good hand and stood up. "Yep. That about sums it up."

7

LABOR TROUBLES

FEBRUARY 1864

The Lewis Boatworks warehouse was filled with people, though they were not building a boat or there to see one launch into the canal. Besides canallers, a good number of coal miners stood clustered in groups inside the empty warehouse. The group was large enough to need all of the space to meet in. Amos had offered his warehouse because he was interested in canal business as both a boat owner and builder.

A dozen Union soldiers stood at the edges of the crowd along the two sides of the warehouse that opened. They weren't there to participate in the meeting, but to watch for any signs of Confederate plotting. Large meetings gave Confederate sympathizers a legitimate reason to get together and talk in small clusters apart from the main meeting. Also, if the talk of canal business got political, the soldiers would certainly end the meeting and maybe even arrest anyone they believed to be a Confederate sympathizer. Gen. David Hunter kept a tight rein on the town. The canallers and miners tried to ignore the soldiers but would steal glances at them from time to time. The soldiers' silent message to the group was obvious.

Despite the warehouse doors being open, the number of people close to each other inside kept the air warm. Alice also thought that it also kept the air pungent. Too many of the men were reluctant to bathe in the winter for fear of getting sick. Even though the coal miners were forced to bathe to keep from turning into human piles of coal dust, they only washed long enough to get the coal dust off their bodies whether or not they were fully clean.

John Harvey, another canal boat builder who had a smaller warehouse along the basin, had called for the meeting and Amos had offered his warehouse as a meeting place because it was currently open. About one hundred men and a few women, of which Alice was one, had turned out to talk about the drayage rates. Harvey stood on the race plank of a boat that wasn't yet finished so he could be seen above the crowd.

"How many of you made a profit last year?" Harvey asked. "Let's see a show of hands."

Less than a quarter of the canallers raised their hands. Alice wasn't surprised to see so few hands. She had raised her hand, but she knew it was only because she didn't have to pay hands. Other expenses like clothing, gear and tolls could be delayed, but the crew on a canal boat needed to eat whether or not the boat was moving.

"The war is causing stoppages of canal traffic nearly every month. It's hard enough to make a living on the canal when it is open." There were murmurs of agreement from the crowd. "Yet, the demand for coal is higher now than it had been in a long time. We should be getting more money for our hard work. If nothing less, we deserve it because it is now so dangerous to boat on the canal."

Harvey then began shouting out prices for items that the canallers had to pay for: food, clothing, tolls and housing. Prices for just about everything were rising because of the war, but not the wages of the canallers and miners. Amos and David had talked about it at length. Amos was able to explain it easily. Once the war started, men who had been farming and creating other goods were drafted into the army. This decreased the supply of goods and foodstuffs. Meanwhile those men were still consuming goods at an alarming rate. In order to feed and supply their armies, governments were spending money easily in order to secure the huge amounts of items that an army consumed. Then because a war was going on, the armies also damaged enemy rail lines, burned warehouses and fields. The combination of diminishing supply and increasing needs drove up the prices quickly.

It was easy to see that what was being paid to the workers wasn't enough to make ends meet. Harvey was using it as a way to work up the canallers into a fit of anger and excitement.

Even when the canallers could haul coal, the canal was shutting down more and more frequently because of damage done to it by Confederate forces. No coal haul meant no payment. The Canal Company had decreased the tolls on the canal to one-quarter of a cent per ton per mile. This meant that it cost canallers forty-six cents a ton to transport coal from Cumberland to Georgetown.

Now there was talk that the tolls would begin climbing again next month when the canal was expected to open.

The owners of the Cumberland Coal and Iron Company had been approached about increasing drayage rates, but not surprisingly, they had said no. Their reason was that if they increased rates for miners and canallers, the cost of the coal would increase to the point where it would be too expensive to purchase. No one would be willing to buy it, which would mean that the company would have to let miners and canallers go.

As the owner of a canal boat, Alice attended the meeting, though she was at a loss for just what to do. She certainly could use the additional income that a freight increase would bring, but the Canal Company would have to keep the canal in good repair for it to mean anything. She saw that as the more critical issue right now. And with attacks on the canal, which increased the cost of repairs and maintenance, the company was unlikely to lower tolls.

"Washington is in the middle of fighting a war. They aren't going to worry about coal prices," Jack Taney, one of the men representing the miners said. "They are just going to want to be warm next winter and keep the navy ships running."

"Maybe, but they could also get coal from Pennsylvania," one captain shouted.

"If they think their ships won't be able to patrol the Potomac and keep the Confederate Navy to the south, the government officials will panic like they did at the start of the war," someone else added.

That all sounded good, but the last time the government panicked, it had started confiscating canal boats and sinking them south of Washington to create a barrier to the Confederate navy. The *Freeman* had been one of the boats confiscated. Alice and Hugh had been lucky, though. Their friend Eli Sampson was a congressman and he had ordered their boat released. Some of the other canallers hadn't been so lucky. Some boats had been sunk in the Chesapeake Bay to create a barrier to the Confederate Navy and other boats were used for floating bridges to allow troops to cross the James River. Something like that couldn't be allowed to happen again.

Right now though, it was more important to find a way to keep the canal open for the entire season. The canallers could make more money by getting paid more per ton, hauling more coal, cutting expenses, or making more runs along the canal. The canal boats already hauled between ninety and 120 tons on their runs. That was as much as they could carry and most canallers were already just barely getting by. So if a rate increase couldn't be gained, then they were going to have to make more runs during the season.

Alice's financial situation wouldn't be as bad as it was right now if she had been able to make more runs during last year's boating season. What the canallers needed was an early spring, late winter and peace on the canal with raiding parties. She could earn enough from the current freight charges if that could happen.

That didn't seem too likely. The newspapers were saying that Gen. Thomas Rosser was causing havoc in Patterson Valley further south in West Virginia. That havoc could easily move north and start causing problems on the canal. This in addition to the fact that the canallers still had to worry about Confederate rangers causing problems.

"Even if they do increase the freight rate, how are we going to get them the coal?" George McHenry called. He was a canal boat captain of the *Pearl Moon*. "I'm having trouble finding hands to help me run my boat. So many men are in the army now and the ones who are coming back are in no shape to work on the canal."

Some of the other captains shouted their agreement, but the comment made Alice think about George going off to fight and how he had come back without an arm.

Alice hadn't considered the need for hands being a problem. She had George and the boys to help her, but some of the canal boats weren't run as family operations. They had to hire hands and most able-bodied men were fighting in the war.

Alice was thinking about leaving the meeting since it was obvious that a decision wouldn't be made tonight until she saw David standing at the rear of the room. He was leaning against the back wall with his arms folded across his chest. Since he wasn't a canal boat captain, he didn't have anything to add to the meeting.

So why was he here?

Hadn't he said something about living here when she had seen him in town the other day?

And what had he been doing with that woman? The meeting between the two of them had seemed innocent enough, but that woman had a look in her eyes that said she was marking David as hers. Had David started courting her?

Not that it was any business of hers. David didn't work for her anymore or live on the *Freeman*. He was no longer a part of her life. He had wanted to leave. It had been his decision, not hers.

She watched David so intently that she didn't realize James Sykes, another canal boat captain, had said something to her.

"I'm sorry," Alice said when Sykes moved in front of her and cut off her view of David. "I didn't hear what you were saying in all this din."

Sykes smiled. He was missing two of his teeth. "I asked, 'What do you think about all of this?'"

"I didn't make enough money last season to refuse the work if I can get it this season," Alice said. "I can't keep doing other people's laundry to pay my bills."

Sykes nodded. "Me, too, but it's getting to the point where I could make more money as a farmer. My brother runs the family farm in Boonsboro now, but I've been thinking about helping him out and selling my boat."

Sykes shifted to the right. When he did, Alice saw that David was gone. Despite herself, she started looking around for him. Either he had gone into his room or he had left the building. He wasn't among the people who she saw.

Alice thought about trying to find him, but what would she say.

No, David was not part of her life anymore. He had found happiness somewhere else with someone else. So why did that make Alice so sad?

The miners and canallers had argued back and forth about what to do for three hours until and the meeting broke up with no decision being reached, though they had decided that they would meet again once everyone had time to digest the situation and possibly think of some solutions.

8

MOTHER AND SON

FEBRUARY 1864

Tony stood on the boardwalk along Wineow Street and leaned against the wall of Murphy Dry Goods. He stood on the side of the building out of the way of people walking along the street. He could catch snippets of conversation from the people who passed him, but he wasn't hearing anything too interesting. Men talked about the railroad conditions, the canal and the war. Tony wasn't there to listen in on people's conversations, at least not if they were as boring as what he was hearing.

From where he stood, he could watch the stairs that led down from his mother's room above the Shanty Town Saloon along the side of the building. He stood under the staircase so he couldn't easily be seen.

He whittled on a piece of wood to pass the time. His carving had started out as a bear standing on its hind legs until his knife had slipped and he had accidentally cut the legs off of the bear. Now he was working to turn it into a snake. He was almost finished, too, which was an indicator of how long he had been waiting.

He knew his mother was upstairs in her room. He had seen her pass in front of a window before he came into the alley. Why didn't she come outside? Was she afraid of the cold? That was a stupid thought. He had to stop coming up with these stupid ideas like standing here for hours watching his mother or rather his mother's room.

One thing was for sure. Tony's toes had gone numb waiting for her. At least the whittling kept his fingers from getting cold and stiff on him.

A few minutes later, Tony had finished the snake and made a decision. He put the carving in his pocket and folded up his knife. Then he quickly stepped out from under the staircase and walked up the stairs to his mother's room. He hurried so that he wouldn't lose his nerve. He knocked on the door at the top of the landing. Even after doing that, he felt like running away. Maybe it was a good thing his toes were numb. If he tried to run, he would probably trip and fall down the stairs.

His mother answered the door. It had been a year since Tony had been this close to her and she looked older than he remembered. The lines in her face were deeper and she looked worn out. Her blue eyes were as hard as he remembered, though. Her black hair was brushed out and still looked lustrous.

"You're a little young to be here, aren't you? What's the deal? Is your father sending you here to become a man?" his mother asked. She cocked a hip and leaned against the door frame. She might have thought it made her look inviting, but seeing her strike the pose made Tony feel a bit nauseous.

Tony just stood there staring at her. He was too shocked to say anything.

"What's the matter? Never seen a real woman before? If your pa gave you the money, I'll show you a lot more real woman." She ran her fingers along the neckline of her red dress and let it dip into the cleavage between her breasts.

Tony backed away a step. How could she not recognize him? He pulled his hat off so that she could see his hair and face clearer.

"I'm Tony," he said.

"Tony, well you can call me..." His mother stopped and leaned closer to him. Her seductive smile turned to a frown. "Aw, it's you. What do you want?"

What did he want? Why had he bothered to come here anyway?

"I want you to see me and who I've become," Tony said.

"What do I care about that?"

"Because I'm your son," Tony nearly shouted.

His mother grabbed him by the arm and pulled him into the room. It wasn't a light grab either. Her fingernails dug into his arm so hard that he could feel it through his coat and shirt. Once he was inside, his mother slammed the door shut. The room was smaller than many of the rooms they had stayed in when he had been with his mother. It probably indicated that she was not making a lot of money since Tony wasn't hiding under the bed and rifling through men's pants pockets. The room had few personal things in it. It was mainly just a bed, small chest of drawers with a lamp on it and a chair. Still, it was bigger than the captain's cabin aboard the *Freeman*.

He glanced unconsciously to the gap between the floor and the bed as if he expected to see himself there.

"Don't be yelling stuff like that around!" His mother snapped. "Do you think I want people knowing I have a kid? I don't want men thinking I'm old enough to have a brat your age."

"Don't worry about that. Not anymore. I call myself Tony Fitzgerald now."

His mother snorted. "I call myself a lot of different names, too, kid, but it doesn't change who I am." She paused and looked him up and down. "Though you have put on some weight and some inches, too. I didn't recognize you. That boat lady must feed you well."

Tony nodded. "I'm happy now. I thought you'd like to know."

"I could care less. Like you said, you're somebody else's brat now."

Not that he had used the word "brat." Mrs. Fitzgerald called him her son.

"I just wanted you to know that I'm all right," Tony said.

He turned and started for the door. His eyes burned with tears that he wouldn't allow himself to shed. He wouldn't give this woman the satisfaction of seeing him cry. He was going to storm out of the room, but he stopped before he opened the door. He turned around and stared her directly into her dark eyes.

"If you don't care about me, why did you have me? Why did you keep me with you?" Tony asked.

His mother—no, not his mother, Carol—snorted. "Do you think I wanted to have a kid? Not me. I thought your father would marry me if he saw that I was pregnant. He wasn't a rich man, but he owned his own store. He did pretty good for himself. I could have had a good life with him. I would have made a good wife." She stopped and Tony wondered if she was imagining a different life for herself. "He didn't want me or you either. Then I thought he would change his mind when he saw his kid, but I was wrong about that, too. He was a heartless bastard. So once I had you, no other man wanted anything to do with me. The good ones thought I was a whore and the bad ones didn't want a woman with a kid. And your father's family, well, they made sure I was run out of Hagerstown."

Tony tried to digest it all. He had just learned how he had come into being and that he had been born in Hagerstown. He had never considered his mother's motivations before or that he had a father somewhere.

"I'm sorry about that," was all he could manage to say.

His mother rolled her eyes. "Don't be. The happiest days of my life have been since you've been gone. So don't be thinking about coming back."

He looked around at the nearly bare room and somehow doubted that.

Tony opened the door and walked out. He certainly hadn't been thinking about coming back to his mother, but he also hadn't been thinking that he would feel sorry for her. He walked down Wineow Street to the canal basin and sat down under a tree. He bent forward and rested his head on his knees.

What was it about him that girls couldn't stand him for too long? First, he had to deal with Laura Anderson ignoring him at school as if she didn't know him and now his real mother didn't even care how he was doing.

The tears he had been holding back broke loose and rolled down his cheeks. He didn't try and stop them since nobody was around to see him crying.

Or so he thought.

"Tony?"

He looked up quickly and saw Mrs. Fitzgerald walking toward him. The cold wind fluttered the skirt on her gingham dress. He wiped his cheeks on his coat sleeve and stood up.

"What's wrong, Tony?" she asked, rushing over to him.

She reached a hand out and gently touched his cheek.

"Nothing, ma'am. I just didn't feel like going to school today," he lied.

Alice frowned. "We can talk about that another time. I'm asking about what made you cry."

He was ashamed to answer her. He didn't want her to think he wasn't grateful for everything she had done for him. He definitely didn't want her thinking that he did not love her. He had felt like he needed to see Carol, though, and let her know that he was doing well. He had thought she might be happy for him.

"Would it have anything to do with you seeing your mother?" Alice asked after a moment.

Tony looked up at her, but he was afraid to say anything. He felt the burning in his cheeks giving him away. How could she know about that? Was she going to be angry with him?

"You're not the only one who played hooky from school today. Thomas did, too, and he and I will also be having a conversation about that later. He followed you and saw you go into Shanty Town, which is one more conversation we'll have. He said he was getting bored standing around watching you 'act like a wooden Indian' and then you went up the stairs to your mother's room. That's when he came and got me."

Tony shook his head slightly. Leave it to Thomas to be curious enough to follow him.

"Don't be mad at him," Alice said. "You would have done that same thing. You two are mirror images of each other."

"I don't know why I went to see her, but ever since I saw her in town the other week, I've been thinking about her. Why did she treat me the way that she did for all that time? Did she ever love me? Was she proud of the person I'd become or at least happy that I was happy?" Tears were rolling down Tony's cheeks again. He didn't want to cry, but he couldn't help it.

Tony saw anger flash in Alice's green eyes, but it wasn't directed at him. He guessed that she was mad at his mother. Alice pulled Tony into a hug. He didn't resist her. It felt comforting and right. He hugged her back as she stroked the back of his head. He felt warm and safe…and loved.

After a few moments, Alice asked, "What did she say to you, Tony?"

"That she didn't love me. She only needed me to try and trick my father into marrying her, but it didn't work so she had no use for me."

Alice had no response for that. She just hugged Tony harder. Finally, he got control of his emotions and stepped back.

"Tony, don't you worry about what she said to you. You're not her son anymore. You're mine, and it was one of the happiest days of my life when Hugh brought you aboard. When he got killed and I didn't know where George was off fighting in the war, I still had you. You were there when I was feeling very alone."

"I love you, too, and the whole family. I'm happy here," Tony told her.

"That's good to know because we're keeping you with us," Alice said as she ruffled his hair.

Tony took a deep breath and smiled. Everything would be all right. He had a family and they loved him.

"Tony, you know that your mother is not my favorite person in the world, but I do think she loves you in her own way," Alice said.

Tony wiped his eyes dry again. "She said that she didn't."

"If that was true, then why didn't she leave you at an orphanage? There are women who many would call better women than your mother and they left their children in an orphanage when their husbands were killed in the war. Your mother kept you. She fed you and clothed you. I can't agree with how she used you before you ran away, but when you were a baby, she took responsibility for you without expecting anything in return."

Tony's brow furrowed. "Are you saying my mother is a good person? That doesn't make any sense."

"I'm not saying she's a good person in the sense of what she does for work or in being a mother. I am saying, though, that in her own way, maybe the only way she knew how, she loves you."

Tony couldn't get his hands around that idea. How could his mother love him and still treat him like she did? It made some sort of sense to Mrs. Fitzgerald, though. Maybe it was an adult thing like what his mother did with men in her bedroom.

"Thank you for coming to get me, but I think I still need to be alone for a while. I've got a lot to think about," Tony said.

Alice put her hand on his shoulder. "Are you sure? I can send Thomas over if it's just me you don't want to be around."

Tony shook his head and smiled weakly. "No, I just need to walk around and think. It's actually one of the things I like about working on the canal. When I'm driving the mules and walking on the towpath, I get a lot of thinking done."

"Don't be out too long. You, Thomas and I still need to have those other conversations about what going to school means," Alice said with a smile.

Tony watched Mrs. Fitzgerald walk away and then he headed back into Shanty Town. He knew that Mrs. Fitzgerald didn't like him being here, but he had grown up here. He felt familiar skulking around the twenty-five saloons and stores that ranged from the B&O Railroad overpass to Footer Dye Works.

He found a couple of boys in an alley and pitched pennies with them for a while. The winner who could bounce his penny off the wall and have it land closest to the wall took all of the pennies. Once he was a few pennies ahead, he quit the game. He walked down Wineow Street and stopped in the Arnold General Store and bought himself a somewhat withered-looking apple. It tasted fine, though.

"Tony!"

Tony heard the shout and spun around. Thomas was running up the street toward him.

"What are you doing here?" Tony asked.

"Mama told me you were here."

"And did she say that you could come get me?"

Thomas nodded curtly. "Yup."

Tony doubted that. "She said that you are already in trouble for ditching school. Do you want to get in trouble for lying, too?"

"I'm not lying. Mama told me that the ice on the river was thick enough for skating and I should find you and we could go sliding across the ice on the river."

Tony stared at his brother, trying to decide if the younger boy was telling the truth or not. "If you get me in trouble, Thomas, I'll cut a hole in the ice and dump you in the river."

Thomas grinned. "I may get you in trouble, but it won't be for lying."

Tony nodded. "Just a normal day then."

Thomas laughed and the two of them headed for the river.

9

FOR THE CAUSE

FEBRUARY 1864

Elizabeth had finished washing the massive pile of laundry at the hospital on 20th Street thirty minutes ago, but her hands still looked like prunes. The wash basins had been filled with hot water mixed with lye. Her skin was red from being in the water scrubbing uniforms and sheets, trying to get bloodstains out of them.

She clasped them together at her waist in front of her as she made her rounds among the recovering patients. She wasn't sure why she wanted to hide her red hands from the soldiers when they lay injured before her with seeping wounds and missing limbs that were sometimes exposed to her view. The hospital was currently full. Every one of the 102 beds and cots available was taken up by a soldier who was recovering. Many of them teased her about trying to hide her hands.

"Be nice to me," Elizabeth would tell them. "Or I may drop a few ants in your bed tonight."

Elizabeth was no longer the same person she had been when she first started working at the hospital. These men had seen enough misery. They didn't need to see more. And truth be told, the more she worked to help the wounded soldiers get better, the less she thought about her own troubles. When she did think about them, Elizabeth realized that having a broken heart was nothing compared to having a lost limb or disfiguring battle scars.

She stopped at the bed of Wilbur Layne, the young soldier who wouldn't speak when he was brought in with leg wounds a couple weeks ago. He still wouldn't talk to anyone, but at least he was more responsive to people around him.

Elizabeth sat down next to the young soldier's bed. He looked at her with wide, blue eyes. Elizabeth patted his hand. He had been bathed. One of the other nurses had done it, not her. With all of the dirt and grime removed, Wilbur looked too young to be a soldier, but then so many of the soldiers did.

"How are you feeling this morning, Wilbur? You look good," she said. Of course, he didn't say anything, but one of these days he would. She was sure of it.

"The cook is making beef stew for supper. He says it's an old family recipe, but I doubt that his mother ever cooked for a hundred soldiers before."

Wilbur stared at her without saying anything.

"If you want to hear him speak, you need to come at night," the corporal in the next bed said.

He was a brown-haired man with a growing beard that made him look older than his mid-twenties, or maybe, it was war that made him look older. He had a seeping wound in his side from shrapnel from a canister shot.

Elizabeth turned to look at him. "He speaks at night?"

The corporal nodded. "He yells."

Elizabeth glanced at Wilbur and then turned to face the other soldier. "What does he say?" she asked.

The soldier shrugged. "It sounds like he saw some pretty scary things on the battlefield. Not that we all didn't, mind you, but from the way he screams in his sleep…well, it's worse than anyone else's nightmares here."

Anyone else's nightmares.

Elizabeth looked around. Some of the men were sleeping. Some were sitting up in their beds and talking to other patients. All of them were waiting to return home or to their units. How many of these soldiers were haunted when they closed their eyes? How many of them would always be?

Elizabeth decided she would have to ask the night nurse about Wilbur's nightmares and whoever else was troubled. She wasn't sure what she could do to help them, but she would have to try. She could do no less than the nurses who had helped George through his fever when he had been wounded. They had worked in a hospital like this and they had cared for her brother. They had saved him and she would save these boys if she could.

She turned back to Wilbur. She smiled and said, "Well, at least I know you can talk. Now we just have to find a way for you to do it more quietly."

Elizabeth patted his hand again as she stood up. She had other patients to visit before supper. That would keep her too busy serving and cleaning up after hungry men to do much else.

When she stood up, Elizabeth noticed a short, stout woman enter the hospital. She was carrying a large basket on her arm and a servant was carrying another one. Elizabeth had seen Mary Todd Lincoln in this hospital twice before coming to visit the wounded. Once she came with friends and the second time she had come with one of her sons, but this time, she was alone except for the servant who was helping her.

Mary Todd Lincoln was a short, slightly chubby woman. Her round face seemed to wear a perpetual frown except when she visited with soldiers.

Elizabeth walked up to her and said, "Good morning, Mrs. Lincoln."

"Good morning, dear. I just brought some treats for the soldiers. Are there any of them who can't have any of these things?" the President's wife asked.

Elizabeth looked in the basket and saw lots of fruit and even sweet rolls and rock candy. Mrs. Lincoln certainly loved to pamper the soldiers, though sometimes her treats could be too rich for soldiers who had lived month on army rations.

"Mrs. Lincoln, if you spoil them with all that, these soldiers will leave here twenty pounds heavier," Elizabeth said.

Mary Todd Lincoln gave her a slight smile. "At least they would leave here."

Elizabeth couldn't argue with that. "I'll let you get started then."

Elizabeth continued making her own rounds as the First Lady

started hers. Elizabeth found the woman somewhat quiet, but not the monster many newspapers seemed to make of her.

She'd been criticized for replacing the shabby furniture in the White House and called a Confederate spy because of her Southern relatives. Yet, rarely, if ever, did Elizabeth read about the First Lady's visits to hospitals to help with the wounded.

Elizabeth watched as the woman handed a soldier a flower and sat down next to the bed to write a letter that the man wanted to dictate to her. His hands were bandaged so he couldn't do it himself. They had been burned when he tried to grab his rifle from inside a burning tent.

The flowers were a nice addition to the hospital. Not only did the color help brighten up the building, but the fragrance helped disguise the less-pleasant smells of waste and decaying flesh. During the winter when there were no flowers and the windows were kept closed, the smell in the hospital could be overpowering. Luckily, the armies didn't fight as much in the winter so there weren't so many casualties.

Mrs. Lincoln continued her work through supper, helping feed the soldiers who couldn't feed themselves. Elizabeth went into the basement to help wash the supper dishes and when she came back upstairs to begin administering the afternoon medications, Mrs. Lincoln was still making her way around the ward. She didn't rush through her rounds and she gave each soldier who she sat with her full attention.

Mrs. Lincoln wasn't ready to leave for three hours. When Elizabeth saw her walking toward the front door, she walked over to the First Lady and said, "Thank you for what you do with the soldiers. We nurses can't spend as much time with them as we would like and I know they appreciate your visits."

"It is very little that I do to repay their sacrifices," Mrs. Lincoln said.

"It's not a little thing. Keeping a soldier in good spirits helps them mend and get well enough to return home," Elizabeth said.

"Then I am glad that I am able to help," Mrs. Lincoln said with a smile. "I haven't always been able to do that."

"Is that because of your son?"

Mrs. Lincoln's breath caught, her face paled and she closed her eyes. One of the Lincolns' sons, Willie, had died two years earlier and it was said that grief nearly killed Mary Todd Lincoln as well.

Elizabeth immediately regretted her comment when she saw the wave of grief sweep across the older woman's face. All her pain was on display in her expression.

Elizabeth put her hand on the older woman's arm. "I'm sorry, Mrs. Lincoln," Elizabeth said. "That was insensitive of me."

The First Lady took a deep breath and wiped away a tear.

"No harm was intended. It is just that Willie is a sensitive subject for me. I suspect that he will always be a wound from which I will never heal. It will be much the same for the mothers of these boys who don't return from the war."

"I can understand a little," Elizabeth said. "My father and a very special young man I knew were killed."

"In this horrid war?"

"The young man was. He was killed while serving to defend the Alexandria Aqueduct." The aqueduct allowed canal boats to cross over the Potomac River to Alexandria, but it had been drained and barricaded at the beginning of the war. "My father was killed trying to help my older brother out of trouble."

Mrs. Lincoln reached out and took Elizabeth's hand in hers. "It sounds like they were both honorable men for you to miss them so. Men I'm sure you have many good memories of."

"They were. I loved them both. It's part of the reason I have come to enjoy my work here in the hospital. If I can help someone else not have to go through what I did or what my family went through when they heard of the deaths, then I know I've done something to be worthy of their own sacrifice."

Now it was Mrs. Lincoln's turn to nod. "Yes, you do understand something of what I'm going through. I'm sorry, child."

"Why do you say that?"

"Because you are a young woman. You should be worried about courting not caring for a room full of wounded soldiers, many of whom will die. You should have had a chance to enjoy life before being weighed down by all of these concerns."

"I'll be happy again someday," Elizabeth said finally.

"Hopefully we all will."

Mrs. Lincoln turned and walked out of the hospital. Elizabeth watched her go and then turned back to her work.

10

WINTER WORK

FEBRUARY 1864

Michael Armentrout stood up from the wooden stool and reached his hands high over his head to stretch the kinks out his back. It made him feel like an old man, though he was not yet twenty. He had been hunched over the desk working on the books of a mill that was located on the Potomac River about a quarter mile outside of Williamsport.

"Sore?" Karl Schmidt asked his voice thick with a German accent. He still had it after more than a dozen years of living in America. He was a short man with a thick, gray beard, but his booming voice sounded as if it belonged with a much longer man.

Michael nodded. "This used to be second nature for me, but after a season of working on the canal, I can't stand to be still for this long. It will take some getting used to."

Michael had found this job a few days after the canal season had ended with the draining of the canal. He made more money doing bookkeeping than he had working as a hand on a canal boat. He was even beginning to save some money.

The problem was he didn't like being a bookkeeper. He found that he didn't like staying indoors any longer. It felt too much like being in college. He had been attending Johns Hopkins to study to be a doctor like his father. Not anymore.

He was used to walking the towpath and being outside where he could feel the sun on his back. He didn't even mind walking in the rain and feeling the mud on the towpath squish between his toes. Like many mule walkers, he had learned to walk the towpath barefoot in order to save the wear and tear on his shoes.

"You do good work, Michael. Your body will get used to it soon enough," Karl said.

Karl was the one who had hired Michael to help him with his work. He also gave Michael a room to stay in at his house. Michael appreciated the kindness and certainly didn't want to disappoint his boss.

But he missed the canal and Elizabeth. He had expected to miss Elizabeth. In a way, she was the reason that he had taken a job on the canal. Missing the canal, though, that surprised him. He felt comfortable with the people on the canal. For the most part, they were honest and open. Certainly they were more honest and open than his parents. His mother was always posturing to play her role in Cumberland society and his father had his own secrets that he tried to hide, though Michael had figured some of them out.

Michael was surprised that he missed his parents and thought about them often. He wasn't sure why that was, which was sad in its own right, but he wondered if it was because of the way he had left. He had simply packed his bag and left without saying goodbye or even leaving a note. He had run away like a little boy.

He sat back down at his desk, dipped his pen in the inkwell and started writing again. He had another hour of work before calling it a day. He usually rode home with Karl in his wagon to eat dinner with the Schmidts. Today was payday, though. Michael would walk to the bank and deposit half of his wages and use the other half to live on for the next week.

About fifteen minutes before five o'clock, Karl laid a small stack of bills on the corner of Michael's desk. Michael looked at the money and then at Karl.

"I've got a bit more to do," Michael said.

"It can wait. Go, get to the bank," Karl said. "You can finish that tomorrow."

Michael nodded. He wasn't going to argue about getting off from work early. He straightened up his books on his desk, scooped up his money and headed for the door.

"Don't wait up for me, Karl. I thought I'd eat dinner in town and catch up on canal news," Michael said over his shoulder.

Karl patted him on the shoulder. "Then I will see you at home."

Michael shrugged on his coat as he headed out of the door. On the street, he walked fast down the road so that he could get into town and make it to the bank before it closed for the day. He got there with five minutes to spare and put half of his pay into his account. By the time the canal reopened, he should have a tidy sum accumulated.

Managing his money was something he had had to learn to do quickly. It wasn't something he had worried about in Cumberland and Baltimore because his father had always been willing to give him money. That wasn't the case now. Very few people were willing to give him money and those who did didn't pay him a lot and expected his hard work in exchange. He didn't mind the work, but he sure did miss the money.

He folded up the rest of his money and shoved the bills into his pocket. Then he headed south along Commerce Street toward the canal basin. Williamsport's Cushwa Basin was much smaller than Cumberland's canal basin, but it only serviced the Cushwa Coal and Brick Warehouse. Most of the boat captains preferred to make full runs along the canal, which meant going to Cumberland. Cumberland's basin serviced not only the Consolidated Coal Company but a number of warehouses that shipped grain and manufactured canal boats. After all, if you had to be tied up with delays offloading in Georgetown, you might as well get full pay for your load.

Michael stopped at the edge of the drained basin. He saw two boats sitting on the clay bed and another half dozen or so along the canal itself. The ground inside the canal prism had been soft and muddy for a few days after the canal had been drained. It was frozen hard now and any puddles of water that had been left were blocks of ice.

Plenty of canallers wintered in Williamsport. It was less crowded than Cumberland and easy to pick up a load of coal at Cushwa's at the beginning of the season and make a short run to Washington and be on the way back to Cumberland by the time most of the other canal boats were still making their way down the canal.

However, Michael had chosen to winter in Williamsport so he wouldn't risk running into his mother or father walking on the street or shopping in a store.

He found the nearest saloon, which was called The Basin Stop, on Potomac Street. As he walked inside, he was enveloped by a fog of cigarette smoke. He blinked and coughed and headed for the bar where he ordered a beer. When the bartender passed him his mug, Michael turned to look over the saloon while he sipped his drink.

The other customers were a mix of canallers and working men from Williamsport. This wasn't a railroading bar. Any railroaders in Williamsport frequented a bar closer to the tracks. Michael watched the canallers to see which ones were deferred to. Those would be the boat captains and the ones who would be looking for hands when the season started.

Michael watched a man sitting at a table with two other men. The other men talked while the third man ate his dinner. However, whenever the third man spoke, the other two listened closely. The men were neatly dressed, which probably meant that the captain also kept a neat boat. Since the man who Michael guessed was the captain was eating at a saloon rather than on his boat or at his house with a family, Michael also guessed the captain wasn't running a family canal boat operation.

Michael finished his drink, set the mug on the bar and walked over to the table.

"Excuse me," he said, stopping at the side of the table opposite the captain.

The men stopped talking and looked up. The captain was in his mid-forties and had a full beard that covered half of his face.

"My name is Michael Armentrout. I'm looking for work on the canal when it opens up, which is likely to be soon."

The captain stared at him and said, "You don't look like a canawler."

"I worked on it some at the end of last season for Captain Howell. I'd like to work on it again when the canal reopens."

"Why don't you work for him again?"

"I don't know where his boat is. I wasn't with him on his last run and I don't want to wait around day and night looking for his boat to come by only to find out he's hired all the hands he needs," Michael explained.

"Look at you, son. You're too good to be a canawler. You look like a towner," the captain said.

"Begging your pardon, sir, but if I like the work and I work hard to do it well, who's to say whether I'm too good to work on the canal?"

The captain chuckled. "You don't even sound like a canawler." He reached across the table and turned Michael's hands over. "Well, you've got some callouses on them so you're not afraid of hard work."

"I got those from running snubbing lines."

The captain slowly shook his head. "You've got the desire, I give you that, son, but you don't have the spirit for this work. It's not in your blood. You weren't born for this work. You've got a good education. I can tell by the way you speak. You can do so much better than this."

"But this is what I want to do."

"Why would you want to is the question," the captain said. "You're probably making at least twice as much doing whatever work you're doing as I am canalling. Hell, son, I wish I could switch places with you and I don't know what you're doing for work."

"I'm just a bookkeeper."

The captain nodded. "A bookkeeper who wants to be a canawler. You were warm this winter, weren't you?" Michael nodded. "And you made yourself some money, right?" Michael nodded again. "Then why would you want to work on the canal in the cold and rain for less money?"

"What you say makes sense, Captain. My father would certainly agree with you, but …well, I started out on the canal just because I wanted to get away from Cumberland. I found that I liked it, though. I spent most of my life indoors and I like being outside. I like talking to the people and the long stretches of quiet in between when you don't see any people. I like having the time to think and to look at the things around me. I like the gentle motion of the canal boat when it's moving and the nuzzling of a mule when it's happy to see you. I just need to be there now. Maybe in a few years I'll want to go back to being a bookkeeper or something else, but for now, I want to drive mules on the towpath."

The captain looked at Michael and scratched his beard. Then he held out his hand to shake Michael's.

"Well, I guess I can always fire you if you don't work out, but you're lucky hands are hard to come by during this war."

"Thank you."

"My name Elijah Harrison. My boat is the *Hannah True*. I can have it ready for the season fine, but I expect you to be aboard when they start flooding the canal. If you're not there when I'm ready to leave, I won't wait."

Michael smiled. "Yes, sir."

11

IDLE BOATS

MARCH 1864

David stood outside of the Lewis Boatworks and stared at the canal boats floating in the Cumberland Basin. The canal had finished filling with water from the Potomac River more than a week ago and the boats were sitting high in the water ready to be filled with coal and head down to Washington for the first trip of the new season. The basin was essentially a small lake with inlet locks to the canal and Potomac River.

While most of the boats took on their loads in the basin, some of them could get coal across the river in Ridgeley, West Virginia. The boats hadn't used the wharf in Ridgeley since the war had started, though.

Of course, none of the boats in the basin were moving either.

What should have been a busy morning with boat captains jockeying for a position in line to fill their holds with coal was still. David heard no men shouting at each other as they worked or clanking of coal cars as they were pulled into position over canal boats. He saw no clouds of coal dust in the air or scurry of activity on the canal boats. In many cases, the captains and crews were still sleeping. Other men were sitting on hatch covers of their boats, smoking and reading newspapers.

Nine days of travel had been lost already. Many of these boats could have traveled to Georgetown, unloaded their holds and be nearly back to Cumberland. The canallers had started out defiant in their strike for higher wages, but now they were starting to get antsy. Every day they sat idle in Cumberland was another day of work lost and wages that needed to be paid, mules fed and wharf fees paid with nothing to show for it.

The Canal Company had raised the canal tolls to 5/16 of a cent per ton per mile which increased the cost of doing business for canallers. The company's justification that although it was an increase in the toll, the previous 3/4 cent toll had only been lowered last November. With so little time at the lower toll rate, a canaller's expenses were essentially the same as they had been last year.

The reasons didn't ring true with the canal boat owners who were struggling to make ends meet. They had reacted by striking. No coal was moving along the canal.

David knew Amos didn't like the increased toll, but they had run the numbers on how much business was being lost because of boats sitting idle. Any benefit to be derived from having a lower toll or increased drayage rate would soon be lost if the strike didn't end.

David turned away from the basin and saw Ruth Abercrombie walking toward him. He had run into her a few times in town over the past weeks and spent more and more time speaking with her. He was beginning to wonder if she was going into town looking for him. David certainly found himself going into town to walk around more often than he needed to do. Ruth seemed to understand the isolation that he felt being a Southerner in a Union city and he certainly understood the similar way she felt.

"What are you doing down here?" David asked with a smile.

"I'm looking for you, of course. You said you worked and lived at this warehouse so I figured I could find you here."

He no longer had to wonder if their meetings were accidental. Not that he minded either way. Ruth was definitely interested in him, but he wasn't sure why. She didn't seem to be romantically attracted to him. David suspected her interest was just because she felt that she could talk more freely around him since he was a Southerner.

"Well, now you've found me. What can I do for you?"

"I've been talking to some friends about you and they'd like to meet you," Ruth said coyly. She apparently valued her friends' opinions of him more than her parents' opinions.

"And what have you been saying about me?'

"I've told them about the kind of person you are. How you helped me in town. Your opinions on different issues like politics. Things like that."

David stared at her for a few moments, trying to read if there was more behind her words. Her interest in him was because he was a Southerner.

"And why would they want to meet me?" he asked.

Ruth gave a quick laugh and put a hand on his arm. "Don't be so nervous. It's not like I'm introducing you to my family. These are just some friends of mine, people I've known for most of my life. I thought that if you're going to be staying in Cumberland, I'd introduce you to some people. Maybe you'll make friends."

Something about this was making David uncomfortable. Maybe it was because it seemed to be taking his relationship with Ruth to a new level or maybe it was because he didn't like the idea of knowing that people around town were having conversations about him. He didn't want people talking and asking questions about him. They might find out how he had come to be here in Cumberland and David doubted that the Union Army soldiers in town would like that answer.

"Is there some time you were thinking about having them meet me?" David asked.

He hoped that it would be a time when he was working. He didn't want a lot of people knowing that he was from the South. Eventually, it would catch the attention of the army.

"Not yet. I thought I'd ask you about it first and see what you wanted to do," Ruth told him.

"I'm not really the social type."

"I can tell that. That's why I figured I would need to be the one to drag you around to meet people and make some new friends. You can't spend all your time in this warehouse or wandering the streets of Cumberland."

David hesitated. How much could he resist without raising suspicions that he was trying to hide something?

"You're scheming something," David said lightly.

Ruth batted her eyes at him. "Why, Mr. Windover. I have no idea what you're talking about."

David rolled his eyes. "Fine, plan your little get-together, but once this canal strike ends, I'll be busy for a few days helping Amos get his boats moving down the canal."

Ruth smiled and gave him a quick hug. David stiffened, thinking it was a bit forward of her. He wondered if agreeing to meet her friends meant more to her than it did to him.

"You won't regret this, David," she said.

He hoped that it was true, but he was afraid it wouldn't be.

Ruth turned and hurried away back toward town. David watched her leave, shaking his head. He hoped that he wasn't getting himself into trouble.

That evening it was announced that the C&O Canal Company agreed to increase the freight rate to the canallers slightly. It wouldn't help much, but it would help. It was also enough to get the boats moving the following day as 120 tons of coal was dumped into the holds of each canal boat before it was sent down the canal toward Georgetown.

David retired to his room that evening. He hadn't done much to it in the time he'd been there. He'd thrown together a makeshift bed and pulled in a desk and chair from another area of the warehouse. It wasn't fancy, but it was more room than he'd had on the *Freeman*.

The workers and Amos had left for the day so David found himself alone as night fell. It was kind of unnerving to him even after weeks of staying in the warehouse at night. He was too used to tight spaces with the Fitzgeralds. Now he was the only person in a space that was larger than a canal boat.

He lit the lamp on his desk and pulled out a sheet of paper. He wanted to write a letter to his father and explain to him in a way that would convince him that David was still loyal to the family if not to the Confederacy. His father had already rejected him once when David had written him. What good would another letter do? He wasn't even sure his father would read it. The man could be stubborn at times. David guessed that his father was also the source of the same quality within himself.

David dipped his pen in the inkwell and wrote out, "Dear Father,". He was completely at a loss for what to write next. He and his father had never been particularly close and now he was going to have to find a way to express emotions in a letter that he could never do in person.

David wadded up the letter and threw it across the room. It wasn't going to happen. If he was going to mend fences with his father, he was going to have to visit him. Perhaps when he had saved up enough money, he would take time off from work and travel to his family's plantation.

How would his family react to that? His father might very well have him arrested and shot for desertion if the war was still going on when they met again.

Despite that, David thought that it was a good idea. He missed his family home. He missed gathering around the dining room at night to each supper with his parents, brother and three sisters. He missed the way the hills rose smoothly across the land unlike the way the mountains of Western Maryland shot up quickly and dropped just as quickly.

He'd been able to fight his homesickness when he was working for the Fitzgeralds, but now that feeling was returning. He was alone too much. He had too much time to think. He wanted to get away from Alice and the canal so why not go to home? Maybe that was where he belonged.

David stood up and went outside his room to the main warehouse. His lantern didn't cast enough light to show the entire warehouse. They were between projects right now so the room was open except for some tools laying out. Sounds tended to echo in the emptiness and the darkness made the warehouse space seem even larger. He walked around the edges of the room to the door that led outside.

He stepped outside in cool night air and leaned back against the building. Funny how he didn't feel as uneasy and alone outside the building as he did inside.

Maybe Ruth was right. Maybe he did need to meet some new people and make some new friends. They would provide him with company and conversation. He wouldn't feel so alone anymore.

"David?"

David jumped up and turned. Alice was standing at the corner of the building. She had a shawl wrapped around her shoulders to stay warm in the cool night. His heart raced faster at the sight of her.

"Alice, what are you doing here?"

"We're going to be leaving tomorrow with any luck and it will be at least a week, probably more, before we get back," Alice said. It hadn't really answered his questions but he didn't want to ask again.

"Have a good journey. I hope you beat the rush to Georgetown."

Alice nodded and moved closer. "We could still use a hand, David."

"You don't need help. You've got the boys."

Alice frowned and looked away. "I just don't understand."

David steeled himself for tears. "Understand what?" he asked.

"What happened? Why did you leave us? Was it something one of us did?" she nearly pleaded.

This was not a conversation that David wanted to have. It seemed like the women he knew were bound and determined to make him talk about what he didn't want to talk about.

"It's late, Alice. You had better get back to the *Freeman* so you can get an early start," David said. He turned to go back inside.

"So you can just walk away and leave us like that."

David stopped and took a deep breath. "It didn't just happen. We both know it wasn't right for me to be on that boat with you. People got the wrong idea."

"I don't care what other people think," Alice said forcefully.

"Well, I do!" he said more sharply than he intended.

Alice stepped back. He'd startled her, but he hadn't scared her.

"I'm sorry. I didn't realize that you felt that way. I never worried about it because I always considered us family."

David leaned his head against the door. "I thought we could have been."

"What's that mean?"

He straightened up. "Nothing. Good night, Alice."

He opened the door and was preparing to step inside when Alice said suddenly, "Are you in love with Ruth Abercrombie?"

"Why do you ask that?"

Alice refused to look at him. "There's talk around the canal. I thought you worried about what people think."

He was tempted simply to say that he was in love with Ruth. It would end the conversation quickly and he wouldn't have to feel so uncomfortable. It would also be a lie and one that Alice would probably recognize. He liked Ruth, but he barely knew her. He certainly couldn't say that he loved her.

"No, I'm not in love with her. I'm still recovering from the last time I was in love," David said.

"That was years ago, David. You should be over her by now. It's all right to let yourself love again."

David shook his head. How could she not know or was it that she just didn't want to acknowledge that he loved her because that would make it real.

"Is that how you feel about, Hugh? Is it all right for you to love again?" David asked.

She frowned. "That's different. Hugh and I were married."

"Of course." He started through the door, but Alice followed him inside the warehouse.

"What is bothering you, David? You're so careful to choose your words like you're afraid to say something or you're holding back a yell. It's like Thomas acts when he's done something wrong, but you haven't done anything wrong."

"Maybe I have, though I didn't mean to."

"What?"

Alice reached out to lay a hand on his arm, but David stepped back out of her reach. She lowered her hand.

"I am afraid to say," David told her.

"Why?"

"Because…because I'm afraid to hear the answer."

Alice put a hand on his arm. "Whatever it is, it's eating you up inside, David. It took you away from us."

He shook his head. "Goodnight, Alice."

She searched his eyes for a few moments and then finally turned and left. David watched her leave, afraid to move. He felt as if he might collapse if he took a step toward her.

David didn't sleep well that night and it wasn't because his pallet was on a hard floor. He kept thinking about Alice and the boys. He wondered about how he would approach his father if he had the chance to speak to him again.

The next morning he walked to the edge of the basin to watch the canal boats try to jockey for position to be the first to fill their holds with coal. The boat captains kept trying to intercept the wharfmaster and convince him to allow their boat to be the next one loaded. The earlier boats to get loaded would be less likely to get caught in back-ups at the locks and Georgetown, which would help them get back to Cumberland quicker for another load. They would get a nice head start to the delayed canal season.

Dark clouds of coal dust rose into the air as the coal cars released the loads into chutes that dumped into empty canal boat holds. The full boats slowly made their way out of the basin and into the canal. Boats were leaving every twenty minutes or so and still there would be boats waiting to be filled with coal tomorrow.

David saw the *Freeman* was fifth in line to take on a load of coal. Alice had managed to get the canal boat in a good position, though it was probably due more to George who still got up before dawn as a leftover habit from his time in the army. They would be on their way before the end of the day. David wondered if Alice was going to try and run the boat twenty-four hours a day to make more trips this season. She and George could take turns as captain while Tony and Thomas served as mule walkers.

David turned away and went back into the warehouse to get himself some breakfast. He wasn't very hungry so he only ate two pieces of bread slathered with strawberry jam and drank a cup of milk. He kept it in a corked bottle that he kept submerged in the canal so that it stayed cool.

It was still too early for the work crew to be in, but David was surprised not to see Amos in his office. The man was usually in well before everyone else. Then he realized that Amos was probably supervising the loading of his canal boats to make sure that they got underway in good time.

David walked back outside. The first three boats had finished loading and were just starting off down the canal. The next three boats, including the *Freeman*, were preparing to move under the coal cars. Mules would haul the cars into place on tracks that ran over the canal over the open holds of the canal boats and dump the coal into the holds.

George stood at the *Freeman's* tiller while Alice, Tony and Thomas waited with the canal boat's mules on the shore.

Alice turned and saw him standing near the warehouse. She didn't say anything or even wave. He guessed that she had talked herself out last night. He certainly had.

Thomas hitched up Seamus and King Edward to the canal boat and Tony had the mules tow the *Freeman* under the coal chutes.

The chutes dumped coal one rail car at a time into the front of the canal boat. As the forward hold filled, the boat tipped forward so that the family cabin at the rear end of the boat rose slightly. Alice would have secured everything in the family cabin to keep it from breaking if it fell. The mules moved the boat forward and another thirty tons of coal was dumped into the rear of the boat. The boat leveled out deeper in the water. The boat moved forward again and another thirty tons of coal rumbled into the front hold and then the rear hold to fill them completely.

Coal falling into the holds sounded like a thunderstorm. The black cloud of coal dust that rose into the air reminded David of storm clouds. At times, he lost sight of the coal cars amid all of the dust.

The Fitzgeralds stood yards off to the side to avoid being completely coated with the dust. Alice had shut the windows in the family cabin, but dust would still coat everything inside the cabin so that she would have to spend a day or two cleaning.

The basin foreman checked the holds, judging the weight against what was marked on his manifest. He signed the drayage certificate for 110 tons of coal at forty-three cents a ton, payable on arrival in Georgetown.

When the holds were finally filled, George waved to his mother who started the mules walking. She would take them across a footbridge where they would be hitched to the canal boat and begin pulling it. Since all four mules were out, Alice intended to harness all of them to the boat. It made it easier to get started, plus she wouldn't lose time getting one pair back into the mule shed. She would do that at Lock 75 outside of Spring Gap when the boat had to stop anyway.

As Alice started to walk away, she turned and waved to David and called out, "I'll miss you."

David's resolve vanished. Something in the tone of her voice and the sad look on her face was more than he could stand.

"Alice, wait!"

He ran along the towpath until he reached her and the boys. Thomas looked impatient, but Tony just grinned.

She stared up at him with her wide, green eyes. His entire attention was focused on those eyes.

"I love you, Alice. There. I said it. You want to know what has been bothering me? That's it," David said in a quick stream.

Alice's eyes teared up and she shook her head. "No."

David took a step back. This was his nightmare. This is what he had imagined happening, but he had let himself think something else.

"Why?" he managed to ask.

"Why? You have to ask yourself why?"

David thought for a moment. "It's not you. You're an amazing woman—strong, smart, resourceful. So it must be me."

Alice shook her head. "No, David. It is me. I'll hurt you. I don't want to do that."

"It's too late for that."

Tears rolled down her cheeks. She turned and hurried off leaving Thomas and Tony with the mules.

"Why did she do that?" Tony asked.

"Because she doesn't love me," David said quietly.

Tony scratched his jaw. "Then I guess I don't really understand women at all."

12

MURDER IN SHANTY TOWN

MARCH 1864

On the *Freeman's* return to Cumberland after its first journey of the season to Georgetown, Tony found himself with free time. The canal boat wouldn't be able to take on a new load of coal until the following afternoon. With boating season now in full swing, the back-ups at the locks, basins and Georgetown had started. Georgetown was the worst because it took much longer to shovel the coal out of the holds than it took to dump coal into the holds or lock through.

Tony found himself in Shanty Town walking down Wineow Street for no reason other than it was a familiar place. He didn't know why he kept coming back here. There was nothing for him here, not even a mother. So why did he keep wandering back here to walk along the boardwalk and look in the store windows?

Mrs. Fitzgerald certainly didn't like it and Tony could understand why. Mr. Fitzgerald had been killed here for simply coming to get George out of a saloon. Mrs. Fitzgerald hadn't liked Shanty Town before then, but after that, she hated it and forbid her children to come here, which is why Tony hadn't told her where he was going.

Tony usually listened to his mother, but here he was still watching and listening to the railroaders, canallers and merchants talk about the war and women, the two most-popular topics in Shanty Town.

He knew he had no reason to be here, but Shanty Town had been the only home he knew for most of his life. Sometimes, he just wanted to come back here to play and talk with other kids who knew what growing up in a place where kids didn't belong was like.

He found himself walking behind three men who were taking up the entire width of the boardwalk as they walked past the shop fronts along Wineow Street. The men probably thought they were talking quietly, but you couldn't speak too softly when you had to speak over all of the noises coming out of the saloons or even just the noises on the street. Besides, these men were angry and angry people talked louder. Tony was going to walk around them, but then he started listening to the conversation.

"There are soldiers around every corner," the man on the left said. He was a head taller than the other two men.

"That's why I wanted to meet here. Not as many soldiers. It feels like the air is a little cleaner to breathe," the red-headed man in the center said.

They all laughed at the small joke. Mainly because the air in Shanty Town was anything but clean smelling. The air was filled with the scent of tar, burning coal, manure, sweat and tobacco.

"There's got to be some way to get…our friends into this city. If they could control the city, they could control the canal, the railroad, the national road. It would be a mighty mess," the man on the right said. He wore blue pants with a stripe down the sides that made him look like a Union soldier, though his words told a different story.

A woman screamed ahead and the men stopped walking so suddenly that Tony almost ran into them.

"Get the sheriff! Get the sheriff!" the woman screamed. That wasn't often a call you heard in Shanty Town. The sheriff and his deputies tended to stay away from this place.

The woman ran out into the middle of the street shrieking. She was dressed like a saloon girl. A man walked over to her to try and calm her down, but the woman pulled away as if the man was trying to kill her.

The woman pointed to the second floor of one of the buildings along Wineow Street.

"She's dead! There's so much blood!" the woman yelled.

Tony looked where the woman was pointing and froze. It was the building where his mother was living. He stepped around the Confederate sympathizers in front of him and ran down the boardwalk to the building. A crowd had started to gather because of the woman's screaming, but they were gathered around her and not the apartment.

Tony ran into the alleyway and bolted up the stairs. The screaming woman had left the door open. Tony stopped on the top landing and looked through the doorway into Carol's room.

Inside, Carol lay on the floor in a large pool of blood. She had been stabbed repeatedly. Tony could see the wounds in her chest and it looked like her throat had been cut, too. Her eyes were wide open, staring at the ceiling and she looked so pale.

He turned away and vomited over the side the landing railing. Then he let himself stumble down to the landing and look away from his mother.

Who would do something like this to her? It was so extreme and so angry.

He sat there trying to wash the images from his memory, but he couldn't. He thought that he would remember the sight of his dead mother until the day he died. He should have taken Mrs. Fitzgerald's advice and stayed away from Shanty Town.

He heard someone coming up the stairs and turned to look. It was a deputy who Tony didn't know.

"You best get away from here, boy," the deputy said.

Tony nodded. "She was my mother."

"Your mother, huh?" His expression softened. "Sorry about that. Did you see what happened?"

Tony shook his head. "I wasn't here. I don't live with her. I was walking down the street when that other woman started screaming."

The deputy looked into the room and then quickly pulled back. He looked pale.

"John, get yourself some help and block the stairs so no one can get up here. It's not a pretty sight," the deputy called down the stairs.

He turned to Tony and said, "You better get down there, too. You got a pa or someone we should notify about this?"

Tony shook his head. "I'm not even sure what my last name

was."

He walked down the stairs and was immediately surrounded by a crowd of people who wanted to know what it looked up there. Tony didn't tell them anything. He just wanted to get away from here. Far away and try to forget.

He stumbled down Wineow Street toward the canal basin, walking more like a drunk railroader than a boy trying to run away. The sounds of shouting, train whistles, wagon chains jangling and simply people talking all blended together into a single sound that bore into his head. It made his head hurt, but even so, it didn't make the memory of seeing his mother's body sprawled on the floor of her apartment out of his head.

He saw the *Freeman* tied to a wharf up ahead and staggered toward it, sometimes looking over his shoulder to look back down Wineow Street.

"Tony, stop!"

Tony obeyed from reflex and then blinked. George was resting on the fourteen hatch covers on the canal boat. The curved covers arched between the race planks covering the huge cargo hold, which took up most of the space on the boat.

"Look where you are," George said.

Tony looked down. He was standing on the edge of the wharf. His toes hung over the water. He would have walked right off if George hadn't stopped him. Tony took a quick step back.

"Sorry, George, I wasn't paying attention," Tony told his older brother.

George stood up and hopped across the gap from the *Freeman* to the wharf. He stood in front of Tony and put his hands on his shoulders.

"What's wrong, Tony? You look pale. Are you sick?" George asked.

"I was in Shanty Town…"

"Tony…" George started to say.

Tony shook his head. "I know what you're going to say, George. It's not a good place. It's dangerous. You're right."

"Did something happen to you?"

Tony shook his head again. "Not me. Somebody killed my mother. Not your mom. Not Mrs. Fitzgerald. Somebody killed my mom.

Carol."

Just saying the words made him feel like a locomotive had been dropped on his shoulders.

"I'm sorry, Tony."

Tony squeezed his older brother's arms. "And I saw her body, George. Someone had stabbed her more than once. She was in her room. There was so much blood, George, so much blood."

George pulled him into a hug. Tony wanted to cry. He felt like he should cry, but the tears just wouldn't come. Was it a betrayal of his mother?

"It was awful, George," Tony said.

"I know it was. I know." George paused. "I remember when Papa was killed. He was just lying in the road like he was horse droppings. He was stabbed, too. I put my hands over the knife hole, but the blood kept pumping out."

Tony remembered the scene, although Mr. Fitzgerald had already been dead by the time Tony arrived. Tony hadn't been sad at the time. He had been angry, so angry that he had burned down the saloon where the men who had killed Mr. Fitzgerald had been laughing and drinking.

This time was different, though. He felt no anger. He was sad; sad that his mother had died hating him.

Tony pulled back from George. "What should I do?"

George shrugged. "I don't know. I didn't handle Papa's death well. It's part of why I ran off and joined the army. Look where that got me."

"So am I going to do something stupid?"

"I hope not. It's all right to be sad. I think you have to be sad before you can be happy again and the longer you don't let yourself be sad, the more likely you are to do something stupid."

13

THE SEASON BEGINS

APRIL 1864

When canal lock tolls rose twenty percent from five-sixteenths of a cent per ton per mile to three-eighths of a cent and as usually happened, it caused a lot of grumbling among the canallers along the canal. Finances were already tight for all of the canallers and now it was costing them about two dollars a ton to transport the coal from Cumberland to Georgetown. This toll increase caught them in a pincer between the Canal Company and coal companies. The Canal Company had already raised the tolls. Now the canallers would need to negotiate new drayage rates with the mining companies and hope that they might be able to not lose money because of the increase. Of course, the coal companies would fight any effort to increase their shipping costs. The canallers' work stoppage earlier in the year hadn't helped their situation. In fact, it had put many canallers deeper in debt.

Captains who had discovered leaks in their boats after their first trip or two down the canal had gotten the boards in their boats caulked. It was a necessary repair. Cosmetic repairs like repainting were delayed in order to save money.

As the weather warmed up, more and more boats appeared on the canal. Many captains had been waiting for consistently warm weather to close up their homes and take to boating. However, there were new boats on the canal that were launched from the builders in Cumberland. War had increased the demand for coal in Washington and people were working to fill it.

The warm weather also meant that there would be more fighting in the war. Though there hadn't been any major actions near the canal since the Battle of Antietam a year and a half ago, there had been plenty of skirmishes as Confederate rangers tried to damage the canal or the railroad or both. In addition, Union troops could often be seen marching along the towpath.

It didn't take long before the rumors spread up and down the canal as the canallers started talking to each other when their boats passed or tied up for the night. They expected another attack or sabotage any day now. Alice wasn't sure how many of the rumors were true, but seeing as how Confederate soldiers had tried to burn the *Freeman* once before, she considered all of them with more than a bit of caution.

A group of sympathizers did try to destroy one of the locks near Cumberland without much luck. They rode up to lock 73 near Spring Gap, scared off the lockkeeper and his family while they pried and hacked out the lock doors.

The attack was only marginally successful. The Confederates were able to knock the doors loose, but it only delayed things for two days while the doors were reseated. Still, the incident put the canallers on edge even more.

Tony hoped that it was the sabotage that the Confederate sympathizers he overheard in Shanty Town had been talking about. He doubted it, though. They had seemed to have bigger plans than to damage one lock on the canal.

Tony leaned back against the railing around the pilot deck of the *Freeman*. One hand rested lightly on the rudder, more to hold it steady than to steer the cumbersome canal boat as it made its way up the canal to Cumberland.

Crickets chirping. Fish jumping. The sound of the boat cutting through the water. An occasional bray from one of the mules. They were the sounds of his job and they told him that everything was fine.

The season had gone well so far. The canal was staying open without any breaks in the berm, sabotage from Confederate raiders or floods. He wasn't sure how long it would last, but he knew that it made Mrs. Fitzgerald happy every time they reached Washington and were paid. They were on their way back to Cumberland now and would probably take on a new load of coal tomorrow.

The canal was quiet as night fell, at least as quiet as the canal ever got. He could hear the water in the Potomac running nearby. Crickets chirped. He also heard an animal rustling occasionally in the brush. It was still quieter than Shanty Town ever got. He could see George and two of the canal mules silhouetted in the distance as they towed the loaded canal boat. Thomas was in the mule shed feeding Jigger and Ocean who would be taking a shift pulling the boat soon.

Tony could hear soft sobs from inside the family cabin. Mrs. Fitzgerald was preparing supper, but she was doing more than that. She was remembering and grieving. She'd been crying many nights when she thought that she was alone or that everyone else was asleep. She never cried in front of anyone, but at times like this when things were quiet, Tony sometimes heard her. It was hard to be truly alone on a canal boat.

The crying stopped and a few moments later, Mrs. Fitzgerald opened the door to the family cabin and poked her head out.

"The stew is ready," she said to Tony. "Find a place to pull over. We'll eat, then switch the mules and get a few more hours in before we quit for the night."

"Yes, ma'am."

Tony couldn't see her face clearly in the twilight, but he knew that although Mrs. Fitzgerald would have dried her tears, her eyes would still be a bit puffy and red from the crying. He, Thomas and George had stopped asking her what the matter was. She always denied any problem. What was the point anyway? Everyone, even Thomas, knew why she was crying.

Why hadn't she told David that she loved him? It was pretty obvious that she did otherwise she wouldn't be crying.

"George, supper's ready!" Tony called. "Is there a place to stop?"

"Not any time soon," George called back. He was walking the mules about thirty feet in front of the *Freeman*. "Go ahead and eat. We're not too far from Cumberland. I want to get there before it gets too dark."

They were only about two hours from the basin at Cumberland.

They had switched mules at the Oldtown locks. The last set of locks before they reached Cumberland were a few minutes ahead, but they were close enough that George felt like he would rather just reach the city and tie up at a wharf.

"Are you sure, George?" Alice called from inside the cabin.

"Yes, Mama. I'm not that hungry. I'll eat once we stop for the night in Cumberland."

"What about the mules?"

"Seamus and King George should be fine to reach Cumberland. It's not nearly as hard on them to pull the boat upstream."

That was an understatement since the holds were empty.

"I'll give them some apples to eat in Cumberland as a reward," Tony added.

Thomas came running across the hatch covers and hopped down the stairs to get into the cabin. He wasn't one to miss meals.

"I'll have Thomas bring you a bowl of stew," Alice said.

"That's fine."

They made it into Cumberland around nine o'clock and tied up at the edge of the basin. The canal office was closed that late in the evening so they wouldn't be able to make arrangements for a new load until tomorrow. They should be able to get on their way before noon, though.

Once the boat was tied up, Thomas took Jigger and Ocean from the mule shed and picketed them on the shore with King George and Seamus. Tony brought the portable feeding trough across. It was a trough mounted on a three-foot long stake. Tony pushed the stake into the ground so that it would stay upright and then went to get some hay for the mules.

The mules stepped up to the trough and began munching on their dinner while Thomas began brushing out King George and Seamus giving them extra attention. They smelled of sweat from their exertions pulling the boat because even when a canal boat wasn't loaded, it was still an effort for them to pull it.

Mr. Fitzgerald had always told Tony that it was important to take care of the mules. They were doing all the work pulling the canal boat. They deserved to be treated well. During the winter, the Fitzgeralds always made sure that the mules were kept warm in a barn and well fed. Thomas even made sure to exercise them regularly.

Tony had seen canal mules that had spent the winter months being taken care of by someone other than their owner. A farmer with extra stalls in his barn just didn't care for what he considered non-productive animals as well as he did his own animals. When it came time to pull the canal boats to Cumberland, those mules were scrawny, sick-looking beasts that were shades of their normal selves. They pulled with less power, lengthening the time it took to make a run up and down the canal. They also slowed other traffic on the canal, particularly at the Paw Paw Tunnel or the narrow paths across the aqueducts.

Tony could see the lights on in Shanty Town and he thought about his mother. Why had someone killed her? Had she tried to steal money from the wrong man? Had the sheriff found out who had killed her? As much as he hadn't liked his mother, his last memory of her shouldn't have to be seeing her lying in a pool of blood.

"Want to do some fishing?" Thomas asked him.

Tony shook his head. "Not tonight, Thomas, I've got some thinking to do."

Tony was up early the next morning. It was already warm outside. He got the oven fire going so it would be ready for Mrs. Fitzgerald to cook breakfast and then went out to feed the mules and give them some fresh water. Once he was finished with his chores, Tony told George that he was heading into town for a bit. Then he hurried off before Thomas saw him and asked to tag along.

Tony walked to the sheriff's office in the center of town. He hoped to catch Sheriff Whittaker before he started patrolling since it was still early. Not that Tony wanted to talk to Sheriff Whittaker, but he was the only one who might be able to help Tony get some answers to his questions.

Tony had been working on the *Freeman* when Mr. Fitzgerald had been killed. He had seen how his death had affected the family. Tony had watched as the hundreds of people attended Mr. Fitzgerald's funeral. Mrs. Fitzgerald, Elizabeth and other women cried. The men, most of them canallers, dressed in their finest clothes that they rarely wore.

Carol had been buried in the potter's field with just a small wooden marker last month. No one had attended her funeral. Tony hadn't even been able to attend because he had been on the *Freeman* somewhere between Cumberland and Georgetown. He wasn't even sure there had been one. He had asked around and no one had known anything about it. He had returned to Cumberland and asked about Carol's funeral. After having three people tell him that they didn't know anything about it, a sheriff's deputy finally directed him to the potter's field.

Someone had hated Carol enough to kill her, but no one had loved her enough to go to her funeral.

The sheriff was sitting with his heels propped up on his desk and his chair tipped back on two legs when Tony walked into the office. The large man was reading the newspaper while he sipped at a steaming cup of coffee. He frowned when he saw Tony.

"What do you want?"

"My mother was killed in Shanty Town two months ago. I wanted to know if you found out who had done it," Tony asked politely.

"I thought your mother was the high-and-mighty canal queen," the sheriff said sarcastically.

Tony knew that he couldn't let himself be baited into an argument if he wanted to get any information.

"I'm talking about my birth mother, Carol. Mrs. Fitzgerald is my mama as far as she and I are concerned."

Sheriff Whittaker set his chair down on the floor and stood up so that he towered over Tony.

"Then why do you care about a dead whore? Go on back to the canal, and on the way back you can trip and fall in and drown for all I care."

Tony wondered if the sheriff would be speaking so harshly if one of his deputies had been around.

"I saw her…I saw Carol after she was stabbed. I may have even seen who did it since I was in Shanty Town," Tony said.

"Did you see who did it?"

"Not that I know of. I didn't see it happen."

Sheriff Whittaker grunted. "The woman was no good, just like you. You didn't even want to have anything to do with her. Why should you care now?"

That comment hurt Tony more than any of the other snide barbs that the sheriff had said. He did care more about his birth mother now that she was dead than he had when she was alive. That wasn't right, but neither was it right that she had been killed.

"Someone killed her, Sheriff. She might have been no good like you say, but she didn't deserve to be killed. Why would someone do that to her?"

"Life doesn't count for much in Shanty Town."

"But don't you know who did it?"

Sheriff Whittaker shook his head. "We questioned some people, but no one saw anything. She was dead and the killer gone before anyone even noticed something was wrong. We don't even know how long she was dead before that woman found her."

Tony had been so close. He had been pitching pennies while his mother was being stabbed to death. That just seemed wrong to him. Very wrong.

Sheriff Whittaker smirked.

"Do you even care who killed her?" Tony asked.

"She was a whore and a worn out one at that. No one cares that she's gone. No one even misses her."

The sheriff sat back down and opened the paper. Tony wanted to ask more questions, but like the sheriff had said, no one cared. She was gone and things went on like nothing had even happened.

He left the office and started walking down Liberty Street not paying much attention to the crowds around him as Cumberland started to come to life in the morning.

The sheriff was wrong about one thing. Someone did care. Tony did. But what did he care about? Was it that he missed his mother or that she had been killed? Or was it that he was offended that no one had been caught?

If one of these people on the street were killed, wouldn't the sheriff search until he found the killer? Wouldn't other people care that someone had been killed in their midst? He wouldn't feel comfortable until he settled the turmoil of feelings inside himself.

Was there any way he might be able to find out who had killed his mother? He was just a kid. But a kid wasn't noticed. Tony knew that from experience. He could go where adults could go, but unlike adults, he wouldn't be noticed.

He started thinking about where he could start his search. Obviously, it would have to be in the saloon where his mother worked. He knew some of the women she worked with. He would have to find that woman who had found his mother.

Tony walked back to basin where he saw George and found out when the *Freeman* would be getting coal. Tony still had a couple hours before he would be needed back on the boat. He hurried away before George could ask him where he was going.

Tony figured the first place to start looking for answers as to why his mother was killed would be in her room. He walked up the stairs and tried to open the door. It was locked so he rapped on it.

A man answered. He had a railroader's look about him, both in his dress and the bulk in his shoulders that came from shoveling coal into the boiler. He was middle aged with deep creases in his face, some of which seem to hold coal dust.

He took his cigar from between his clenched teeth. "What do you want, kid?"

Tony noticed a large rug in the middle of the floor when the man opened his door. He was sure that it was covering a large bloodstain that the landlord probably couldn't get out of the wood.

"I'm looking for the woman who used to live here," Tony lied. "Her name was Carol."

"You're a little young for the company of women who would live in a place like this, aren't you? Which one is Carol?"

"Which one?"

The man nodded. "Yeah, there were two women living here. I don't know where the one got to, but one of them still works at the Railroader's Rest."

"Can you describe her?"

The man frowned and blew a cloud of cigar smoke in Tony's face.

"She was kinda plain. She has brown hair and eyes." The man smiled. "And a big set of..." He held his hands out in front of his chest. Then he noticed Tony staring at him and let his hands drop. "Anyway, she's about this tall." The man held his hand up to his chin.

Tony wondered for a moment if his mother had started using a young girl to help her fleece her men "friends," but that didn't make sense. Although his mother had also worked in the saloons serving food and offering men more if they would follow her to her room, this man had said that one of the women was still working in a saloon.

That couldn't be his mother. Nor could it be a girl.

Tony thanked the man and headed down Wineow Street to the Railroader's Rest. It was dark and filled with smoke like just about every saloon Tony had ever seen. It was a railroader's tavern, though. He would have to keep quiet the fact that he worked on the canal or they would notice him, child or not.

He waited outside on the boardwalk until he saw two men go inside. He slipped into the saloon with them. Heads would turn to look at whoever came in. A group of adults would be noticed and their faces looked at. Tony was lower down. If he came in behind the men, not many people would notice him unlike what would have happened if he had entered alone.

He moved around the bar slowly, looking at the people who were drinking, eating and playing cards. He didn't recognize any of them, but they were railroaders so it wasn't surprising. He stayed away from loners. They were men who came to get drunk, but they were also men who wouldn't be talking amongst themselves. Tony wasn't planning on asking questions so he needed to be around men who were talking.

After a few minutes, he saw the woman he was looking for come out from the back where the kitchen was located. She was the woman who had found his Carol's body, the one who had run down the stairs screaming. That explained how she had found the body in the room. She had lived there with Carol.

The woman set a plate of chicken, biscuits and beans in front of a man at a table. Tony walked over to her. She was older than Tony had first thought. She tried to hide it with make-up, but Tony could see wrinkles around her eyes and on her hands.

"What do you want?" the woman asked.

"I was there when you found the dead woman," Tony reminded her.

The brown-haired woman trembled. "Don't remind me. I've been trying to forget that day."

"The dead woman was my mother."

The waitress stared at Tony. "Carol never said she had a kid."

Tony sighed. "She wouldn't have. Plus, I haven't been living with her for a couple years."

"I'm sorry about your mother. I liked her."

Tony realized that it was the first time he had heard someone say something nice about his mother in a non-sexual way.

"The sheriff still hasn't found out who killed her," Tony said.

The woman nodded. "Not that he's looking. The sheriff and his deputies don't want to come to Shanty Town unless they have to. I bought myself a derringer. A woman can't be too safe around here."

"Do you know who might have killed her?"

The woman snorted. "Probably any of the men she robbed. I've seen some of them leave our room pretty mad."

"Mad enough to kill her?"

"No. A man goes with a woman like your mother should know what he's getting himself into. It's not like she was the only woman who did it." The woman paused, staring at Tony. "I've got to get to work."

She pushed past Tony and left him standing alone. Tony turned and looked over the crowd in the saloon. The place smelled of smoke, whiskey and sweat. The men were loud and dirty. One of them might have murdered his mother. He needed more information.

He looked around the room and settled on the men playing cards. He moved close enough so that he could hear one group of card players talking, but far enough away that it wouldn't be thought he was helping someone cheat.

At one table, the men were bragging about how brave they were to face the dangers on the railroad.

"All it takes is a Johnny Reb pulling up some rails and I could wind up dead," one man said.

"Awww, Charles, you haven't had to worry about Rebs for a year," another card player told him. "The army's controlling the lines pretty well."

Tony knew that was true. It was easier to transport troops west on the Baltimore and Ohio Railroad, but in the early years of the war, the Rebels had taken great joy at tearing up track south of the Potomac River in Confederate territory and disrupting a major transportation route for the army.

At another table, Tony heard a more-interesting conversation.

"I've no love for the canallers, but you're talking about something a lot more than blowing a whistle to startle mules," one man said.

One of the ways that railroaders would torment canallers was to blow their train whistles along the stretches of the canal that paralleled the train tracks. It gave them a good laugh to watch the normally docile canal mules jumping and kicking in fright. It made the mule driver's life miserable as he tried to calm the mules down without getting kicked and then get them pulling the canal boat again.

"I'm just saying if you stop the flow of coal into Washington, you would slow down a lot of things, including the ships that use that coal," another man said.

"A thing like that could get you shot."

"Well, think about what I'm saying. All the other times that the Confederate Army has tried to shut down the canal by burning boats, all of the coal has gone to waste. When the rangers have tried to take over the boats, it's always been on a small scale. That grain in the holds of one of two boats doesn't last forever when you're trying to feed an army. But combine the two. Commandeer the boats and take the coal while the army is diverted trying to repair an aqueduct or a breech."

Tony couldn't see the face of the man who was speaking. He wanted to move around the table, but he was afraid of drawing attention to himself. These men were talking about treason and they wouldn't want that known.

The second man shook his head. "I don't know. You'd need a lot of men."

"You'd be surprised how many men are willing to help. Ol' Abe may be able to make Maryland stay in the Union, but that don't mean everyone in the state has to like what he's doing," a third man said. "You've been talking pretty big that you're one of them."

Tony backed away. He surely didn't want to be noticed by these men. However, he had to admit that this was the place for them to talk. It was unlikely someone would pay attention to their conversation in such a noisy place. And with Cumberland half full of soldiers, a railroad was a pretty safe place to talk when you were a Confederate sympathizer.

Tony slipped out of the saloon and stood on the boardwalk for a few minutes. What should he do with this information? He didn't know who those men were, though a couple of them looked like railroaders.

He took off at a trot down the street and ran to the Lewis Boatworks. When he stepped inside the warehouse, he saw David supervising the framing of a new canal boat. The keel had been laid and some of the hull had even been attached. David kept glancing between papers in his hand and the workers who were nailing additional supports to the keel.

"David," Tony said.

David turned around and smiled at him. "Hi, Tony. When did you get back from Georgetown?"

Tony nodded. "We got in last night. Can I talk to you about something?" Tony asked.

David walked toward him. "Is something wrong?"

"I was in the Railroader's Rest and…"

David grabbed him by his arm. "What were you doing in a saloon? Alice will whip you something fierce if she finds out."

"I needed to go. I was trying to find out who killed my mother and that's where the woman she shared a room with worked."

David's grip loosened. "Did you find out anything?"

Tony shook his head. "Not about my mother, but I listened to some men playing cards and they were talking about destroying part of the canal and commandeering a lot of canal boats to take across the river to the Confederacy."

David leaned in closer. "Are you sure?" Tony nodded. "Did you hear any other details? Did you know any of the men?"

"I didn't know them, but two of them looked like railroaders and it was the Railroader's Rest. I'm not sure about the other two, but they are definitely Confederate sympathizers."

"Would you recognize them if you saw them?" Tony nodded. "Would they recognize you if they saw you?"

Tony shook his head. "I don't think they really noticed me. I was trying to not be noticed by anyone."

"What about a time or a place where this was going to happen?"

"They didn't say, but it sounds like it was already set up and they were trying to get one of the railroaders to help them somehow."

David ran his hand through his hair and stared at the window at nothing. He said nothing and Tony let him think.

"I want you to take me back to the saloon and see if those men are still there. If they are, you'll point them out to me."

"What if they aren't?"

"I'll worry about that when it happens."

David called up to one of the men working on the canal boat and told him that he needed to leave for a few minutes but he would be back soon. The man waved and David headed out of the warehouse with Tony.

"What are you going to do, David?" Tony asked.

"I don't know. First, I want to see these men for myself so I can recognize them," David told him.

As they approached the saloon, Tony stopped suddenly. He stared for a moment at three railroaders walking down the street and pointed. David pushed his hand down.

"Those are the men walking down the boardwalk," Tony said. "I recognize one of them."

"Fine, but don't draw attention to yourself by pointing to them," David said as he gently pushed Tony's arm down to his side. "That's one way to have them remember you."

Tony nodded and shoved his hands in his pockets.

The men walked away with their backs to David. There were three of them and he needed to see their faces. He and Tony moved in closer.

"Play along," David told Tony.

"What are you doing here, boy?" David suddenly said loudly.

Tony looked up at him confused. What was going on? "What…"

"Don't try to make up some excuse. Your ma will be beside herself when she finds out where you were."

David grabbed Tony by arm and hauled him off down Wineow Street. As they got closer to the basin, David let go Tony. The boy jumped away and turned to face David.

"What was that all about?" Tony demanded.

"I needed to see those men's faces."

"How does yelling at me help you do that?"

"When I suddenly started yelling, what do you think they did?"

Tony thought for a moment and then it occurred to him. "They turned around to see who was yelling. And you were facing them with the way you were standing. I couldn't see them because my back was toward them."

"We were also close enough so I could see their faces," David said.

"Did you know any of them?" Tony asked.

"No, but I'd recognize them again. That's what I needed. David clapped a hand on Tony's shoulder and gently squeezed. Now you get back to the *Freeman* before Alice finds out where you've been," David said.

"What are you going to do?"

David rubbed the back of his neck. "I don't know. I've got to think about this a bit."

"What should I tell, Mrs. Fitzgerald?"

David froze for a moment and a frown crossed his face. Then he shook his head.

"Don't tell her anything. Just make sure that everyone keeps watch and you keep the rifle near the rudder where you can grab it quickly. Tell George about it. He's got a good head on his shoulders and he may have some other ideas."

Tony nodded that he understood. He started to walk away, but then he turned and asked, "Are you going to come back?"

"No," David said flatly.

"She cries at night." Tony didn't have to say who. David knew. "When she's in her cabin, she cries and doesn't think we can hear."

"This was her choice, Tony. I told her how I felt and she…she didn't want me."

"Maybe that's what she said, but it's not how she acts."

Then he turned around and headed back to the canal basin. He had to help get the *Freeman* ready.

14

EYES OPEN, HEART CLOSED

APRIL 1864

George walked along the towpath with Seamus and Jigger trailing just behind him. He didn't have to whip them or tug on their harnesses to keep them moving. They were experienced canal mules. They knew their job and did it. George could control them with simple voice commands.

The ground was still moist from a rain yesterday so it was more pliant than the dirt path usually was and it felt cool under his feet. He knew they were somewhere near Oldtown, but he wasn't paying too much attention to his surroundings to know exactly where along the towpath that they were. He was letting his mind wander and keeping the mules moving more from habit than anything else.

He jumped when he heard his mother blow "Lock Ready!" on her canal horn to let the lockkeeper know they were coming. The mules raised their heads and surged forward to get to the lock quickly so they could rest. His mother hadn't needed to blow the horn, though. There was already a boat waiting to enter the lock, which was emptying of water.

Now that he was paying attention, George knew where they were. They were approaching the odd locks just past the Paw Paw Tunnel: 66, 64 2/3, and 63 1/3. The reason for the odd numbering of the locks was that the Canal Company had decided to eliminate Lock 65 to save money on their over-budget project when the canal was being built.

The lock house for Lock 66 sat back from the canal, more so than other lock houses tended to be. The carpenter shop where the canal gates were manufactured and repaired occupied the lot where a lock house would usually sit next to the lock.

"We're going to get through this lock and then pull over for the night," Alice called to George.

It took about eight minutes for the *Harvest Moon*, which was the canal boat ahead of them to lock through. It didn't go too far down the canal before it pulled over to the side of the canal for the night. It was getting on to dusk and there wouldn't be many boaters still traveling.

Lucas Crabtree reset the lock and then the *Freeman* moved into it while George manned one of the snubbing lines to help keep the canal boat from bouncing and scraping against the stone sides of the lock. The locks closer to Washington City were actually made from granite cut from the same quarry as the granite used to construct the White House.

If a canal boat slammed into the sides of the lock, it could damage the lock or the canal boat; most likely the canal boat.

Since George couldn't hold onto the snubbing line with his one hand, he looped the thick rope around the snubbing post in the ground next to the lock wall and pulled it tight by wrapping the rope around his waist, bracing his foot against the post and leaning backwards. The tension from the snubbing lines on both sides of the lock would steady the canal boat as it was lowered so that it didn't hit the lock wall. As the boat was lowered in the lock, Lucas and George would let out more of their snubbing lines.

"Any word from Washington?" Lucas asked from across the canal where he was manning another snubbing line.

"Too many wounded soldiers; too many dead," George told him. If George never saw another dead man in his life, it would be too many. As unlikely as that was, he only prayed that he wouldn't have to see them the way that he had on the peninsula in Virginia where he had lost his arm.

"It seems like things have turned for the Union, though."

"For the Union, maybe, but not for the families of the soldiers who are killed in the fighting."

The *Freeman* slowly moved into the lock and Lucas and George tightened the snubbing lines. The lock was just long enough to hold a ninety-two-foot-long canal boat when both the east and west gates were shut.

George leaned on the long swing beam to shut one of the west canal doors while Lucas shut the other door on the north side of the canal. They then walked out on top of the massive canal doors and turned the lock keys to shut the sluice valves.

Now the *Freeman* was entirely contained within the 100-foot lock.

Lucas and George walked to the east end of the lock and used the heavy, metal lock keys to open the sluice gates at the bottom of the lock doors so that the water within the lock would drain out. Once the *Freeman* was level with the water level outside the east gates, the doors would be opened. It would take about eight minutes. The surge of water being released between locks helped create the two mile per hour current that helped carry the canal boats to Washington.

Once the water within the lock was at the same level with the water on the western end of the lock, Lucas and George pushed opened the lock doors. George started the mules moving to pull the *Freeman* out of the lock where Alice steered it to the north side of the canal. This would allow any other canal boats, such as those that traveled all night, to still move along the canal without having to worry about getting their towlines around a sitting canal boat.

George unhitched the mules, pulled their harnesses off, and picketed them while Tony walked the other two mules off of the *Freeman* to picket them on the opposite side of the canal.

"George, why don't you and your family join us for dinner tonight?" Lucas asked.

George suddenly realized that it had been hours since his mother had served up chicken pot pie for lunch and his stomach was rumbling.

"Sounds good. Can we bring anything?"

"You don't need to, but if you've got anything extra like one of those pies your mother bakes, I wouldn't say, 'no,'" Lucas said with a grin.

George walked across the tops of the canal doors to cross the canal. Then he walked over where he could board the *Freeman*. He told his mother of Lucas' offer.

"Tony, go help your brother feed the mules and then get some fresh water from the Crabtree's well. I want you and Thomas to wash up before dinner," Alice told her adopted son.

Tony frowned, but he didn't say anything. At least she wasn't making him take a bath. Tony complained that there was nothing more embarrassing than sitting in a tub of lukewarm water and feeling like the chicken in a pot of chicken soup. Oh, and then there was the time Thomas pissed in the water and then let Tony take his bath in it. George had laughed at that, but he wondered if he had ever been an unknowing victim of that prank by one of his brothers.

Canal lock houses were all generally the same size, about 30 feet by 18 feet. They had two floors and a basement. The Crabtree house had two bedrooms on the second floor. Lucas and his wife, Virginia, had one bedroom and the two Crabtree girls stayed in the other. Ben Crabtree was left sleeping on a cot in the family room on the first floor since the girls outnumbered the boys in the family.

The kitchen and the family room were on the ground floor of the house. Besides serving as a bedroom for Ben, the family room also had to serve as a dining room when guests or family stopped by for a meal.

Virginia Crabtree had a long dining table set up in the center of the room with a bench on either side. The other furniture in the room had been pushed to the edges of the room. She was setting platters of food on the table when the Fitzgeralds walked through the open door.

Virginia set a roasted chicken on the table and smiled at Alice. She had long, brown hair like her daughters, but at the moment much of it was hidden beneath a head scarf to keep the hair out her eyes.

"I've got the apple pie that Lucas asked for, Virginia," Alice said as she lifted the pie higher. "I put it together this afternoon and it's fresh out of the oven."

"It smells wonderful," Virginia said. "Follow me back to the kitchen and I'll show you where you can set it."

The kitchen was cluttered with dishes, vegetable scraps and flour. Two pots were still on the stovetop cooking.

"Everything smells great," Alice said.

Virginia took the pie from Alice and set it on a high shelf. "The boys will still find it, but hopefully not until after we've eaten."

Alice laughed. "I'm not sure I would bet on that," she said.

Virginia leaned out the open kitchen window and shouted, "Dinner's ready!"

Tony, Thomas and Ben were the first ones into the house. They ran inside racing each other and Virginia pointed out the window.

"Wash your hands first," Virginia ordered.

The boys groaned and then reversed direction to head back out the door. They pumped water into a bucket and used a bar of lye soap sitting next to the pump to wash their hands clean.

Dinner was roasted chicken, fresh bread, mashed potatoes and lima beans. George and Lucas Crabtree spent most of the dinner talking about either the canal and coal or the war while Alice and Virginia Crabtree talked about the differences between living on a canal boat and in a house.

"I miss my house in Sharpsburg," Alice said at one point as she looked around the roomy kitchen. "Even though it was larger than the family cabin on the *Freeman*, it was easier to keep clean. I'm always wiping coal dust off things on the canal boat."

"You could rebuild your house," Virginia suggested.

"I suppose, but it wouldn't be the same. The old house had a lot of memories of Hugh and the children when they were little. A new house wouldn't have those memories."

During the meal, George would glance over and see Becky Crabtree staring at him, more precisely, staring at the stump that was his arm. George was wearing a long-sleeved shirt with the end of his left arm folded back and pinned to the shoulder. She usually looked away when he saw her staring; however, by the end of the meal, she had stopped looking away.

Her long, brown hair was pinned on top of her head, showing off the gentle curve of her neck. She had been a slender girl, but now her body had filled out to show her feminine curves. George still thought she was beautiful, but he was no longer interested in her as he had once been. He had changed in two years and he hoped it was for the better.

Her stare made George uncomfortable, and he tried to keep himself interested in the conversation with Mr. Crabtree.

"The Union will have this wrapped up before too long. I'm thinking it may even be before year's end," Lucas said.

George glanced at Becky. She smiled at him.

"Maybe," he said.

"You don't think so?"

Becky twirled one of her brown ponytails around her fingers. She was a slender girl who was showing definite feminine curves. Her blue eyes were penetrating.

"The Johnny Rebs are tough. They can take a lot," George said.

"You sound like you admire them."

George nodded. "Yes, I do. That doesn't mean I don't think they're right, but I do think they're tough."

They went on to talk about the flooding of the Potomac River and the problems it caused at both Williamsport and Monocacy. A rock slide at the marble quarry near Lock 26 had damaged the gates there. It had taken a week to repair them, which, of course, had slowed down traffic on the canal. At Williamsport, the flooding had washed sand bars from the river into the canal. The Canal Company had had to dredge the canal in the vicinity of Williamsport to ensure that no canal boat would get stranded and block traffic on the canal.

For dessert, Mrs. Crabtree served doughnuts coated with honey and Alice's apple pie. Tony, Ben and Thomas gobbled up as many of the doughnuts as they could get a hold of, which was tricky, seeing as how Alice and Virginia kept slapping their hands. Thomas managed to stuff one in his pants pocket, but he was forced to take it out when the honey soaked through his pants.

When they finished eating, the boys ran off to play near the canal.

"I'll keep an eye on them," George said. What he really wanted to do was get away from Becky.

George watched them chase each other across the top of the lock doors. He wondered how long it would be before one of them fell in. It would probably be Thomas.

"How are you doing, George?"

George's head snapped around and he saw Becky standing next to him. She had followed him out of the house without saying anything.

"I'm fine, Becky."

She moved up to stand so close to him that they were almost touching. He noticed that she stood on the side of his good arm. George hoped that he didn't expect him to hold her hand.

"I don't remember the last time we talked."

George did. It had been the night he had listened to her talk about the Union soldiers who happened to have stopped by the Crabtree house at the same time as the Fitzgeralds. All Becky could do that night was swoon over the soldiers. It had driven George mad with jealousy so much so that he had soon run off to join the army and made the second-biggest mistake of his life. Sure it had cost him his arm, but the biggest mistake of his life had been going into a saloon in Shanty Town. That had cost him his father.

Since George had returned to his family after recovering from his injuries, he had avoided talking to Becky. Part of the reason was that he had had trouble adjusting to having only one arm and part of the reason was that he didn't particularly care to see her. She reminded him of how stupid he had been.

He had lost more than his arm during the war. He had also lost his interest in Becky. She seemed more like a girl now than she had ever seemed.

"It's been awhile," George finally said.

"Would you like to take a walk? It's so nice out tonight and my father is going to tell the little kids stories so he'll be busy for a while."

"I like your father's stories. Maybe we should go over and listen."

He moved back toward the house, but Becky squeezed his arm. "I can hear them anytime. I'd rather hear your stories."

She wrapped her arm around George's good arm and pulled. George reluctantly stood and followed her outside. The air was cool but not uncomfortable. The moon was full and he could see it reflecting off the surface of the water in the canal.

He could hear the younger kids laughing and playing somewhere in the dark. Lucas must have been telling a funny story rather than a scary one.

Becky led George across the top of the lock doors—a path about six inches wide—so that they could walk along the towpath on the other side. At least she couldn't hold his arm and walk next to him across the lock door; however, she grabbed his arm again as soon as they were on the towpath. George stopped where the mules were picketed and patted their necks. It allowed him to pull his arm free from Becky as he slipped between the mules to keep King George between him and Becky.

"What's the matter, George? You're very quiet tonight," Becky asked.

"I guess I've got a lot on my mind."

"Like what?"

"Like the canal and the war."

"Oh."

She was quiet for a bit and then said, "Don't you think it's a lovely night?"

"Yeah. I'm glad it's warming up. It can get cold sleeping in the hay house at night when the temperatures drop. I wind up burrowing into the hay to try and stay warm."

At least the family cabin had a stove. When you slept in the hay house, all you got were extra blankets to try and keep warm.

"George, did it hurt when you lost your arm?" Becky asked suddenly.

He stopped walking. "What?"

Suddenly the end of his left arm was throbbing and he shook it.

"Did it hurt?" Becky repeated. "I can't imagine what that would be like."

George wasn't sure how to answer her. He wasn't sure he wanted to. How could he explain it to her? Yes, it had hurt, but no more than some of the other pains he had been feeling at the time. Mostly, he had been afraid. That canister shot changed how he saw everything.

"I'm sure it must have hurt an awful lot, but you probably just gritted your teeth and bore it like the hero you are," Becky said when George didn't answer.

He almost laughed in her face right then and there. He remembered gritting his teeth for about a second before he started screaming and crying.

"I'm no hero. I was in the army less than a year and most of that time, I spent in a hospital in Washington trying to recover. On the day I was injured, twelve other men in my company died and twice that many were injured. Getting shot is nothing special. Staying alive is."

"Well, you stayed alive."

"It still doesn't make me a hero."

"But you did your part to help save the Union."

"For what little good it did."

It was hard for George to imagine that he had once thought he was in love with Becky. Yes, she was pretty, but she cared about so little about what was going on around her. He couldn't imagine her ever being able to stand on her own like his mother had after his father had died.

What disturbed him even more was that, in a roundabout way, he had given up his arm for her. She had been one of the reasons that he had run off to enlist and that enlistment had led to him being in battle and getting wounded and losing his arm. Did that mean that the loss had been for nothing?

He hoped that Becky would eventually mature enough to be a fine woman, but she would never be the woman for him.

When Alice crossed the fall board later that night, she saw George lying on top of the family cabin with his good arm behind his head staring at the stars.

"I thought you might still be walking with Becky," Alice told him.

"We did for a little ways, but I wasn't really in the mood," he said as he propped himself up.

Alice sat down next to her oldest son.

"Really? Becky's a cute girl and she seemed mighty interested in you." She paused, and then added, "And she wanted to take the walk. Conditions don't get much better for a little sparking in the shadows."

"I wasn't interested in kissing her."

"Really? I thought that you really liked her."

George nodded. "I used to. I really used to, but not anymore."

"What happened?" Alice asked.

George shrugged. "I don't know. It's not her fault that I lost my arm, but I kept thinking tonight that if she hadn't been fussing over those soldiers, then I wouldn't have tried to strut around like I was someone special, Pa wouldn't have gotten killed and I wouldn't have run off to join the army and lose my army."

"That's a lot of blame to put on that nice girl," Alice said as she stroked his hair.

"I'm not blaming her," George said quickly.

"Sounds that way to me. I think it sounds that way to you, too, which is why you're so mightily disturbed. You want to blame her because then you won't have to blame yourself, but you're too good a person to do that."

"So how do I stop feeling this way?"

"You don't. At least I wouldn't. Guilt is something that helps keep up from making mistakes. When you feel bad about something, you aren't likely to do it again."

"What about you, Mama? Do you feel guilt about a lot of things?"

Alice chuckled. "All the time. A lot of its little things that will fade after a while. But there are other things that weigh on me every day. I feel guilty about not providing better for you, that your sister felt like she had to go to Washington and that I couldn't help your father."

"David?"

She nodded slowly. "Him most of all."

15

MUDSLIDE

APRIL 1864

The rain woke Alice sometime in the night. It wasn't actually the sound of the rain drumming on the roof of the family cabin that she noticed but the rocking of the boat.

Rocking?

She sat up in bed. The *Freeman* rocked back and forth so roughly that the lantern sitting on the bedside table was beginning to slide across the smooth top. She quickly grabbed it and sat it in the wall bracket so that it wouldn't fall off the table and break.

Alice pulled her blanket around her shoulders and stepped through the curtain that served as her door to the family cabin. The boys were still asleep in their bunks as far as she could tell, though Tony's leg dangled off the side of his bunk. She wondered if the rocking boat had caused that or he had simply rolled over too far. Probably the latter. The boys could sleep through most anything.

She opened the outside door and climbed the steps to race plank. The rain fell heavily with dull thuds against the wood. It smacked her repeatedly in the face with dull thuds. She ignored it to look over the edge of the boat. The water was choppy from the rain, but she could still see surges of water coming in small waves from upriver.

Alice couldn't see anything in the night and rain, but she looked toward the west anyway. The rain must have caused a breach in the canal berm opening it up to the Potomac. She didn't think that enough water would be coming through the outlet locks to cause this kind of motion in the boat.

She walked slowly along the race plank to the hay house where George was inside sleeping. She knocked on the shutters and George opened one of them. She could barely see his face in the darkness of the hay house.

"Mama, you're soaked. Get in here before you're washed overboard."

He held out his hand. She took it and stepped through the window onto the hay. She gathered her sopping hair in her hands and wrung some of the water from it.

"It's not as bad as the storm last year, but I don't want to try boating until it stops, which I hope will be by the morning. Anyway, I wanted to get you to tighten down the lines on the shore so the waves can't throw us against the berm."

"I just getting ready to do that, Mama," George said. "I was getting dressed first." He glanced out of the window. "Not that it will help any in this rain."

Alice nodded. "I'll go check on the mules and make sure that they aren't getting too nervous about all this movement."

She climbed back out the window and made her way to the front of the canal boat where the mule shed was located. She opened the door and saw the four faces staring back at her.

"I hope I didn't wake you all," Alice said to the mules.

She reached inside and stroked their noses. Seamus stepped closer and nuzzled her hand.

"You'll be all right, though you might not get much sleep tonight," she said.

Alice checked to make sure that they had plenty of oats and water. They'd rest easier if they weren't hungry.

"Goodnight," she told the mules.

She closed the door on the shed and headed back to the family cabin. She could see the light from George's lantern on the towpath as he tightened the snubbing ropes against trees. If the water got too rough, the boat could be smashed against the berm, damaging it.

Keeping the boat tied down gave it less room to move around and less of a chance of being damaged.

She didn't want a repeat of when the *Freeman* had been caught in the river during a storm a year and half ago. The canal boat had been tossed around worse than what was happening now, but it would only take a couple of leaks from being battered against the shore.

"Are you almost done?" Alice called.

"Just finishing now," George called back.

Alice headed back to the family cabin to change into some dry clothes before she caught a cold or pneumonia. It had happened to her last year so it wasn't outside the realm of possibility. She had been sick and delirious for days with pneumonia. David and the boys had nursed her back to health.

David. Just thinking about him brought an odd pain to her chest. It was an odd feeling of someone missed, although thinking about Elizabeth in Washington didn't cause her the same feeling.

Once Alice was inside the cabin, she stoked the fire with half a bucket of coal to fight off the chill in the cabin. Once that was done, she slipped into her room to change into dry clothes. George would be coming in soon and he would need to change, too.

As expected, when George came in a few minutes later, he was dripping wet.

"It's like the entire river got sucked into the air and dropped on us," George said as he took off his shirt and wrung in out. He held one end of the shirt between his side and his upper arm and twisted the other end with his good hand.

"Over the bucket, George, that way I can dump the water out the window," Alice said.

She hung up her sopping wet clothes on a rope line she had tied across the cabin. They still dripped rainwater freely despite their wringing out.

"Yes, ma'am."

"Be quiet!" Thomas called from his bunk. "There are growing boys over here who are trying to sleep."

"Sorry to wake you, Sunshine, but it's raining out." George walked over and shook his still wet body onto his brother.

Thomas screamed and thrashed under his blankets. "Go away, George!"

George laughed and went back to wringing out his clothes. He hovered near the stove trying to warm himself while he worked.

"I don't think we have too much to worry about," George told his mother. "It looks like it's just a heavy rain. No wind or lightning. Things will calm down when the rain stops."

"We may have to wait a bit until the water drops down to normal. The locks will be kept open to help the excess water flow through. So no boats will be able to pass until the water calms down."

George nodded. "Well, at least we can visit with the Johnstons to pass the time."

Alice glanced over at George when he said it. George frowned over the comment, but he didn't say anything to explain his reluctance.

"Things will be backed up in Georgetown because of this. I guess that means I can visit with Elizabeth for a bit when we get there."

She might not feel the same thing about Elizabeth's absence that she felt about David, but Alice still missed her daughter.

"Unless she is working at the hospital," Tony said, joining the conversation.

Alice tried not to think about that a lot. While she admired her daughter's determination to help with the cause, it was hard for Alice to visit the hospital. Seeing all of those torn men reminded her of how Hugh had looked when she found him lying in the street in Shanty Town, stabbed and dying. It also created images in her mind of how George must have looked in a similar hospital.

"I hear that they are talking about something that will help speed things up in Georgetown," George said. "It sounds pretty odd, if you ask me, but they want to slide the boats down the side of the bank from the canal to river."

"What?" Alice said. "That can't be done. A loaded boat would be too heavy and it would damage the boat."

George shrugged. "I'm not an engineer. I don't even know if what I'm hearing is the truth, but it's not just canal boats that they want to slide down the embankment to the river, it's the boat inside a portable lock."

Alice's eyes widened. "Now I know you're funning with me."

George shook his head and grinned. "It's the truth."

Alice looked at Hugh's pocket watch and saw that it was four o'clock in the morning.

"Well, since everyone's awake, I think I'll start breakfast," Alice said.

The high waters surging along the Potomac River, and by extension the canal, kept rocking the canal boats throughout the night and into the morning. The canal wasn't nearly as turbulent as the river, but it was still too rough to boat on. Though the feeder locks controlled the flow of water into the canal, they couldn't be shut off completely otherwise the canal would drain. Either way, there would be no boating on the canal until the water calmed.

She would have to wait until the water level came down and Lucas was ready to start locking boats through again. When Alice saw smoke coming from the chimney in the morning, she walked over to house to have a cup of coffee with Mary Johnston, the lock keeper's wife.

The rest of the family, except for George, followed her. George helped Paul Johnston appraise whether the water was calming down and the boys just wanted to play with the Johnston boys.

They were able to move on about mid-afternoon. By then three other boats had lined up behind them to get through the lock. The Fitzgeralds were the first through, though. Alice kept them boating through the night since they had lost most of the day.

They came into Williamsport in the morning and were surprised to not see much activity. A good number of boats took on coal at the Cushwa Basin to make short runs between Williamsport and Georgetown. Alice preferred the longer runs, not so much because she made more money per trip. After all, it took longer to boat from Cumberland to Georgetown. No, she liked the longer runs because it meant that she wouldn't have to clean the family cabin as much when the coal was dumped into the holds.

She sent the boys into town for groceries while George switched mule teams.

"Might as well just wait here, Alice," John Henninger, captain of the *Hancock* called over from his boat.

"I want to get to Georgetown before it gets to crowded," Alice told him.

"Won't happen. All them rains last night caused a mud slide down near the marble quarry. All that mud and rock came off the mountain right into the canal."

Earlier in April, the same thing had happened and Alice began wondering how unstable that mountainside was.

"Was anyone hurt?" she asked.

"Not that I hear, but they shut down the level from twenty-six to Seneca. The lock gates were damaged so they need to be fixed and the canal needs to be dug out."

"How long are they saying that will take?"

"They aren't."

Alice leaned back against the railing that surrounded the pilot's deck. More delays. Sometimes it seemed like they spend more time sitting around waiting to boat than they spent boating.

Since they were stranded for the time being, Alice would normally have gone into town to do some shopping for needed items, but money was too tight right now. Nothing was necessary at the moment so she stayed on the boat and kept it going as far down the canal as they could.

She wound up stopping the boat just below Lock 44, just outside of Williamsport. The Fitzgeralds spent the day with the Jackson family. Alice helped Eve Jackson cook up three cherry pies, which everyone enjoyed after dinner.

John Stuart, captain of the *1492*, came riding a mule upriver on the towpath the next day.

"Aren't you missing a boat?" George asked him.

"I'm riding back to Williamsport for a few things and passing along word about the canal," Stuart said.

"So when are they going to get us moving again?" Alice asked as she came out of the family cabin.

"You would have thought that after April everything that could have rolled off the mountain did, but this one brought down a lot of boulders. The Company is going to use powder to blast it to smaller pieces and then haul it out by wheelbarrow. If you want to make a little extra money, Geo..." Stuart glanced at George's stump. George tried to pretend that he didn't notice. "David could get hired to help haul or blast."

"David's not here," George said.

"That's a shame," Stuart said. "He and your ma have a falling out?"

George shook his head. "No, not really. He just wanted to stay in

Cumberland."

"That don't seem fair seeing as how…"

"What?"

"Well, he came aboard and had…" Stuart started to say.

"He what?" Alice said from behind Stuart.

Stuart spun around and shifted uncomfortably. He couldn't look her in the eye.

"Nothing, ma'am," he said. "It was just idle talk."

"Foolish talk is what it was."

Stuart sighed and nodded. "But you have to know there was a lot of talk about you two and a lot of the talk was saying that you and David…"

Alice's face turned red. "David was just a hand and a friend."

Stuart's head bobbed up and down. "Yes, ma'am, I'm sorry to make it sound otherwise." Stuart decided to change the subject. "The more folk who help out, the faster we'll all get moving again."

He kicked the mule in the sides to start it moving again. "I'll be on my way now. I want to get back to the boat before it gets too late. My wife is fixing up a big pot of turtle stew and needs the vegetables from the store."

Alice watched him walk away and then said to George, "Are you all right?"

George nodded. "I'm fine. John's right not to include me. I can't shovel or work a wheelbarrow properly. It's true and being polite wouldn't have changed it."

Alice was surprised that George really did sound all right about it. When he had come home from the hospital, he had been determined to pretend that he still could do everything that he had been able to do before he had lost his arm.

It appeared that he had finally come to terms with what he could and couldn't do.

She went back into the family cabin to work with Tony and Thomas on their reading. Since there was nothing else to do with the canal closed, she kept on the boys to do school work. It would help keep them from getting further behind. It was a frustrating job, though. Thomas especially did not want to sit around reading, writing and doing sums when there were woods to explore.

Tony was hard to work with as well, but for a different reason. He was willing to write, but he wanted to work on a project of his own that he wouldn't talk about. He showed no interest in doing the assignment and work that Alice gave him.

By the time the canal reopened after a week, Alice felt more exhausted than if she had actually been working on the canal during that time.

16

THE WAR ENDS FOR ONE

MAY 1864

Relieved that boats were moving once again along the canal, Alice had collected her earnings in Georgetown once the *Freeman's* holds were empty and then headed to the Carter General Store. The store was far enough away from the wharf where the *Freeman* was tied to not charge inflated prices. The wharf stores near Georgetown were like the Shanty Town stores in Cumberland. They were convenient and had everything a canaller needed, but the items were either expensive or low quality. For instance, she could buy kerosene for a third less at Carter's than any of the wharf stores. Alice preferred shopping at the store owned by a Quaker family to restock food supplies that she needed for both her family and the mules. What little money was left over after the shopping trip, she tucked into a wooden cigar box that she kept under her bunk in the captain's cabin.

At the beginning of the season, Alice had worried whether she and the boys would be able to handle running a canal boat on their own. Having a man to hunt for fresh game or run snubbing lines at the locks wasn't necessary, but it certainly made things easier. When she ran the snubbing lines, her arms ached the next day and she was certainly no hunter. George had learned to run the snubbing lines with only one arm, but you needed two arms to hunt with a rifle. Tony and Thomas still struggled with the snubbing lines. Everyone had worked hard and did what they could and things had worked out.

The boys had managed well. They had made it back to Cumberland with money in their pockets.

She wanted to take on a load and be back on the move. The wharf workers were getting a dozen and a half boats loaded each day and on their way and still the basin was crowded with canal boats around the edges of the basin waiting to be loaded. It seemed like for every dozen boats that left Cumberland, fifteen more arrived.

Although there was a war going on, the canal's business was surging. Alice had noticed a new store going up near Lock 29 and another set of derricks had been built at Georgetown near the foundry in order to off load coal that was purchased to heat the foundry furnaces. Even in Cumberland more coal cars were being used to speed up the loading of the boats at the basin. It was as if everyone knew that the war would interrupt traffic on the canal before too long and wanted to get as much done as they could.

Alice had also seen more Union blockhouses going up along the canal and railroad. The blockhouses were essentially log barns that were about forty feet square and twelve feet tall. A large portion of the walls were reinforced with earthen walls. The ceilings were timbered as well. The thick logs provided protections from bullets and small artillery shells. The logs that made up the walls were notched in various locations to allow the soldiers inside to fire at enemy troops.

All of the blockhouses told Alice that the army expected more attacks on the canal, which didn't make her feel too comfortable since she and the children wouldn't be behind reinforced walls. The blockhouses served as a constant reminder that the war was still going on. She was secretly relieved that someone, probably George, had thought to put the rifle near the rudder of the *Freeman* where it would be within easy reach.

With more and more boats on the canal, many nights it seemed like small cities had sprung up along the towpath. Alice missed the early years when the canal had been quiet; no marching, no shots, no shouted orders. Back then, the sounds on the canal had been braying mules, the gentle lapping of water against the boat and the laughter of children. Of course, then she hadn't lived on the canal boat with

Hugh. She had stayed at home with the children in Sharpsburg.

Alice hung up the laundry on the roof of the family cabin to allow it to dry. Now that she was only washing clothes for herself and the boys and not a dozen different people, it was almost relaxing.

Almost.

What would be fully relaxing was that if she didn't have to do it all.

The *Freeman* was making its fourth run to Georgetown this season and the canal was definitely in full operation.

He loved her.

The thought had come to her so unexpectedly that Alice stopped what she was doing. She put her hand to her cheek as she felt herself blush.

What was she doing thinking about David when there was work to be done?

Things, well, some things, made sense to her now. It had troubled her that David had left them because it didn't seem like him. But he had left because of her, because of his feelings for her.

David had caught her off guard when he had told her that he loved her. Alice hadn't known what to say, but then she had felt herself pushing him away and hearing herself telling him that it couldn't be. It was almost as if she had been watching someone else do those things.

But it had been her.

Her head told her that she had been right to push him away. She didn't have time for romance. She had a family to take care of and a canal boat to run. On top of all that, the war was going on around them.

Her heart was telling her something different, though. It was saying that she was foolish. David wasn't just some handsome man she had once loved like Henry Danforth, the railroader who had courted Alice before she had met Hugh. David had been there through the rough times with her. He loved the children and got along well with them. When he had lived on the canal boat with them, he had been more than a boat hand. He'd been her partner, perhaps even more than that.

She left her empty laundry basket on the roof of the family cabin and walked down the stairs into her cabin. She squatted down and pulled a wooden box out from under her cot. She opened the box and lifted her family Bible out of it. It had been passed down through four generations of her family. Marriages, birth, christenings were all listed at the beginning of the book, including her wedding to Hugh. She set the thick book on her cot and flipped it open to an old daguerreotype that she and Hugh had had taken on their wedding day. Alice was wearing a light blue dress, though you couldn't tell it in the picture's sepia tones. Still, Alice remembered the details. She would always remember the details from that day. Ribbons hung from her hair and she was holding a small bouquet of wildflowers. Hugh was wearing his Sunday suit and looking as handsome as she had ever seen him.

She touched his face with her fingertips as tears rolled down her cheeks.

Tony and Thomas had started talking about bone hunting at the beginning of the season. More than once over the years, they had come across the skeletons of a canal mule that had died on the canal. The mules worked until they couldn't pull heavy loads any longer. Many times the canal boat captains simply turned the mules loose to live along that narrow strip of land between the canal and the Potomac River.

Over the more than twenty years that the canal had been open, hundreds of mules had died along the canal.

The boys had overheard captains talking that there were people who ground bones into flour and mix it with vitriol oil to make lime.

"We can make two or three dollars a ton," Thomas said.

"Do you have any idea how many bones it would take to make a ton?" Tony asked.

Thomas shrugged. "Who cares? We'll just collect bones in a pile somewhere and collect them at the end of the season to sell to whoever buys bones. Someone along the canal must buy them."

And so, the boys built themselves a wagon and one afternoon they pulled it off the towpath into the woods and fields between the canal and river.

"It shouldn't be too hard to find the bones," Tony said. "All you have to do is take a deep breath."

They found a mule skeleton that was nearly intact. The flesh was gone. Tony wasn't sure whether it was because of scavengers or the natural result of being left to decay. They gathered the bones and tossed them into the wagon.

"How many pounds do you think that is?" Thomas asked.

"No idea, but where are we going to store them?"

"I say we keep them near Great Falls. That way they are close to Georgetown. If there's someone who buys bones, he'll most likely be near Washington."

They started to head back to the canal boat. It took both of them to pull the loaded wagon over the uneven ground until they reached the graded towpath. Then Thomas was quick to leave Tony to pull the wagon by himself.

"I smell another skeleton," Thomas said.

"How can you tell?" Tony asked. He was still smelling the skeleton in the wagon and couldn't tell the difference.

"Wait here. I'll find it."

Thomas ran off into the high grass to find the skeleton. Tony heard Thomas scream. Tony looked around frantically.

"Thomas!" he called.

"Over here. It's horrible," Thomas answered.

"I can't see you."

Thomas started jumping up and down. Tony saw him and ran over to him. Thomas pointed to the ground. A dead soldier lay on the ground, but the only way Tony could tell it was a soldier was because of the uniform. The man's remains were nearly skeletal. A few scraps of skin still clung to the bones beneath soldier's uniform. The bones that they could see had obviously been gnawed on by animals.

"He must have been shot and died here. Nobody found him because of the tall grass," Tony said.

Tony tried to remember hearing about a skirmish on the canal at this location, but it could have been a while ago judging by the soldier's body.

"That's a horrible way to die," Thomas said. He stayed well back from the body. "What should we do? Do you think he died right away?"

Tony looked at the man. He had never seen a human skeleton before, particularly one with its clothes still on.

"I don't know," Tony told him.

"I hope it was right away. I'd hate to think that he was laying there calling for help and no one came."

Tony sniffled. Tony thought his brother was on the verge of crying.

"We should bury him. We would be doing something for him," Tony said. "He's got a shovel on his pack. We can use that."

"I think he would have like that." Thomas paused. "Should we tell someone? Won't they be missing a soldier?"

Thomas was right. Tony started searching the soldier's pockets and making a small pile out of whatever they found. It wasn't much. A watch, a small diary, a couple dollars, a knife and a tobacco pouch.

"What are you doing?" Thomas asked.

"I'm searching his pockets. We can probably find some identification in there. If not, we'll drop everything off with the next group of soldiers that we see. They can decide what to do with them."

"I'll start digging the hole then."

Thomas pulled the shovel from the pack and walked a couple yards away. Then he started digging. The ground was soft so it wasn't a struggle.

"How do you think he died?" Thomas asked.

"I guess he was shot. It's not like we can see the bullet hole with him being all bones."

"Do you think he was afraid while he was laying there?" Thomas asked softly.

The loose earth gave way to harder-packed ground that forced Thomas to work harder to get the shovel to cut into it.

"Maybe. It depends on how quick it happened," Tony said.

Thomas took a break from his digging and sat down on the ground near the skeleton.

"It's sad that no one found him. It's like no one cared," he said.

Tony wondered if it was any sadder than having lots of people know you were dead and none of them caring. He stared at the body and wondered if that was how his mother looked now. Had she decayed in a cheap coffin in a potter's field? Tony shivered.

It took the boys about an hour to dig the grave. Tony traded places with Thomas when he got tired. The grave wasn't that deep when they were finished. It would have to do, though. They had to catch up to the *Freeman*.

Tony wrapped the body in the blanket from the soldier's backpack and then pulled it into the shallow grave. While Thomas buried the body, Tony scavenged around for rocks that they could set on top of the grave to serve as a marker.

In the end, Tony thought that the two of them did a fair job with the grave. He wondered if anyone would ever see it hidden as it was beneath the grass in the field.

They had to run most of the way back to the canal boat. They were both exhausted and panting hard when they caught up with George who was walking the mules along the towpath. They fell into step beside him.

"Where have you two been?" George asked. "We're coming up on a lock and Mama wants to switch the mules."

"We found a dead soldier, George," Tony said.

George stopped walking momentarily and then had to hurry to catch up to the mules, which had kept on walking out of habit.

"A dead soldier. Are you sure?" he asked.

Thomas nodded his head vigorously. "He was wearing a Union uniform."

"What did you do about him?"

"We collected the things in his pockets so they could be given to someone in the army and we buried him as best we could," Tony told him. He held out the bundle of items that he had tied up in a kerchief.

George didn't do anything. He simply stared off in the distance.

"Did we do the right thing, George?" Thomas asked.

George nodded.

"Yeah, I'm sure he would be grateful. You two did just the right thing."

The *Freeman* rounded the curve in the canal near Snyder's Landing in Washington County. Alice pushed the rudder to the side and the canal boat slowly moved to the side of the berm.

"Let's stop here," Alice called to George who was walking the mules.

George pulled to the mules to a stop and the *Freeman* slowed until its own weight halted its movement.

"Why are we stopping?" George called. "It's still early."

"I need to go into town to buy a few things," Alice told him.

Snyder's Landing was the closest spot on the canal to Sharpsburg. Hugh Fitzgerald had always wintered the canal boat near here so that they were close to their home in town. Of course, that home no longer existed. It had burned down during the Battle of Antietam.

Tony climbed out of the hay house and laid the fall board out. George brought the mules across the foot bridge while Thomas set the portable trough in the ground. Alice went into her cabin and took the saved money from her cigar box and put it in her small purse.

She told the boys that she would be back in a while and headed out along the landing road until it intersected with Main Street.

Five roads came together in Sharpsburg, which made it a popular stopover point with travelers. Sharpsburg also had its own fire company and newspaper. Farm families grew wheat, rye, and hay. They also raised sheep, geese, and beef. The farm lanes were well rutted from wagons going to Hagerstown, Harpers Ferry, Bridgeport, Boonsboro and Shepherdstown. Of course, legal trade with Virginia had been cut off for a year so travel on the roads to Harpers Ferry and Shepherdstown stopped at the river.

Alice hadn't been back in town since she had made arrangements to sell their lot in town after the battle. It looked better than it had that last time. Most of the signs of the battle were now gone. The damaged buildings had been repaired and the buildings that had burned like her own home had also been rebuilt or the lots had been cleared.

The boys rushed into the first general store that they saw to spend their pennies on candy. Alice let them go and continued walking along the dirt road. She recognized many of the people she passed and waved to them.

Sarah McNichols stopped her. Sarah and her family lived across the street from the Fitzgeralds when they had still lived in Sharpsburg. The McNichols home had been undamaged during the battle while the Fitzgerald home had burned to the ground.

"Alice, it's so good to see you back. It's been so long."

"It's good to see you, too," Alice told her. "How is your family getting on?"

"Brian is with the 2nd Maryland. I get letters from him now and then, but I miss him so and the children do, too."

"I can understand that loss."

Sarah frowned and suddenly hugged Alice. "Oh, I know you do.

I'm so sorry. I forgot about what happened to Hugh."

"Thank you."

"Are you staying long? I'd love to have your family to supper."

"No, I won't be staying more than an hour or so, but thank you. I had a few things I wanted to do and then we need to be off. It's hard to know how long the canal will be open nowadays so we need to get as much boating in as we can when it is."

Sarah kissed her on the cheek. "Well then, do try and stop by this winter when it's closed."

"I will. I promise."

Alice continued walking down the street. After a few minutes, she stopped and stood in front of a new, two-story wood-frame house. It was painted white with blue shutters and door. The paint was fresh enough that it hadn't started peeling.

This was where her house had stood before the battle. A stray shell from the fighting had caught it on fire and it had burned to the ground. Luckily, her family had had the canal boat to move onto, but they had lost so much in the fire. Selling the property had brought in some money but not nearly as much as had been lost.

Had selling the lot been the right thing to do?

It had seemed so at the time, but she missed Sharpsburg. She missed her friends here like Sarah McNichols.

Sharpsburg had been her home for so long. She had been married to Hugh for twenty years before he had been killed. They had been married for eight years and had two young children before the canal had even opened. As the opening day for the canal approached, Hugh had sold their farm outside of Sharpsburg in in 1849 and had had the *Freeman* built for $1,200.

They had lived on the boat year round for six years until they had enough money to buy the house in town. At that point, Alice and the children had moved into the house.

Maybe she should have sold the *Freeman* after Hugh had been killed and found work in town. At the time it had seemed like that was a betrayal of Hugh. She had also been afraid of not finding work if she had stayed in Sharpsburg.

It was too late to change things now, though.

How would she feel living here now? Hugh was gone and this had been their home town, but without his companionship, it would feel empty. Everything she would see would just remind her that he was no longer with her. But then, that is how she felt on the *Freeman*, though she hadn't boated with him every season. Even Elizabeth wasn't here. She wasn't even sure that she could find work here.

Maybe she could find a place to live in Washington. At least there she would be near Grace and Elizabeth. She really didn't like living in the city. It was too large and too pretentious.

"You should be pleased that there's a good family living there now."

Alice turned and saw John Arnold standing next to her. She had been so lost in her thoughts that she hadn't heard him approach. He was a wiry thin man whose hair was as white as snow, though he was only forty one years old. He had been a friend of Hugh's and Hugh had allowed him to rent the mule barn and house when they were canalling. Alice had asked him to sell the house lot last year.

"How are you, Mr. Arnold?"

"I'm doing quite fine, Alice. It's good to see you back in Sharpsburg. To what do we owe this honor?"

Alice shook her head. "I'm not sure why I came back. I just felt the need to walk down the street again."

"Home sick?"

"Perhaps. The house looks nice."

"I thought so, too. The family had a farm in Boonsboro that they sold after the husband was killed. He was in the army. His widow felt the need to be away from there, but she didn't want to move too far from her family unlike you."

"And how is your wife?"

"She is doing well. Would you care to come to house for the tea? Rebecca would be very disappointed with me if she found out that you were in town and didn't call on her," John told her.

Alice smiled. Yes, she felt comfortable here. It did feel like she had come home.

"Have many families sold out and moved since the battle?"

Arnold nodded. "Some. Most of the ones who moved were in a situation like yours. Their homes were destroyed. Others were just afraid that it would happen again."

Alice turned around in a slow circle taking in as much of the town as she could see.

"What about in town? Are there properties for sale in town?" she asked.

"A few. Are you interested in buying?"

That was the question, wasn't it? It was the one that needed answering and the reason she had come here today. Unfortunately, she didn't have the answer.

She smiled and said, "You know, I think tea with you and your wife would be nice. I would like to hear more about the properties that are for sale."

17

FAMILY REUNION

MAY 1864

Elizabeth trudged into the First United Methodist Episcopal Church hospital in the morning feeling tired. She had walked to the church hospital hoping that the exercise would get her blood moving and re-invigorate her. It had always worked for her before when she had driven mules on the canal. She had walked the towpath so many times that she didn't have to think about where she was going. She would let her mind wander and think about whatever she wanted. The mules would follow the towpath and she could follow the mule.

The same was true with her relatively short walk to the hospital. She had taken the route so often that she could do it with her eyes closed. In fact, she may have done just that a few times after a long session caring for the wounded at the hospital. Sometimes she arrived home not remembering anything about the journey home. Walking wasn't helping her clear her head now. She just wanted to shut her eyes and go back to sleep.

She had worked late into the night and hadn't slept well last night. She kept having dreams about battles and soldiers being torn apart. She'd awakened tossing and turning in bed. She had gotten up in the middle of the night and gone into the sitting room of the

Sampson house to read *Great Expectations* by lantern light until she was tired. The horrors that Pip faced in the novel almost made her feel better about her situation. Almost.

Mrs. Carlyle was waiting for her when Elizabeth walked in the front door. She frowned and clapped her hands to speed Elizabeth up.

"Come on, Elizabeth. These men want to see a smiling face, not someone who is going to fall into the first empty bed and go to sleep," the hospital matron said.

Elizabeth nodded. "I'm sorry."

"Don't apologize," Mrs. Carlyle said. "Smile."

She put a hand on Elizabeth's shoulder and turned her so that they faced each other.

"Is something the matter?"

Elizabeth shook her head. "I'm just tired. I'll be fine."

"Then get to it," the middle-aged woman said.

When the church had first been used as a hospital after the First Manassas, the wounded soldiers had been laid on the pews and the nurses had slid sideways down the narrow space between the pews to reach them. Once the wounded had started being returned to their units or buried, the pews had been removed to the basement and cots had been brought in. Now the chapel was filled with four rows of fifteen cots with additional space that could be used in the balcony if needed.

Elizabeth picked up a pitcher of water and a glass. She had discovered that many of the men asked for something to drink when she made her rounds so she simply carried a pitcher with her and filled the glass when asked. The cots were laid out in four rows of ten with aisles between them that allowed the nurses and doctors to move easily among them. Elizabeth started at one end and worked her way down the aisle.

She stopped by the bed of Wilbur Layne. The young soldier still wasn't speaking, but at least he was alert. Plus, the men on either side of him said that he wasn't screaming in the night anymore.

"How are you doing, Wilbur?" Elizabeth asked happily.

He didn't say anything, but he smiled at her. He wasn't looking as pale as he had for the past few weeks. His wounds had started healing, but she kept a careful eye on them like she did with all of the soldiers' wounds.

"Would you like something to drink?"

He nodded and raised his head up. Elizabeth poured a glass of water and held it up to his mouth. He put his hands around hers and slowly drank the water. When he had finished, he fell back against the bed, but he still held onto her hands.

"Do you want something else, Wilbur?" Elizabeth asked.

His lips moved but no words came out. Then he simply let go of her hand.

"I'll see you again later," she said as she moved away.

As she walked away, she rubbed her hand. Michael used to hold his hands around hers like that when she had worked as a servant in his parent's house. His hands had always felt so soft and warm.

It had been months since she had thought about Michael. She had finally gotten over Abel's death two years ago and then Michael had started to court her last year. Elizabeth had been happy until Michael's mother had put an end to their relationship. So was Elizabeth finally over Michael or that she had simply been too busy to think about him?

Hours later, Elizabeth finished her shift and then headed home. She rode in a small surrey with Mrs. Carlyle who had finished her shift at the same time. Elizabeth sunk into the seat and listened to the clip-clopping of the horse's hoofs.

"Still tired?" Mrs. Carlyle asked.

Elizabeth nodded. "I haven't been sleeping that well." The cool air helped her stay awake, but she was looking forward to taking a nap when she got back to the Sampson house.

"You work hard." She paused. "You are a good nurse, Elizabeth."

"Thank you." However, even the compliment didn't do much to rejuvenate Elizabeth.

Mrs. Carlyle looked over at her. "Why are you here, Elizabeth?"

"I wanted to help."

"I don't mean at the hospital. Why are you in Washington? You don't sound like someone who grew up around here. Are you looking for a husband?"

"No, of course not," Elizabeth said quickly.

U.S. Secretary of War Simon Cameron had appointed Dorothea L. Dix, a Boston schoolteacher, as the superintendent of the U.S. Army nurses on April 23, 1861. Dix had a reputation of being hard-nosed about who served as a nurse in the hospitals that she oversaw.

If she knew that Elizabeth was working here, she would probably ban her from the premises. Dix required that her nurses be at least thirty years old, plain looking and plain dressing. While Elizabeth could control how she dressed, she couldn't do anything about her age or the way she looked.

"I grew up in Sharpsburg, but I came here to learn to be a lady," Elizabeth admitted.

"Well then, why are you here in this hospital?"

"I want to help these soldiers stay alive. My brother lost his arm in the war, but he survived, in part, because of the care he was given in a hospital like ours. I want to help other soldiers be able to go home like my brother did."

"And you think you taking care of wounded soldiers will help them do that?" Mrs. Carlyle asked.

"I don't know. I do know that learning to be a lady is something I want to do, but helping at the hospital is something I need to do."

Mrs. Carlyle patted Elizabeth's leg. "Well said, Elizabeth. Well said."

"Why are you here, Mrs. Carlyle?" Elizabeth asked suddenly.

The older woman was silent for a few moments. "Like you, I want to help. My husband was killed at the battle of Manassas. Not immediately, though. They brought him here to this hospital and amputated his leg. I searched the hospitals after the battle and watched the newspapers to see if his name would appear on the casualty lists. When I finally found him, he was delirious with fever, but I saw how well the nurses took care of him."

"So did you start nursing by taking care of your husband?"

A tear rolled down Mrs. Carlyle's cheek. "I was going to, but he died before I could. I helped other soldiers, though. I felt like it was the least I could do since someone else's wife had cared for Josiah until he died."

The two of them didn't say anything after that until they stopped in front of the Sampson brick house and Elizabeth thanked Mrs. Carlyle for the ride.

"Get some sleep, Elizabeth. You're no good to our patients if you can't stay awake," Mrs. Carlyle said.

"Yes, ma'am."

Elizabeth climbed out of the carriage and waved goodbye. When Elizabeth walked into the kitchen, she didn't see Chess hard at work as he usually was. She walked into the dining room and still didn't see him.

"Chess, I'm home from the hospital," she called out. "But I'm going to take a nap. I'm done in."

Chess stepped into the kitchen and wiped his hands on his apron. "Yes, ma'am, but I think you might want to come to the sitting room first."

Elizabeth yawned, then asked, "Why?"

"There's some people here and I think they want to see you," Chess said with a slight grin on his face.

Elizabeth sighed. Her shoulders sagged. "Really? I'm not in the mood for company. I'm exhausted."

Chess just shrugged and waited.

Elizabeth held up her hands. "Fine. Lead on." With Grace Sampson still at the hospital, Elizabeth needed to be the woman of the house and that included greeting any callers.

She followed Chess into the sitting room and saw her mother, George, Thomas and Tony sitting with Mrs. Sampson. They were all grinning at her.

"Mama!"

Elizabeth rushed into the room and hugged her mother. Her mother squeezed her hard and tears ran down her cheeks.

"Chess should have told me it was you," Elizabeth said. She turned to Grace and added, "I thought that you were still at the hospital."

Grace chuckled. "Chess came and got me earlier after your family arrived."

"I wanted to surprise you, ma'am," Chess said, chuckling. "It looks like it worked."

"I haven't seen you since last month," Elizabeth said to her mother as she hugged her brothers one by one. Thomas squirmed around a bit under her grip.

"That's why we came to see you. We missed you," Alice said.

"They are going to have dinner with us, too," Mrs. Sampson added.

"Yes, Chess said he would cook us something to make us forget about the cooking that we eat on the canal," Alice said.

"He can, too," Elizabeth told her mother.

"So, sit down and tell us how you're doing."

Elizabeth collapsed beside her mother onto the couch as if she was a sack of wheat. She felt tired from her work and a sense of relief at seeing her family. Combined, those feelings as didn't leave her with much energy.

"Actually I'm exhausted. I thought learning to be a lady would be different. I would learn the right things to read, the correct manners and the perfect things to say. Instead, I'm spending most of my time working in the hospital," Elizabeth said.

"You may want to be a lady, but you're a Fitzgerald and we have never sat on the side when there's work to be done," Alice told her.

Elizabeth nodded. "I don't mind the work. I feel like I'm doing good, but there's just so much to do."

"She could run the place if she wanted to," Grace said. "She's a hard worker but a tender caregiver."

"I would like to visit the hospital," Alice said. "I could bake some things tonight and take them to the soldiers tomorrow morning."

Elizabeth hesitated. "I don't know."

"Why not?" Grace said. "The soldiers always enjoy visitors and they definitely enjoy food."

"That's true," Elizabeth agreed.

"I just want to do a little something to help. The wharf is backed up so it may be the day after tomorrow before we can offload and head back to Cumberland," Alice told her daughter.

Elizabeth gave up the battle. Besides, she wanted to go up to her room and sleep. "You win."

The carriage pulled up in front of the church hospital with Elizabeth, Grace, Alice and George in it. Tony and Thomas sat up front with Chess and watched him drive the horses. Each of them had a basket filled with fruit and small cakes for the soldiers.

"It's a church," Alice said.

"We have to use places where there's enough space to set up soldiers' cots. Hotels, churches, meeting halls and even mansions have all been turned into temporary hospitals," Elizabeth explained.

Alice's mouth fell open a bit. "There's that many wounded?"

Elizabeth nodded. She still felt tired, although she had had gotten a good night's sleep, more than a good night. She had slept twelve hours.

"More," Elizabeth said. "Remember this is just one city. Baltimore, Frederick, Philadelphia. They all get shipments of wounded soldiers. Remember all the hospitals in Cumberland and there wasn't even a battle fought there. Just about every major city has its war hospitals. I'm sure the Southern states have to deal with the same thing."

"So many men," Alice murmured.

"Too many."

The group climbed down from the carriage and walked toward the hospital. It still looked like a white, wooden church from the outside. They walked into the area that had been the chapel and stopped to look over the beds filled with soldiers. George suddenly turned around and walked back outside.

"Where are you going, George?" Alice asked.

He didn't answer her.

"Let me go get him," Elizabeth said. "Mrs. Sampson can show you around and get you started talking to the men."

Elizabeth walked outside and saw George leaning against the side of carriage and facing away from the hospital. A sheen of sweat covered his face and he was breathing heavily.

"I'm sorry," Elizabeth said. "I should have thought this would bring back bad memories for you."

George shook his head. "Bad memories? No, the battlefield brings back bad memories. When I think of my time in the hospital, I remember the nurses who took care of me and made sure I got better."

"Then why did you come outside?"

George didn't say anything for the longest time. Elizabeth let the silence fall between them. She had learned from her work that it wasn't good to badger someone into talking. The answer you would get would just as often be something to change the subject as it would be something to explain how they felt. She noticed a thin film of sweat beginning to shine on his skin.

"I was delirious for my days in the hospital. I had a fever that wouldn't break. My...my arm had been amputated at the battlefield. Not that I realized that at the time. I was in pain and I was seeing all kinds of disjointed memories. When I woke up in the hospital and saw I didn't have an arm, I thought it was another fever dream. I mean, I could feel my arm so it had to be there."

"A lot of amputees feel that," Elizabeth said softly.

George nodded. "I know that now. Then when I realized things weren't going to change, I realized how stupid I had been."

"Stupid how?"

He sighed and said, "I ran off and joined the war because of a girl. So, I lost my arm because a girl wouldn't look at me. That's what I thought of when I woke up in the hospital."

"You're wrong. You ran off because of a girl and that was stupid, but you lost your arm because you were shot in your arm. You were fighting for your country. That's an honorable thing. And in that war, sacrifices are sometimes asked of the soldiers and the civilians, too, for that matter. What was it President Lincoln called it, 'the last full measure of their devotion?'" Elizabeth said.

"But I didn't die."

Elizabeth nodded. "You were lucky. A lot of soldiers die after an amputation. Their wounds turn gangrenous or they never come out of their fevers. Too many. You were willing to give that last full measure that the president talked about, but God had a different plan in store you. You weren't stupid, George. You were chosen to live."

He slumped against the wheel of the carriage. "But why? If God had a different plan for me, I wish he'd tell me what it is."

"I don't know why. You may never know the reason why, but obviously God had a reason to keep you alive when so many other men die from the same type of wound. I do know it wasn't so you could feel stupid. You've got to live the best life you can and hopefully, when you are about to die an old man, you'll be able to look back and see why you were chosen and you'll be thankful you were."

George thought on that and then smiled at her with a lopsided grin.

"How did you get so smart?" he said finally.

Elizabeth smiled. "I've always been smart. You've just been too stupid to realize it."

George took on a look of mock seriousness. "I'm not stupid. I'm chosen. You said so yourself," Then he nudged her with his shoulder.

"That was girl stupid. This is brother stupid. It's a whole different type of stupid."

"How do you know that?"

"Because I'm smart. You said so yourself."

George moaned. "You're not going to let me forget that I said that, are you?"

"I only wish there had been witnesses around so you couldn't deny it," Elizabeth said.

George laughed.

"What you're doing here is a good thing," he said. "It's an important thing. The nurses meant a lot to me when I was recovering. They were kind. They were caring. They didn't look at me weird because I was missing my arm. They kept me from feeling depressed. I'm sure you mean as much to these soldiers."

"I try, but it breaks my heart when one of them dies. I have to tell myself that it was their time to leave and that they're happy again."

George put his arm around his sister's shoulders and hugged her.

"So are you going to come inside?" she asked.

"I can't let this food go to waste," her brother told her.

"I want to introduce you to some of the soldiers."

"Why?"

"I want them to see that there's life after this war. They can go home and lead normal lives even if they are missing an arm or leg."

"I thought we were just here to give them some good food," Elizabeth said.

"Anybody can give them something to eat. I want you to give them something to think about and dream about."

Elizabeth looped her arm around George's good arm and led him into the church. As he walked up the stone stairs, he hesitated. Did he really want to do this? Elizabeth kept gently leading him forward and soon they were inside.

George looked around the hospital and sucked in his breath. His mother and brothers were already moving around between the cots. Tony and Thomas seemed to be especially successful at making the soldiers laugh and smile. Thomas was probably talking about pets while Tony seemed to be playing cards with one of the soldiers. George just hoped his brother wasn't cheating.

Images flashed through his mind of him lying in the open near a tent. He could hear the explosions of fighting still going on in the distance. His nose was filled with the smell of blood and gunpowder.

George could hear the screams of wounded men and men going under the surgeon's knife. George had been lucky in that regard. He hadn't had to deal too much with the surgeons.

The canister shot had taken his arm completely off. Another soldier had tied the stump off to keep him from bleeding to death. The surgeon had washed away the blood to see what he dealing with, cauterized the blood vessels with a glowing hot metal brand and stitched him closed.

George had passed out shortly after he had gone into the tent and awakened on a stretcher on a rail car that had carried him to a hospital like this one. That hospital had been his home for a month.

"I want to introduce you to Wilbur," Elizabeth said from beside him.

"Who is he?" George asked.

"He's a young soldier who seems nice, but he is scared."

Elizabeth led him to Wilbur's cot. He was awake and watched them approach, but he didn't say a word. Elizabeth sat down on a stool next to the cot. She patted Wilbur's hand.

"Wilbur, this is my older brother, George," she said. "He fought in the war, too."

"Not for too long. I was wounded in my first battle," George said.

"They brought him to a hospital like this and took care of him," Elizabeth said. "He got better, too. They sent him home and we'll get you better and send you home, too."

George saw Wilbur's eyes move to the stump of his arm. He was used to people staring at it more than his face.

George held up his stump. "Well, not all of me went home."

"Do you miss it?" Wilbur whispered.

Elizabeth's mouth dropped open and she jumped to her feet.

"Well, it's nice to see that you can talk after all the times I've tried to get you to say something," Elizabeth said.

"I'm sorry," Wilbur said, blushing.

"No, no. Don't be. I'm just happy you're saying something." Elizabeth turned to George. "Thank you, George." Her face beamed with delight. He wasn't quite sure why.

"I didn't do anything." George looked at Wilbur and said, "She overreacts a lot."

Elizabeth punched him in the arm.

"See what I mean?" George said, smiling. Wilbur actually laughed.

Elizabeth turned away and said, "I'll let you two talk."

"You don't have to go," Wilbur said.

Elizabeth didn't say anything, but George could see tears streaming down her cheeks as she walked away.

18

INVESTIGATIONS

MAY 1864

David walked into the Railroader's Rest and stepped up to the bar. He had spent the last few years trying to get past the fact that he had been a spy for the Confederate Army and now here was acting as a spy again.

Railroader's Rest wasn't that crowded so he didn't have to risk getting into an argument with a railroader as he wove through the smelly men to reach the bar. He asked the fat bartender for a beer. When he got it, he picked up the mug and turned around so that he could look over the room.

He hoped that working in the boat warehouse kept him from looking so much like a canaller. Railroaders and canallers seemed to have a cats-and-dogs sense about each other. The problem was that both of them considered themselves the dogs. That meant that David didn't want a room full of railroaders knowing that he had worked on the canal or even helped build canal boats. He would be a dog bone to them if they did recognize him.

Of course, looking like a bookkeeper wouldn't win him any friends, either. This was simply a place where he didn't fit in. Just like he hadn't fit in on the *Freeman*. Well, not the *Freeman* so much.

David had felt very much at home there. Even George had come to accept him. It was Alice's life in which he didn't have a place.

The barroom was as empty as the bar. Four men played poker at a table near the fireplace. A pair of men in filthy coveralls drank and talked at another table and a single man with a bushy white beard sat at a table eating a steak dinner reading a copy of the *Alleganian* that was on the table next to his plate.

None of them seemed to be the Confederate sympathizers whom he and Tony had seen here. David had thought that would be the case, but this was where he had first seen the three men so it was where he had decided to begin his search for them.

Most of these men looked like railroaders, but two of the poker players were Union soldiers. That would definitely keep away Confederate sympathizers or at least anyone who would speak in support of the South.

If Confederate sympathizers were planning a large coordinated attack on the canal, then there would have to be a group of them; at least two for every canal boat that they planned to hijack and a group to damage the canal. That would be a lot of men. There couldn't be that large a group of sympathizers in Cumberland ready to risk going up against the 8,000 or so troops in the city.

David needed details to decide whether the sympathizers' talk had just been men blowing off steam or men planning treason. And if the men had been serious, then how realistic was their plan?

They had to be planning something that would cause problems but wouldn't require the manpower of a direct attack on the canal. When David had been spying for the Confederate Army, he and two other men had tried to blow up one of the aqueducts on the canal without success. The stone work on the canal aqueducts was tight and solid. Could the sympathizers be planning something like that? Sabotage rather than piracy?

David turned back around and grabbed his mug of beer for another drink. He needed to find those men.

He paused with his glass halfway to his mouth. He knew where he could find the sympathizers or at least he knew how he could find people who knew them.

David finished off the beer quickly and headed out of the bar. Once out on Wineow Street, he turned to head back to the warehouse and saw Amos staring at him.

David walked over to him. Amos shook his head and rolled his eyes.

"What were you doing in a railroader's bar?" Amos asked. "They'll jump you as easily for building the boats as sailing them."

David shrugged. "That coming from a man who smells of money and looks like he couldn't defend himself?"

Amos grinned and glanced down. David's eyes widened as a small derringer slid into his boss's hand from under his sleeve.

"They would be surprised then," Amos said.

"I know that I am," David told him.

Amos used his other hand push the derringer back into its hiding place. He looked up and saw David's wide eyes and laughed.

"Don't be so surprised, David. I'm not a fool."

"I didn't think so, but I also didn't think that you were a magician either. You certainly made that derringer appear from nowhere."

Amos pulled a cigar from his pocket and bit off the end. Then he lit it with a wooden match. After a couple puffs to get it going, he said, "That was just an old Mississippi River gambler's trick. I spent a lot of time on the riverboats out there years ago."

Amos used his hand to turn David and start him walking down the street in the direction that Amos had been walking.

"Now why did I just see you coming out of a railroader's bar?" Amos asked.

"I was looking for someone," David replied.

Amos shook his head. "I didn't think you were dumb."

"I'm not."

Amos smirked. "First, you let the Fitzgeralds leave without you and now you're trying to get yourself killed."

"Amos, I'm trying to protect the Fitzgeralds and all of the other canallers."

The old man snorted. "From railroaders? That's like trying to protect all of the cats from all of the dogs in the world."

David shook his head. "It's not like that, Amos. Someone I know and trust told me he heard a group of men in there talking about damaging the canal and hijacking canal boats."

David figured that Amos would be concerned about that since he owned half a dozen canal boats whose captains worked for him. He wouldn't want to see his investment damaged.

"The railroaders are bad, but even they wouldn't do that," Amos said. "Besides, they aren't devious. They think like the trains they drive. Keep going forward in a straight line."

David knew that he could trust his boss and he decided that now was the time to see just how strong that trust was. "Not the railroaders. They were Confederate sympathizers."

Now it was Amos's turn to be shocked. He frowned as he gnawed on the end of his cigar. Finally, he pulled it from his mouth and blew out a large stream of smoke and nodded.

"They're around, I won't deny that, but do you think they would do what you're talking about?" he asked.

"They've already been doing that. This is a question of scale. They apparently have a plan to destroy a good portion of the canal and hijack many boats. It could end the boating season before it has barely even started."

Amos rubbed his chin. "And what do you think you can do about it?"

"I know what the men look like, but I'm trying to find out their names and some evidence that I can take to the sheriff. He will need hard proof before he believes me."

"You're treading on dangerous ground, David. You could wind up getting yourself in trouble if the sheriff or the army should discover your past."

David stopped walking and turned to face Amos. "What do you mean? My past?"

Amos patted his arm. "Don't worry, David. I won't tell anyone that you used to be a Confederate soldier."

David was more shocked at Amos's admission than he was at seeing a derringer up the man's sleeve. "You knew? How long?"

"Since close to the time I met you. You can't hide the accent or the military bearing, David."

"Why didn't you do anything about it?"

"Everyone knows that the Fitzgeralds are abolitionists and strong supporters of the Union. If Alice Fitzgerald saw no harm in having you on board her boat, then I figured she knew something about you that I didn't. I told you, she's a good woman. I trust her opinion."

"Thank you."

Amos shrugged. "Besides, you're too good a bookkeeper to lose and that includes losing you because you do something stupid now."

"And if I do nothing, it will be dangerous for everyone on the canal. I've got friends who work on the canal now."

"And the Fitzgeralds."

David nodded. "Yes. Like I said, I've got friends on the canal."

"And the Fitzgeralds are just friends," Amos said with a grin.

They walked in silence for a few yards, both of them lost in their own thoughts.

"We could warn the canallers and have them stay on watch," Amos said.

"I don't think that would stop the plan. It would just mean that there will be some shooting and canallers could still get hurt. I'd rather no one get hurt. There's enough of that going on already."

Amos scratched his head. "Fine. I can't stop you from doing what you want, but for God's sake, be careful. These sympathizers won't take kindly to you even if you are a former Confederate soldier. If those men you're looking for are planning violence, then they won't mind adding one more person to the list of those they want to hurt. My impression is that they're no-goods looking to steal and using the war as an excuse."

David left Amos at one of the many wharfs in along the basin. Amos had business to conduct with the wharf owner. The owner was threatening to raise his rates because of the war and Amos needed to stop that.

David turned back to walk to Cumberland. He thought about how he should approach the situation as he walked into town. The streets seemed nearly devoid of soldiers, which probably meant that soldiers were on a patrol outside of town.

He needed to find out a specific time and place where the sympathizers would be meeting. Only then could he take the information to the sheriff.

Ruth Abercrombie lived with her parents on Mechanic Street in a brick two-story house with a wide front porch. The shutters needed a fresh coat of paint, but otherwise the house was well kept. It was a well-kept house of a family of moderate means. The house didn't stand out in the residential area and did not distinguish the family from any other. David walked up to the door and knocked.

Ruth answered and smiled when she saw him at the door. He liked her smile, but he worried about some of the sentiments behind it.

"David! What brings you here?" she asked.

"Well, I find myself feeling somewhat lonely staying in Cumberland with so much time on my hands. I know you've been trying to get me to meet your friends. I think I'm ready to do that."

David hated lying, but he had to get a look at the saboteurs and they were people whom Ruth knew. Even if she didn't know them, someone she knew did. The sympathizers couldn't be that large a group in Cumberland.

Ruth's smile widened. "That would be wonderful!"

"One thing, though, none of these friends of yours are soldiers, are they?"

Ruth looked around nervously and then stepped outside onto the porch, closing the door behind her. She took David by the arm and stepped to the side so they weren't standing in front of the door.

"David, Union soldiers killed my husband. Why would I make friends with them?"

David shrugged. "You said your parents support the Union and I would guess that your friends do, too."

Ruth looked around. "Not necessarily. Not everyone in Cumberland supports the Union. Some are more open to free thinking than others, and there are many of us who would love to see the Union fail and the states prevail."

"Because of slavery?" David asked. "That's what they say in Virginia. Northerners are trying to force their way of life on the South."

Ruth chuckled. "My family doesn't own slaves."

"Your family is pro-Union."

"Well then, my late husband's family didn't own slaves, but they did believe that each state had the freedom to govern itself for the most part. After all, the Constitution says that any rights not given the federal government in the Constitution were reserved for the states. The federal government is seeking to take what isn't theirs under the law."

David nodded. "I'm not arguing with you."

"If the federal government's position was so strong, Lincoln wouldn't have to send generals like Hunter to bully peaceful citizens."

David couldn't argue with that. He had heard stories about how unsympathetic Gen. David Hunter was with citizens with Confederate sympathies. He had driven them out of Cumberland and allowed them to be terrorized. With Cumberland essentially under martial law and him as the commanding military authority, he could almost do whatever he wanted.

"I wouldn't mind seeing Hunter get his comeuppance," David said.

Ruth grabbed his arm. "See, I knew we had a lot in common. You'll like my friends, David. They think like we do. Plus, I know they are always looking for men in town who can keep them up to date on what is going on." She spoke quickly with a lot of excitement.

"You mean they're looking for information about the canal?"

"About the canal, about the railroad, what's going on in courts, what the soldiers are doing. All of it. They try and keep tabs on everything in case the Confederacy needs the information. Many of us have family serving in the Confederacy and want to keep them as safe as we can."

These were just the people whom he needed to meet. He was starting to feel less guilty.

"I'm sure we can find a lot to talk about then," David told her.

"We're meeting tonight to talk about something a group of the men want to do. Why don't you come pick me up here at seven o'clock and I'll take you to meet them? It will also keep my parents from asking about where I'm going if they see me with you. They'll think I'm being courted."

David nodded. "I'll be here then."

"I look forward to it," she said and flashed her smile again. This time David wasn't so happy to see it.

By the time David had walked back to the warehouse, he was wondering what he was getting himself into. He was leading Ruth Abercrombie on, making her think that he was interested in deepening their relationship when he only wanted her to point out possible saboteurs to him. She would be hurt when the truth came out. Not only that but the Confederate sympathizers in town might stop trusting her, and then she would be ostracized by both Union and Confederate supporters. In other words, everyone.

Ruth wasn't a bad person. She had a good reason to hate the Union Army. What would happen if he took away her faith in the Confederate Army?

The idea worried David so much that he nearly hit his thumb twice while he was hammering because his mind wandered off his work.

"You look worried, David. Actually you look dangerous, at least to yourself," Amos said after the second time David nearly smashed his finger.

"I'm nervous. I'm meeting with a group of sympathizers tonight. I don't know if the men I'm looking for will be there, but I can't imagine there would be too many groups of sympathizers in town."

Amos frowned. "You be careful. You won't be much good to the Fitzgeralds if you're dead. They don't need another tragedy like that in their lives."

"I'm not in their lives anymore and I'm doing this for them."

Amos winked at him. "Right. So you're putting your life on the line for the good of the canal, which I remind you, you aren't boating on anymore."

David didn't say anything at first. Finally, he said, "She doesn't want me, Amos."

Amos chuckled and shook his head. "For someone who is in love with the woman, you certainly don't seem to know her heart."

He walked away, leaving David to figure out a way to not injure himself.

David dressed himself in a clean white shirt and brown vest and pants for the party. He had to buy the vest and pants that afternoon because all he had ever needed on the canal were work clothes. Luckily, he was able to buy clothing off the shelf at a mercantile on Baltimore Street that Amos had recommended. That saved him the cost of needing to have a vest and pants tailored to fit him, which wouldn't have been ready in time.

If Ruth wanted her parents to think that their daughter was courting, he needed to play the part. The only way he could do that was to imagine that he was meeting Alice. It was wrong, but it was necessary if he was going to be convincing. David took a deep breath and closed his eyes. He knocked on the door for the second time that day and waited.

Ruth answered the door. She had also changed clothes into a nicer dress than she had been wearing this afternoon. Her dark hair no longer hung loose but was done up in a stylish bun on top of her head.

"I'm ready, David."

She stepped onto the porch and took hold of his arm.

"So where are we going?" David asked.

"Washington Street. We'll be meeting everyone at a get-together there." Washington Street was the wealthy neighborhood in Cumberland where presidents of large companies in the city and politicians lived. Behind the tree lined street were lots of large homes of people like the C&O Canal President, bank presidents and the mayor of Cumberland.

They walked along Mechanic Street and turned onto Baltimore Street then crossed the chain bridge over Wills Creek. The night air had just a hint of chill to it, which was not uncomfortable. It kept David alert.

They walked up the hill past Emmanuel Episcopal Church. It sat on a high hill above the intersection of Washington Street and Greene Street. It was a gothic stone chapel built on the location of the original Fort Cumberland where the city had gotten its start. Once the hill leveled off, they walked past the courthouse and the Allegany Academy.

The Academy was a private school that had been used as a hospital in the early years of the war. David remembered that Elizabeth Fitzgerald had gotten her first taste of being a nurse by helping care for wounded soldiers at the academy. It had become an emergency hospital to help with the excess of wounded after the battle of Antietam. David chose not to say anything about it to Ruth. He didn't think that talking about the daughter of a woman he loved would be the best topic of conversation.

They talked about some of the things happening in Cumberland and the weather, but they walked alone in silence for much of the time. David was worried he was getting into something over his head and it kept distracting his thoughts from Ruth. He hoped that she wouldn't notice since it was so impolite.

They reached the house after a twenty minute walk. It was a large three-story home with a peaked roof and wide porch. The gas lamps were all lit inside and David could see a crowd of people. He paused at the beginning of the walk to the house. Such a crowd would have certainly attracted the attention of the army if they had been in town. Most of them were in New Creek on maneuvers, which was a day south of Cumberland. A minimal detachment had been left in town to watch over things. That was probably the reason they sympathizers had waited until now to host a party.

"I didn't know it would be so many people," he said.

He was surprised that this large a group of sympathizers would gather openly. If General Hunter had known about the party, he would have surrounded the house, arrested everyone inside and shot those who resisted.

Ruth patted his arm. "You should be happy. That means that all of the attention won't be focused on you. Besides, having so many people together helps us feel like we aren't alone among the enemy," Ruth told him.

"Is that how you see all of the people who support the Union?" David asked.

"Yes."

"Then why stay in Cumberland?"

"It's my home and it is occupied by the enemy. I have to endure just like a woman in Virginia, Georgia, Alabama and all of the other Confederate States do," Ruth said simply.

They walked up onto the porch and David rang the bell. He could hear the noise of a party inside the house and he wondered if anyone even heard the knock and bell ringing. A tall, bearded man answered. He was dressed in a well-tailored black suit, which made David feel shabby in comparison. The man frowned when he saw David, but then he noticed Ruth.

"Ah, Ruth, so this is the gentleman you told us about," the man said.

"Samuel Hendershot, this is David Windover. David, this is Samuel Hendershot. This is his home," Ruth said.

David shook the man's hand.

"Ruth tells me you hail from the South."

David nodded. "Virginia. My family has a plantation in Culpepper County."

Just talking about it made him see it in his mind. He could see his bedroom with its large bed and closet full of clothes. He could see the second-floor porch outside of his room. He would sit outside in the spring and fall looking over the tree-lined drive that led up to the house and the field of corn and tobacco.

Samuel's eyebrows rose. "So what caused you to be stuck on this side of the border?"

"Quirks of fate." Which certainly wasn't a lie, David thought.

Samuel stared at him for a few moments and then stepped aside. "Well, come in, and enjoy some punch and cookies. Nothing more fancy than that, I'm afraid."

"Samuel's wife bakes the best sugar cookies," Ruth said.

They walked into the foyer. David could see a crowd of people filling the rooms on either side of the foyer. Some of them glanced his way, but most people continued their private conversations.

Ruth took him by the arm and led him into the sitting room on the right. She began introducing David to different people. He shook their hands and tried to pay attention to what they were saying while he scanned the crowd looking for the faces of the men he had seen in Shanty Town. These people were well dressed, though. The men he had seen hadn't been. He wondered if the class system held for a small group like Confederate sympathizers.

"David, this is John Tallen. He's a banker in town," Ruth said as she introduced him to and older man with a bald head and thick fringe around the sides. He wore round wire-rim glasses and looked like a friendly grandfather.

David blinked. "And he's a ..." he started to say to Ruth, but didn't want to finish the statement in case it wasn't what he thought.

Ruth smiled and nodded. "Yes, he's a southern supporter? He has spent a lot of money getting supplies to the rangers."

"Yes, the rangers aren't part of the regular army so they have trouble getting supplied sometimes. I've been known to help them out at times."

Partisan ranger units were organized under the authority of the Confederate Congress. They cooperated with the Confederate Army but operated independently. They were smaller units that could move quickly attacking Union outposts and supply trains to disrupt operations of the Union Army.

David nodded, trying to hide his surprise at the information. He didn't know why he should be surprised. People from different walks of life supported the Confederacy for different reasons. The same could be said about many people in the South supporting the North. Of course, that didn't stop the class system. While this group was made up of middle and upper class people, David didn't see farmers and day laborers in the group.

David fetched punch and cookies for himself and Ruth. He had to admit that the butter cookies were delicious. He estimated that there were about thirty people in the house. With half of them being women, that left a small amount of faces he needed to check. It helped that Ruth introduced him to most of them. Being the new person in the group, everyone turned to look at him at least once during the evening. Some people avoided him because he was a stranger, but most of the group was friendly. None of the men were the ones he was looking for.

Now what would he do? Where else could he look for those men? He had to be able to find them somewhere in the city.

"You look bored, David," Ruth said when she noticed how much he was looking around the room. They had only been at the party for an hour.

David shook his head and patted her hand. "I'm not bored. I'm just a little uncomfortable. It's like I told you before. I'm just not one for big get-togethers."

"Don't worry. This is mainly so these people can recognize your face. Then when they see you on the street, you'll be able to talk safely about the important things we believe in."

"Safely?"

What kind of life did these people lead to fear speaking their minds? General Hunter had exiled Priscilla McKaig and her family shortly after the Battle of Gettysburg last year. The McKaigs were a family of strong Confederate sympathizers. One of the McKaigs was a state senator who had been imprisoned in Fort McHenry for his sympathies and some of the older McKaig boys were fighting for the South. Priscilla and her family spent four months wandering homeless through northern West Virginia until Gen. Benjamin Kelly allowed them to return to their home.

"You know, talk about things you wouldn't want a stranger to hear. We have to be careful, David. If you don't know who you're talking to, you need to be very careful about what you say. The army isn't concerned about imprisoning Confederate sympathizers."

"It seems like you might want a deputy on your side to make sure that anyone who is imprisoned is cared for."

"Oh, there is someone like that. Unfortunately, most of the arrests made in Cumberland are military. The people they arrest don't stay around Cumberland too long. The army ships them east to Fort McHenry or Point Lookout."

David shivered. He had heard about Point Lookout prison camp in Southern Maryland with the Potomac River on one side and the Chesapeake Bay on the other. The camp was actually named Camp Hoffman, but most peopled just identified it by its location Point Lookout. Point Lookout was the largest Confederate prisoner-of-war camp. It was built to hold 10,000 prisoners, but during much of the war, it housed close to twice that much. Because of this, there wasn't enough housing, food and proper sanitation. Prisoners there died daily from starvation, disease and exposure.

It was not a place where David wanted to wind up if it was discovered that he was a former Confederate soldier.

"It seems like you are fairly organized here," David said.

Ruth shrugged as she wrapped her arms around one of David's. "Not quite. We look more organized than we are. Still we do our part."

"Like what?"

"There's a plan in the works now that should deal a blow to the canal when it happens," Ruth said with a smile.

David stopped walking for a moment. Ruth was a part of the conspiracy? He found it hard to believe, but how many plots were going on against the canal?

"Maybe I can help you. I used to work on the canal, you know?" he asked.

"You probably could help us, but you're not the only canaller who is Confederate at heart."

"No, I suppose not, but I would like to help some way."

"I'm happy to hear that, David and I'm sure we can find a way to put your talents to use."

19

UNFAIR FIGHTS

JUNE 1864

The mood in Cumberland definitely changed when Maj. Gen. David Hunter, who was in command of the Union Army in the Cumberland region, headed south with most of the soldiers in the city. Michael Armentrout didn't envy any of the residents of the towns that Hunter would pass through, but the tension in Cumberland lessened. Although Hunter was a harsh commander and especially hard on Confederate sympathizers, without him around, it would be an invitation to any of the remaining sympathizers to cause trouble. Hunter was worrisome to people. He had burned homes of Southerners, destroyed their crops and tore up their railroads. The Southerners would certainly want their revenge against him.

It was something that was on everyone's minds. Canallers and railroaders were tense. Everyone was waiting for something to happen and imagining the worst.

Michael Armentrout had been working as a hand on the *Hannah True* since Capt. Harrison had started limited trips from Williamsport in January. He had only expanded his trips to reach Cumberland during the last month.

This most-recent trip had ended on a Thursday evening. The captain checked in at the Canal Company office and was told that he wouldn't be able to take on a load of coal until the morning so he let the crew relax for the evening.

Michael considered staying on board the canal boat and getting a good night's sleep. Besides, he was nervous about walking around in Cumberland. He didn't want to run into his parents, especially his mother. It was safer to stay on the boat. If his mother saw him on the street dressed as a canal hand, she was likely to start crying loudly to try and make herself into a martyr for having a son who was a common laborer.

"Mike, I'm going into Shanty Town to get some decent beer and steak," Levi Donnelly said. Levi was the other crewman on the *Hannah True*.

"Have fun," Michael said as he filled the portable trough with oats for the mules. Capt. Harrison took good care of his canal mules and he made sure that his hands did, too.

"Come with me. I don't like to eat or drink alone."

"You won't be alone. Now that it's dark out, the saloons will fill up. You might have trouble finding a place to sit down and eat."

"You know what I mean," Levi whined.

Michael considered it. He was hungry and he really didn't want to stay on the boat if he didn't have to. Levi probably only wanted him along, though, to buy a round or two of beers. Levi had a hard time holding onto his money.

If he stayed in Shanty Town, he certainly wouldn't run into his parents. He chuckled just thinking about seeing his mother in one of the Shanty Town bars.

Michael threw up his hands in surrender. "Let's go. I'm feeling hungry."

They walked into Shanty Town. Levi picked out the Wharf & Rail as a place to eat. They walked into the tavern and Michael coughed from all of the cigarette smoke. As Michael had said, the tavern was full. Levi found a table near the door and they sat down. Michael quickly realized why it was vacant. It caught every gust of air when the door was open. He could smell horse sweat and manure from the street.

Michael and Levi ordered dinner, steak and potatoes. Their beers came first and Michael was pleased to find that it wasn't too watered down. It would help him calm down and get to sleep easier when he finally went to bed.

When the meals finally came, Michael was also pleasantly surprised. He had certainly eaten worse. The food smelled delicious and nearly overcame the stench from the street.

"You made a good choice, Levi," Michael told him as he tried to chew steak and talk.

Levi nodded with his mouth full of steak. He swallowed and said, "I eat here every time I'm in Cumberland. The captain told me about it. The steaks are good, but the apple pie is even better."

They were nearly finished eating when three men opened the door to the tavern. Judging by their dirty coveralls, Michael guessed that they were railroaders.

One of the men bent over their table and started smelling the steaks.

"Those slabs smell pretty good," one of the railroaders said.

"Excuse me," Michael said, pushing the man back.

"Nope, nope, nope," the man said.

"What's it taste like?" another one of the railroaders asked.

"Don't know," the first man said. He reached out and grabbed what was left of Michael's steak and shoved it in his mouth. As he chewed, he mumbled, "It's good. We should get some."

"That was my steak."

"Right. It *was* your steak."

Michael stood up. "You owe me for a portion of my dinner."

Michael realized why the railroaders had picked on him. Each and every one of them was taller and heavier than Michael. They had also probably guessed that he was a canaller, which made Michael and Levi their natural enemies.

The Baltimore and Ohio Railroad was the canal's biggest competitor and a thorn in the side of the canal directors and canawlers. Both the canal and railroad began building on July 4, 1828 and raced toward Cumberland. Charles Carroll, one of the owners of the railroad, had kept the canal tied up in legal battles to win the right-of-way at Point of Rocks and the right to pass through land he owned. By the time the canal finally opened in Cumberland in 1850, the railroad had already been operating there for eight years.

The canal had already lost most of its flour trade to the railroad, or rather, been tricked out of it by trying to work with the railroad.

Now the railroad and the canal fought for the coal business in western Maryland. Because the canal and railroad ran side by side in many areas, railroaders took pleasure in blowing their whistles to spook mules as they passed canal boats. It was something that Michael had been warned about his first season on the canal.

"Won't happen," the man who had eaten his steak said.

"That was my steak you ate."

The man just laughed and Michael could smell alcohol on his breath. This wasn't going well. He glanced around and didn't see any help nearby. Levi was concentrating on finishing his meal before one of the railroaders took what was left of his steak. He probably figured that he was the next target for the railroaders after Michael since Levi wasn't any bigger than Michael.

Unlike most canallers, Michael didn't have a hatred of railroaders. They were doing their job and the canallers were doing theirs. The ones who did it best would succeed. Michael didn't mind the competition or even good-natured rivalry.

These men, however, were looking for a fight and they had chosen Michael as their target, most likely because he still looked like a clerk and not a barroom brawler.

They weren't going to let him go. They would either humiliate him or beat him up or both.

Michael punched the man who had taken his steak in the mouth. The man staggered and would have fallen if his companions hadn't caught him.

"How's that taste?" Michael yelled. He had to yell something or he would have screamed from the pain in his hand.

The man regained his feet and said, "You're about to find out."

Michael took a step back, but he could feel the table at the back of his legs. The man swung at his face. Michael tried to duck and only succeeded in getting punched on the side of the head. He fell over the table and felt someone grab him by the back of the shirt. He instinctively kicked backwards. He connected with the man's knee and heard him yell.

Michael tried to push himself to his feet, but someone hit him in the jaw, slamming him back to the table. A hand grabbed his hair, pulled back and then slammed his head against the table. Michael saw starbursts, but he stayed conscious.

He drove his elbow back hard. Instead of connecting with the man's ribs, he only hit the man's arm. The man's fist hit his side and Michael grunted.

Michael felt himself being turned around. As he did, he swung his fist and hit the man in the face. The railroader fell backwards, but he was quickly replaced by one of the other railroaders.

Other people crowded around Michael, yelling and wagering on the outcome of the fight. Michael heard a shot fired and wondered if he had been hit. He hadn't felt anything, but he wondered if he would, feeling like he was feeling.

The crowd fell silent.

"Enough!" Michael heard someone shout.

He heard grumbling. The crowd wanted blood. Unfortunately, they seemed to want *his* blood.

He felt a hand on his shoulder. "Michael, are you all right?"

Michael couldn't feel his face and his lips wouldn't work to allow him to form any words. He got his hands under him and pushed himself slowly to standing position. His body didn't feel so bad. He had taken the beating on his head and face.

He turned around and saw a man waving a hand in his face. Or maybe he was just holding his hand up. Michael's vision was blurry.

"Michael, do you know your last name?" the man asked.

Michael nodded and whispered. "Armentrout."

"Do you know me?"

Michael squinted, trying to bring the man into focus, but he couldn't quite manage it. Still, the man seemed familiar. He should know him. This man had helped him and was someone he should know. If he could just get a little more focus.

"David."

And then Michael passed out.

Michael woke up on a canal boat. He could tell because he could feel the boat moving beneath him. He could see that it was morning, too. The shutters on the window were open and the sun was streaming in. He thought that the brightness was what had awakened him.

Michael's whole face ached. He reached up and touched it. It was swollen in places, but at least his eyes hadn't swollen shut. He ran his tongue over his teeth and was relieved that they all seemed to be in place, though one or two felt a little loose.

He sat up and swung his legs over to the deck. He reached out his arms and stretched. He felt sore, but at least he didn't think that he had any broken bones.

Michael stood up slowly and opened the door to the cabin. He was in the captain's cabin. When he stepped inside the family cabin, he was alone. He paused momentarily as he realized that he wasn't on the *Hannah True*. The layout of the room was wrong and it was much neater than the boat that he worked on.

He tried to remember the fight at the tavern last night, but it was fuzzy. He had been eating dinner with Levi and he thought that it was Levi who brought him back to the *Hannah True*. That hadn't happened, though.

So who had brought him here? And where was here?

Who was it who had stopped the fight?

He tried to remember. It had been a man. No, not one man, two. The man who had spoken to him was…David…David Windover. Yes. And the other man had been… The second man had one arm. It had been George Fitzgerald, Elizabeth's brother.

They had probably brought him to the *Freeman*.

Michael slowly walked out the door and onto the race plank.

"Good. You're awake."

George was resting on the roof of the cabin sipping a glass of water.

"I was wondering if I was going to have to wake you up before we took on a load of coal," George said.

"What time is it?" Michael asked.

"Around eight o'clock in the morning. We've still got a couple of boats ahead of us before we fill our holds."

"You were there last night?" Michael asked.

George nodded. "David and I were eating dinner at another table when the fight started."

"Thank you for helping me. I'd like to thank David, too. Where is he?"

"He is back at the warehouse where he's working. My mother is in town running errands. She should be back soon."

Michael walked up onto the quarterdeck and sat down on the railing that ran around the edge of the deck beside George.

"I guess I look a mess," Michael said.

George nodded. "But I've seen worse," he said as he waved his stump around to indicate what he had meant.

"Did I put on as pitiful a showing as I think I did last night?" Michael asked.

"It made for a quick fight and that's a good thing seeing as how bad you did. Even I could have done better than that with one hand tied behind my back," George said with a smile.

Michael frowned. "Well, excuse me for not growing up in Shanty Town." Michael stood back up. "I guess I'll head back to the *Hannah True*. Capt. Harrison will probably be wondering what happened. Thanks again."

"Don't you want to wait around and see my mother?"

"Is Elizabeth with her?"

George stopped and looked at his feet.

"What?" Michael asked.

"Elizabeth is not with us. She's living in Georgetown with some friends of Mama's."

Michael felt something within him collapse. The one thing he thought that would make getting beat up last night worth it was that he would get to see Elizabeth again. He would have a chance to explain things to her.

"Why did she leave the *Freeman*? I would have thought that your mother would want her to stay with the family especially after everything that happened with you."

"She did want her to stay, but after …well, after everything that happened with you and your family, she insisted on leaving. She wants to learn to be a lady from the Sampsons."

"Learn to be a lady? She is a lady!"

George shrugged. "Your mother made her feel like she was no better than a slave."

Michael shook his head and sighed. "I'm sorry."

"Why are you on the canal? It's no place for you."

"I had to get away from my mother. She was making me feel almost as bad as she made Elizabeth feel. This seemed like a good place to get away until I can decide what I want to do."

"Have you figured it out?"

Michael shook his head. "I obviously don't fit in here. We saw that last night, but I also don't want to go home and become like my father."

"He's been coming around the canal basin looking for you, by the way. He's talked to my mother a couple times."

Michael's eyes widened. "Don't tell him which boat I'm on."

George shrugged. "If you want, but your father seems like a decent guy. Why torment him?"

"Because I can't be me if I'm living in that house."

David came walking up to the boat, but he didn't come aboard. "I came by to check on you, Michael. It's nice to see you standing up for yourself."

"Thanks to you."

"Glad to help." He paused and turned to George. "I just heard some news that I wanted to pass on. General Early crossed the Potomac with 14,000 men."

Crossing the Potomac also meant that the canal was being crossed. And if the Confederate Army was moving north into the Union again then it could be the beginning of another major offensive like Gettysburg had been.

"Has anything happened to the canal?"

"Not yet, but they are bound to try and do something to either the canal or the railroad. They always do when they get near the canal or railroad."

Michael walked across the fall board to the shore and shook David's hand.

"Thanks, I'd better be getting back to my boat."

He stepped across the fall board to the shore.

"Uh, George, where is my boat?" Michael asked.

George chuckled. "The *Hannah True's* about half a dozen boats back. It still hasn't taken on a new load yet." He pointed over his shoulder.

Michael tipped his fingers to his forehead and headed off.

20

BETRAYAL OF DUTY

JUNE 1864

David walked into the sheriff's office in Cumberland with a frown on his face. He couldn't help it. He didn't like Sheriff Whittaker and he didn't want to be here, but his own investigations into what the Confederate sympathizers were planning had hit a dead end. He knew something was going to happen, but he couldn't find out any more details. He didn't want to put off saying something any longer in case there was really something to their plans. David couldn't risk having the sympathizers blow up an aqueduct or sink canal boats. He didn't want innocent canallers wounded or killed. The sheriff needed to know what was happening so he could watch the canal for trouble and alert the army without involving David.

He stopped when he saw one of the city deputies sitting at the desk reading a copy of *The Civilian and Telegraph*, a Union newspaper. The city also had a Confederate-leaning newspaper called *The Alleganian,* but a mob worked up with Union fervor had smashed the presses back in 1861. David guessed that was the only reason that the deputy was reading *The Civilian and Telegraph* since he was one of the Confederate sympathizers for whom David had been searching.

David had seen this man before in Shanty Town when he was

with Tony. The deputy was one of the three sympathizers whom Tony had heard plotting to cause havoc on the canal. David had come to warn the sheriff about this man and his associates.

"Can I help you?" the deputy asked, looking up from the newspaper.

David forced himself to remain calm. He reminded himself that the deputy didn't know him or that David knew about the deputy's plotting.

"I was looking for the sheriff," David said.

"He's out patrolling around the town right now. Even with the army in Cumberland, there's still work for us to do. I'm not sure when he'll be back, but I'm his deputy, Deputy Michael McKay. I can help you if you have a problem."

David shook his head. "No, this is something I need to talk to him about. I'll come back another time."

The deputy stood up and tucked his thumbs in his waistband. "Aren't you a canaller?"

David stopped and quickly considered how to answer. "I used to be. Now I work in town." He wasn't sure he wanted to tell the deputy where he worked so he kept it vague. The answer seemed to satisfy the deputy, though.

David turned and walked outside, happy to be away, though it raised another problem. Now what was he going to do? Ruth had said Confederate sympathizers could be found where you wouldn't expect them. Now he had found one. He was going to have to talk to Sheriff Whittaker, and only the sheriff, about his deputy. David had expected the conversation with the sheriff to be difficult, but this would make it nearly impossible.

He walked back to the basin and found the *Freeman* back from its latest run to Georgetown. It was tied up to a wharf waiting its turn to take its next load of coal. David walked to the shore beside the boat and called out, "Tony."

The young boy poked his head out of the mule shed.

"I need to talk to you," David said.

"Give me a minute."

Tony disappeared back into the shed, probably to put away the brushes and hoof picks. He reappeared a short time later and jumped off the *Freeman* and landed on shore.

"Hi, David."

"Any trouble on canal?" David asked.

Tony shook his head. "None for us. I haven't heard about anything happening somewhere else."

"I found out who one of the three sympathizers is that you overheard in Shanty Town."

"Who?" Tony said quickly.

"Deputy McKay."

Tony put his hand on his face and groaned. "That's going to make it hard to get the sheriff to help. He's not going to want to admit that his deputy is trying to sabotage the canal, especially since he doesn't like canallers either."

"There's also the problem with where this attack will happen. The planning may be happening here, but it could happen anywhere along the canal," David added. "It will probably happen close to Cumberland, though. I mean, why plan here with people from Cumberland if you are going to attack somewhere more than a day away."

"Then it's the army's problem."

David nodded slowly. "I know and I have no desire to talk to General Hunter about it. That's why I finally decided to turn it over to the sheriff."

Gen. David Hunter was in command of the Union forces in this region. He had only recently taken over command of the army in the area from General Benjamin Kelley, who had been granted a month-long leave of absence.

"What do you want to do?" Tony asked.

"Just keep watching carefully for now. If the sheriff doesn't help, then I'm going to let the deputy know that his plan is known and that the canallers are watching for trouble. I'll say that the canallers will fight back and they will come for him if something happens on the canal," David told him.

"Why do you want to let them know what's going on?"

"I think it will force them to change their plans. I don't want to see this turn into a shooting battle. That is likely to happen if we get the army involved. Just keep everyone on the alert. I think you should talk to George about this, too. He's got some military training. He'll know what to do to keep the *Freeman* safe."

David waited until suppertime and headed back into Cumberland to the sheriff's office. As he had hoped, he found Sheriff Whittaker eating a chicken sandwich at his desk, which sat off to the side of the office. It faced the deputy's desk, which was next to the door.

"Sheriff, can I talk to you?" David asked as he looked around to see that they were alone.

The sheriff looked up but kept on chewing on his sandwich. He swallowed and said, "I know you."

"We've met."

David nodded. "You work for that Fitzgerald woman."

David shifted uneasily as he stood in front of the sheriff. Would his relationship with the Fitzgeralds cause him to turn a deaf ear to what David had to tell him?

"Not anymore," David told him.

"What do you want?"

"I've come across some information that a group of Confederate sympathizers in town is planning on sabotaging the canal."

The sheriff nearly dropped his knife and fork. "What's that you say?"

"Confederate sympathizers are planning to sabotage the canal and attack as many of the canal boats as they can."

Sheriff Whittaker stood up. He was taller than David and outweighed him by twenty or so pounds. However, the sheriff was a bit overweight from a lack of vigorous work, while David was still lean from his time working on the canal.

"Where did you hear this?" Whittaker asked. He began pacing the office, walking from wall to wall.

"Some of the sympathizers were overheard talking in a saloon in Shanty Town," David told him.

"What you were doing in a railroader's saloon? You're a canaller," David asked.

"It wasn't me. It was…wait, how did you know it was a railroader's saloon?"

Sheriff Whittaker punched him in the face. Caught unaware, David was knocked off his feet. He had barely registered the pain from the punch before the sheriff began kicking him. David tried to roll away, but there wasn't a lot of room to move around in in the office. He got stuck when he rolled up against the bars in the jail cell. Then the sheriff's boot caught him solidly on the head and it was the last thing David felt before he blacked out.

David came to lying on his back. He turned his head to the side and saw the bars of a jail cell. He was on the wrong side of them. He tried to sit up, but his side hurt from where the sheriff had kicked him. He probably had a broken rib or two. He slumped back down onto the straw mattress on the cot that he was laying on.

He'd been stupid. He had thought that he could trust Whittaker because he was the sheriff.

"What am I going to do with you?" the sheriff asked from outside the cell.

"How about letting me go?" David said as he held his side.

He tried not to breathe too deeply because it only made his ribs hurt more.

Sheriff Whittaker chuckled. "I can't do that at least for now."

David didn't need to ask why the sheriff was doing this. He was doing it for the same reason as any other Confederate sympathizer. He believed that the federal government was running roughshod over the states and their ability to control their own borders.

"The canallers know that an attack is being planned. They'll be ready. Your people will be shot," David said.

Sheriff Whittaker shrugged. "Do you think I care about that? We are fighting for the cause. Besides the canal boats are generally too strung out to be much of a problem if a dozen men attack at once. We can burn two or three boats at a time and work our way down the canal."

"What about the canallers who are sympathizers?"

"If we know who they are, we'll make sure not to hurt them, but they should be willing to provide their boats to the Confederacy if it helps the cause," Whittaker said.

"Maybe, but are they willing to let them burn?"

Whittaker shrugged. "It's war."

"You can't keep me here without charging me with something," David said.

The sheriff snorted. "I'll say I found you drunk and asleep in an alleyway. Not that anyone will care enough to wonder. No one will probably even think to look for you here."

David sat up quickly. He felt a stab of pain in his side and saw the cell swirl around him.

"That won't hold water," David said, suppressing a groan.

"It just needs to be good enough to keep you from the army until after we take action," Whittaker said.

"When will that be?"

The sheriff smiled and shook a finger at David. "You don't know as much as you made it sound."

Whittaker picked up his plates off the desk and carried them into a back room. At least David knew he hadn't been unconscious for too long if the sheriff was just finishing his meal.

David looked around wondering if there was a way out. If the sheriff and one of his deputies were Confederate sympathizers, would the other two deputies be as well? If not, David might be able to convince one of them to let him out or at least to alert the army. Not that David wanted the army looking into his own life too much.

The door to the jail opened and David watched Tony poke his head inside. He saw David and rolled his eyes. Tony stepped inside and began searching for the keys to the cell without saying a word. He moved quietly across the floor so that even the floorboards weren't creaking.

"What are you doing here?" David asked.

"Getting you out. Where's the sheriff?"

"He's in the back."

"Where are the keys?"

"I don't know."

"I've got them."

David and Tony looked up and saw Sheriff Whittaker holding the key ring in his hand. He walked through the door from the back room in the jail. The keys jangled against each other whenever the sheriff moved.

"Well, Tony, I was hoping I had seen the last of you and your mother," the sheriff said with a large smile on his face.

The sheriff dropped the keys into his pocket. Tony darted for the front door, but the sheriff got there ahead of him and blocked him. He swung his huge arm backhanded Tony across the mouth. The young boy actually flew into the air before he fell backwards on to the brick floor.

"Tony!"

David looked around for something that he could throw at the sheriff, but there just wasn't anything within his reach. He shouted for help, but he doubted that anyone would come. They had probably heard prisoners shouting before. He was helpless as he watched the sheriff kick Tony in the side in much the same way he had done to David. Tony cried out and tried to crawl away, but the sheriff followed him.

"I'm going to enjoy this. You and your mother caused me a lot of trouble last year. Now you both want to cause me more trouble this year. I won't have it."

He punched Tony in the face and David saw blood burst from Tony's nose.

David grabbed the bars of his cells door and yanked on them, ignoring the pain in his side.

"Stay away from him!" David yelled.

The sheriff ignored him and grabbed Tony off the floor. The boy looked so small compared to Whittaker. Tony punched at the sheriff, but his punches didn't faze the larger man.

"Tony get over here so I can help you," David called.

Tony began to crawl in his direction, but Sheriff Whittaker grabbed him by the ankle and pulled him back from the cell. David reached through the cell, hoping to grab Tony's hand. The sheriff simply stepped on his fingers. David screamed.

"Stop it! He's a boy," David called.

"He's a troublemaker. He wants to stop me. His mother tried that. She wanted to blackmail me about being a sympathizer and trying to destroy the canal. I wouldn't let her do that and I won't let him either."

The sheriff kicked out again, barely missing Tony's head.

The front door slammed open and George stepped through holding his army pistol. It was pointed at the sheriff. He glanced at Tony and David, but he kept his eyes on Whittaker.

"Back away now!" George shouted.

The sheriff paused and looked from the pistol to George and then back at Tony. George pulled the hammer back and the barrel didn't waver from the sheriff's chest. The sheriff backed off.

"I'm the sheriff here," Whittaker said.

"I know who you are. Now sit down in that chair and keep your hands where I can see them," George told him.

Sheriff Whittaker did as he was told.

"You're making a mistake. This boy was a prisoner who was trying to escape," Whittaker lied.

"I don't think so. Give me the keys to the jail cell. Move slowly," George ordered.

The sheriff looked at David and then back at George.

"You're one of them," the sheriff said.

George allowed himself to smile. "I'm George Fitzgerald. Tony is my brother and David is my friend."

Whittaker glared at George and grumbled, "So what are you going to do? Shoot me?"

"Only if I have to. Now give me the keys to the cell," George said.

The sheriff hesitated. "I'm the sheriff."

"You think that will matter when people see what you've done to Tony? You'll be lucky if they don't hang you."

Whittaker pulled his key ring from his pocket and tossed the keys toward George. With only one arm, George couldn't pick them up and keep the pistol trained on the sheriff at the same time so he kicked the keys across the floor to David. David reached through the bars, grabbed the keys and found the one that unlocked his cell.

"Get Tony to a doctor," George said.

"In a second," David said.

He walked over to the sheriff and smashed his fist into the man's nose. David felt the nose break under his fist and he had to admit that it felt good. Sheriff Whittaker's body flew back against the floor and he cracked his head on the floorboards. David put his shoe on Whittaker's neck just hard enough to keep him on the floor.

"If you ever go after Tony or any of the Fitzgeralds like that again, I will find you and I will kill you," David said and he meant it. He had felt so powerless watching Tony being pummeled by the much larger sheriff and only because Tony had wanted to help David.

"What are you going to do with him?" David asked George.

"I'll take him to the nearest soldiers and let them deal with him. My guess is that they'll ship him off to Fort McHenry or some other military prison. You should have gone to the army to start with," George explained.

Fort McHenry was famous for its role in the War of 1812 because of the British bombardment and Francis Scott Key penning the poem that became "The Star-Spangled Banner." During this war, it was being used as a military prison. Some of Maryland's Confederate sympathizers had been sent there, too, including Thomas Jefferson McKaig, a Cumberland resident and Maryland state senator.

David arched an eyebrow. "You know why I couldn't go to the army."

George sighed. "Yeah, I suppose I do."

Not that it made David feel any better about things. He bent down and scooped Tony up in his arms. One of Tony's eyes was swollen shut and he was bruised and bloody, but he was alive.

"Thank you for coming," David said to George as he passed him on the way to the door.

"Thank Tony when he wakes up. After he told me what was going on, I figured it would be better to get the military involved so he and I came looking for you. Unfortunately, he found you first."

David hurried out the door and started down Centre Street where he knew where a doctor's office was located a few doors down. He knocked on the door and when the doctor answered, he showed David and Tony in immediately. The doctor used the first floor of the three-story building as his office and lived on the upper floors.

David laid Tony on the hard examining table. Tony looked so fragile and still. He had to be all right. He had to or David would never be able to forgive himself.

"What happened to the boy?" the doctor asked as he began examining Tony.

Tony must have been semi-conscious because he groaned when the doctor poked and prodded him. His eyes didn't open, though.

"The sheriff beat him up," David said.

"The sheriff?"

"We found out that the sheriff is a Confederate sympathizer," David added.

The doctor began wrapping Tony's ribs with bandages. Tony groaned, but his body was still limp, which worried David.

"Being a sympathizer is not necessarily news in Cumberland," the doctor said. "I have friends who are sympathizers. They wouldn't do something like this only to keep it a secret."

The doctor finished wrapping Tony's torso. He walked over to his cabinet and began searching through the bottles on the shelves. He pulled one out, unstoppered it and dumped out some pills on the table. He cut one of the pills in half and handed it to Tony with a glass of water.

"Here, take this. It will help with the pain," the doctor said.

Tony swallowed the pill with a slight grunt.

The doctor put the pills that he dumped out into a new bottle and passed it to David.

"When the pain gets bad, give him half of a pill," the doctor said.

David nodded and slipped the pill bottle into his pocket.

"These sympathizers are planning on burning canal boats and destroying parts of the canal. Tony found out that the sheriff and other sympathizers are planning to do that. That's why the sheriff beat him."

The doctor looked at him suspiciously. "That's hard to believe," the doctor said.

"It's the truth," Tony mumbled.

His eyes were open, but he didn't seem to be able to focus on much.

"It's good to see that you're conscious," the doctor said. "You've got some cracked ribs that need to heal. Not to mention plenty of bruises. No other broken bones, though."

"I have a very hard head," Tony said. He even managed a smile, which gave David hope that the boy wasn't badly injured.

"I hope you at least landed a few blows," the doctor said.

"Not a one. David did, though."

The doctor nodded curtly. "Good for him." He faced David. "If what you say is true, then you need to report the sheriff to General Hunter."

"That's what we're planning on doing," David said. "What kind of care does Tony need, Doctor?"

"He's going to need rest for a day or two until the swelling from the bruising goes down. He'll be in pain for a while. Make sure to give him the pain killer when it gets bad."

David paid the doctor as Tony slowly sat up. He was a mess. His face was turning purple with bruises and his clothes were bloody and ripped.

"What are you doing?" David asked.

"Well, I'm not going to let you carry me all the way through town. Now that I'm awake, I can walk. Slowly, but I can walk."

"Is it all right for him to walk, Doctor?" David asked.

The doctor shrugged. "He's got to get home somehow. If you don't have a horse or carriage, then I suppose he can walk. If he needs to rest along the way, then let him do it. Don't rush. Don't have him move around too much. It won't feel good."

They left the doctor's office and started into town. They walked in silence with David keeping a careful eye on Tony. Tony winced with each step he took. David walked beside him with his arms hanging loose but ready to reach out and catch Tony if he started to fall.

"Thank you for coming for me," David said.

"George thought you should be talking to the military and not the sheriff."

"Well, he was right." David didn't add that it was because he didn't want to risk getting on General Hunter's bad side. David wished now that he had just done to Hunter to start with. Then Tony wouldn't be in the state that he was in.

"What happens now?" Tony asked, trying not to wince as he walked.

David shrugged. "I hope that when word gets out that the sheriff is a Southern sympathizer, other sympathizers who were plotting with him will realize that word of what they want to do to the canal is known and they'll call it off. I still think the canallers should be armed for now."

When they reached the *Freeman*, David helped Tony onto the race plank and nudged him toward the family cabin.

"We need to get you into your bunk so you can rest," David said.

"That might be hard to do with Thomas around," Tony said.

Alice was in the family cabin of the canal boat preparing a soup when David and Tony walk in. She noticed David first and smiled, but then she saw Tony's face and the smile turned into a frown. She stepped toward him and looked closer.

"Tony, what happened to you?"

She reached out and gently touched his cheek. Tony winced. She led him gently to his bunk. Tony slowly lowered himself into the bunk and managed to keep from groaning.

"I'll be all right," Tony said.

Alice grabbed a rag and dipped it in the bucket of water sitting in the cabin. Then she began dabbing at the bruises on his face and generally fretting over him. Tony tried to twist away. He looked nearly as uncomfortable as when the doctor had examined him.

And so Tony and David told her the story of the sympathizers and what had happened with Sheriff Whittaker. Tony stopped partway through the story and said, "David, I think the sheriff might have had something to do with my mother's murder."

David nodded. The sheriff had said something about not letting Tony's birth mother cause him anymore problems.

"I heard him make the comment, too," David said. "It does sound like he may have played a part in it. I was planning on talking to the army officers about looking into it. I wasn't going to say anything to you until I knew something more definite."

"You're going to the army, but what about..." Tony said.

David shrugged. "I can't avoid it. Look what happened. You worked hard looking for your mom. You deserve to see something come out of all that work."

"Could he have killed her?" Tony asked, meaning Sheriff Whittaker.

"This morning I would have said, 'no,' but since then, the sheriff nearly killed you, so 'yes' he could have done it, but it doesn't mean he did do it."

Tony grabbed David's arm. "Please find out. I need to know."

"I'll ask around. Right now, you need to rest. You heard what the doctor said."

Tony nodded. "Lying down in bed will feel good right about now. I am aching all over."

"Can you eat? You need nourishment if you're going to get better," Alice said.

Tony shook his head. "Not right now. Maybe later."

He walked over to the lower bunk and slowly lowered himself into it. Alice held him by his arm so that he wouldn't fall.

"Tony, I will check on you before you leave for Washington and thanks again," David said.

He turned and headed out of the cabin and up the three stairs to the race plank. Alice followed him outside.

"David." He stopped and turned to face Alice, trying to hide the conflicting emotions he felt at that moment. "I want you to come with us."

That surprised him. "You know that wouldn't be smart," he said. Why did she have to keep trying to put him into a situation where he would be constantly frustrated?

"David, we care about you."

"We?"

Alice nodded. "All of us. Tony, Thomas, George."

"I care about them, too, but it's you that I love."

Alice looked away. He could see her cheeks flushing.

"Don't say that, David."

David reached out and stroked her cheek. He was surprised and happy that she didn't pull away. Her cheek felt warm and soft under the backs of his fingers.

"Why not? It's true. I avoided saying it for so long because I was so afraid to face up to it. You made me face up to that and now you want things to go back to the way they were?" he told her.

"No. Yes. I don't know," she tapped her foot in frustration.

"You have to make a decision, Alice. I made mine. Now you have to make yours," David said as he carefully watched her face.

Alice shook her head. "I can't. I'm either betraying Hugh or hurting you."

"You're doing both of those things now anyway. When you make your choice, let me know."

Then he turned and jumped to shore from the boat. However, his side still hurt and it made him slip on the shore. He went to his knees.

Alice rushed across to him. "David!"

She put her arm around his waist to help him to his feet. It only made David feel worse and he groaned.

"My ribs," he mumbled.

She let him go and he slumped back down to his hands and knees.

"What's wrong?"

"The sheriff may have broken some of my bones when he was kicking me," David admitted.

"George, help me get David into the hay house," Alice called over her shoulder.

David waved her away. "No, Alice, I need to get back to the warehouse."

"You're hurt, David. Let me help you."

George walked out of the cabin. He stood on the race plank watching his mother and David.

"George, help me carry him," Alice said.

George walked over and grabbed David under the armpit and helped haul him to his feet. David tried to shake them off, but his side and head were throbbing. Not to mention the fact that he was probably covered in bruises by now.

"I've got a job to do," David said.

"You won't be able to move tomorrow without hurting. If the sheriff took after you like he did Tony, you're probably lucky you've made it this far."

"David, stop being stubborn. You won't be able to work for a while. Let us help you," Alice said.

"She won't stop, you know," George said.

He was probably right about that. David finally nodded his consent. They helped him walk back onto the boat and got him settled onto the hay pile in the hay house.

It felt good to lie down, but his sides burned with each breath. Despite that, he was surprised that he fell asleep.

He awoke to a knocking on the shutters of the hay house.

"I'm awake," David said.

One of the shutters opened and David closed his eyes against the bright sunlight. When he could see again, he saw Amos staring at him.

"Well, George certainly wasn't lying about how you look," Amos said.

"How do I look?"

"The right side of your face looks like a bruise and your eye might be swelling up. Probably serves you right. I did warn you," Amos said, grinning.

David reached up and gingerly touched his face. He had gotten off lucky. Whittaker's kicking could have killed him once he lost consciousness.

"I can make it back to the warehouse," David said.

"Really?" Amos obviously didn't believe him.

"Maybe," David admitted.

"It's all right, David. Mrs. Fitzgerald said she wanted to take care of you until you heal up. I think it's a good idea."

David shook his head. "No, she can't afford to keep me on if I'm not helping."

"You can try telling her that, but all she has to do is look at you to know you're in no shape to go anywhere. It's all right, David. I understand."

"I'm sorry."

Amos shrugged. "You belong here, David. There's nothing to be sorry about. Besides, you helped us get rid of a couple of bad people. George told General Hunter what was going on. He ordered the sheriff and the deputy who you recognized arrested. They must have taken off, though, right after you left."

"So he didn't catch them?"

"No, but they are definitely without employment right now."

"They're getting off easy if they aren't caught. Whittaker could have killed Tony," David said.

"And you."

"I'm an adult, though. Tony's just a boy who Whittaker has a particular dislike for."

Amos held out his hand. "I just wanted to check on you before you leave. I would say take care of yourself, but I think Mrs. Fitzgerald has taken on that task."

David shook his friend's hand. "I am sorry, Amos."

"I know, but maybe that kick to your head will have knocked some sense into you and you'll see that this is where you belong."

Amos chuckled and then he turned and walked away.

21

LIFE AFTER BECKY

JULY 1864

As the summer temperatures rose, so did Confederate attacks on the canal. On July 4, Col. John Mosby and his Confederate rangers crossed the Potomac River near Point of Rocks, Maryland. Though it was a small community, it had been the site of the large legal battle between the railroad and canal. The fight had been over the tight area between the Catoctin Mountains and Potomac River that either the canal or railroad could pass through it but not both of them. The legal battles had raged for years and the C&O Canal won the final decision.

Mosby's Rangers attacked an excursion boat on the canal with Treasury officials on it. The rangers took the passengers' valuables and made prisoners of the Treasury officials. Then the Confederates burned the boats, which blocked the canal.

They then went into Poolesville, Maryland, which was a town near a shallow ford across the Potomac River. Usually, Union troops were stationed there to protect the ford, but they had been deployed elsewhere, leaving the town open for the rangers. They burned a Union warehouse, robbed stores and burned equipment. The destructive raid complete, the rangers returned south to the safety of the Potomac River.

Other skirmishes broke out along the canal near Shepherdstown, the South Branch bridge, the Patterson's Creek bridge and Frankfort, West Virginia. Most of these skirmishes didn't affect the C&O Canal, though the foot bridge at Lock 38 was burned. The canallers did start keeping their heads low, though.

David didn't associate any of this with the plan that the sympathizers in Cumberland had. He hoped that they had given up their plan since Sheriff Whittaker had been exposed.

Gen. Jubal Early crossed the Potomac River from Shepherdstown at Boteler's Ford and burned some of the nearby canal boats before retreating back across the river in July. A week later, the Confederates crossed again at Conrad's Ferry and Edwards Ferry and left the canal badly damaged.

Tensions were high. Canallers either wore a pistol on their hip or kept a rifle close at hand. All of the problems caused by the Confederate soldiers slowed traffic on the canal, sometimes to a standstill, but the canal remained open.

During one of the times when traffic on the canal slowed, Alice decided to leave the *Freeman* at Snyder's Landing. It was no use sitting on the boat for hours until things started moving again. Plus, she wasn't so anxious to move towards the fighting on the canal. She worried about the *Freeman* becoming another one of the boats that the Confederate raiders had burned further east.

David winced whenever he heard shots and cannon fire. It reminded him that he was no longer part of this war, but men were still dying. Though he hadn't been that great a soldier, he still had had a duty to perform, which he turned his back on.

For the most part, he didn't regret his decision. He felt more at home with the Fitzgeralds than he did with his own family. He believed that he had helped them and he knew that they had helped him.

"David, I'm going to walk into Sharpsburg with George. I'm not sure when we'll be back. The boys are off somewhere hopefully not getting into trouble so you'll be here alone," Alice said as she walked out of the family cabin.

David waved to her. "Enjoy yourselves."

"Do you want to come along?"

David shook his head. "No. I'm going to relax and do some reading or I can look over your books if you want. I got good at bookkeeping in Cumberland."

"No, we're fine for now. I might ask you to look at them once we leave Georgetown…if we ever get there."

George walked out of the cabin behind his mother. He didn't look too happy to be going into town and Alice had to urge him along. They walked along the hard-packed dirt road from the landing and came into Sharpsburg from the south.

"Why are you dragging me along, Mama? If you need help carrying things that you buy, I'm only half good to you," George said as he flapped his arm stump. He was wearing a long sleeve shirt with his left-arm folded back and pinned. It hid his stump, which he had found made people around him more comfortable. No one wanted to stare at the puckered and scarred flesh where his lower arm had once been, but eventually all of their eyes drifted in that direction.

"I needed to talk to you about something, George," Alice told him.

George glanced back over his shoulder toward the boat. "Is it about David?"

Alice was so startled by his comment that she stumbled. "Of course, it's not about David. It's about our family."

"What about it?"

"What do you think about me selling the *Freeman* and getting work in Sharpsburg?" she asked hesitantly.

"Why would you want to do that?"

"It's dangerous on the canal, George."

"It's dangerous here, too, or did you forget that an army battle caught our house on fire?"

Alice frowned at her son. "How can I forget about that?"

George shrugged. "It sounds like you may have. I don't think it is any safer here than on the canal. Shepherdstown is just a short distance away. The next time the raiders attack, who's to say they stop at the canal? They might come into Sharpsburg and burn it like they did at Poolesville."

It was hot out and she was beginning to sweat. She waved a paper fan with her hand to try and keep cool.

Houses and stores appeared more frequently to show that they had moved into downtown Sharpsburg. George ignored some of the stares coming in his direction from people he knew. However, since they were staring at his arm, he wondered if they realized who he was.

"Maybe, I'm tired of boating on the canal and wondering if we're going to be able to make ends meet," Alice said.

"If that's the case, then sell the *Freeman*, but I don't think you'll find making ends meet any easier here."

Alice hooked her arm through her son's as they walked.

"Don't you ever miss not moving around all the time?"

"You forget, Mama, I grew up on the canal. I'm used to moving around. I spent more time each year doing that than living in our house here. I'm a canawler, Mama."

"And I'm not?"

"Sure you are, but it sounds like you don't want to be anymore and that's fine. I'm old enough now to be out on my own so I'm going to stay on the canal. I'm not a farmer. I don't know how to run a store. I definitely don't want to work on the railroad. I want to be a canal boat captain."

"Do you think the boys would miss the canal?" Alice asked.

George shrugged. "Probably, but they would also make friends who they would be able to see for more than a couple months in the winter."

Alice walked into the Hays' Grocery, but George stayed outside. No need to crowd the narrow aisles following his mother around. He sat on the bench outside the store and leaned back against the wall.

It felt odd. He felt like the wall was moving behind him like it would if he was resting on the canal boat.

It was a warm day with a gentle breeze blowing from the east. He scratched his stump absent-mindedly and then closed his eyes.

"I know you."

George opened his eyes. He wasn't sure if he had fallen asleep or not. The young woman standing next to him was staring at his face.

"You're George Fitzgerald, aren't you?" the woman asked.

George tipped his cap to her and stood up.

"Yes, ma'am, I am."

The woman grinned. He liked her smile. It set off her blue eyes and the freckles on her cheeks. Those freckles made her look young, but he thought that she might actually be older than him.

"You don't remember me, do you?" the woman asked.

George stood up so that he had a better view of her. He tilted his head to the side as he stared at her and mentally ran through some of the faces that he could recall.

"Nancy," he said finally.

The girl smiled again. "Nancy what?"

George shook his head. "You are making me work for this, aren't you?"

"I don't know about you. I'm having fun."

"Greene," George said suddenly, snapping his fingers. "Nancy Greene. You had two twin brothers my age. You sat two rows behind me in school."

"Very good," the woman said. George grinned, proud of himself. "But wrong, sorry."

George's smile collapsed and the woman in front of him laughed. Despite being the one laughed at, George still enjoyed the sound of it. It was energetic and happy.

"I give up then. I'm sorry I forgot you."

"My name is Nancy Fleming. I got married two years ago."

"Hey! That's not fair then. How was I supposed to know that?"

"It's all part of the game, Silly."

"Do I know your husband or am I supposed to guess his name, too?"

Nancy suddenly frowned and George wondered what he had said wrong.

"His name was Nate." Nate Fleming. George didn't recognize the name.

"Was?"

"He was killed in the fighting at Fredericksburg."

George closed his eyes and shook his head. "I'm sorry. The war has not been a friend to families."

Nancy nodded slowly.

"So what are you doing back in Sharpsburg?" she asked.

"Waiting for my mother who is shopping. Otherwise, we're working on the canal," he said.

As if hearing her name, Alice stepped out of the store carrying a full basket. She paused, taking in Nancy and George.

"Hello, Mrs. Fitzgerald," Nancy said.

"Hello, Nancy. You get prettier every time I see you."

Nancy turned to George and said, "You see, your mother remembered my name."

"She said, 'Nancy.' I remembered that much. Ask her your last name."

"Too late. I've got shopping to do. It was nice seeing the both of you. I hope I'll see you again."

She stepped through the door to the store and disappeared into the dimly lit interior. George watched her go, not sure of what to think.

"Still think you don't want to live in Sharpsburg again?" Alice asked.

George snorted. "She's married, Mama, or she was."

"Widow?"

George nodded.

"She's so young to be a widow," Alice said.

"So are you."

Alice swatted his good arm. "What a flatterer you are. We'd better get back to the boat and see if things are moving."

22

MAKING AMENDS

JULY 1864

It seemed to Elizabeth that she always heard cannon fire whether or not a cannon was firing. The booming faded when someone was speaking to her, only to roar back in moments of supposed silence. It was just that seeing so many injured soldiers every day and having battles fought so close to Washington had turned her into a bundle of nerves. She had seen the damage that warfare inflicted on the men she cared for.

In early July, Confederate Gen. Jubal Early had moved his army south from Frederick with the intention on taking Washington and federal government. The news of the army's approach had scared all of Washington, Elizabeth included. Nothing stood in the general's way of attacking the capital city from the north. Union Gen. Lew Wallace rushed his small army to stand as a human wall against Early's men, although Wallace had less than half as many men as Early. His goal was more to slow down Early and buy time for Gen. U.S. Grant to get troops to Washington to defend it.

The battle near the Monocacy River on July 9 was bloody, leaving 1,294 men dead and wounded. Usually, they would have been sent to hospitals in Washington but Early's men were in the way.

Elizabeth had nothing to keep her mind off the sounds of the fighting, as selfish as that sounded.

The federal government had been building up its defenses around the city with forts, detached batteries, rifle pits and blockhouses. What they lacked right now were men. With word of Early's approach, General Grant had to give up his position around Richmond and rushed his men north to defend Washington. If it hadn't been for the delay that Wallace caused, he might not have made it in time.

Early's advance stalled at Fort Stevens, one of the Civil War forts built to defend the city against enemies approaching along the Seventh Street Pike. The reinforced defenders at the fort held off Early until he retreated back into Virginia.

The retreat loosened the tension in the city as wounded soldiers once again began filling the hospitals. Elizabeth hadn't been in Washington during the Battle of Manassas so the sounds of the cannons firing unnerved her. It seemed as if the smell of blood filled her nostrils constantly as she made her rounds in the hospital.

When she closed her eyes to sleep, she dreamed nightmares of being hit by a cannonball and ripped apart like so many of the soldiers she had seen. She started getting dark rings under her eyes from a lack of sleep. One time, she fell asleep standing up and collapsed onto the floor.

"Are you all right?" Josh Montgomery, one of the soldiers in the hospital asked her. Josh was an older man in his mid-forties who tended to treat Elizabeth as if she was his daughter.

Josh had lost a leg when a minie ball shattered his thigh bone. He had lost the leg, but he was lucky to be alive. As many soldiers died from amputations as lived, though his recovery had taken awhile.

"I'm just tired, I guess," Elizabeth told him.

"Everything will be all right, Elizabeth."

"How can you be so sure? It's certainly won't be all right for the men I see who die here," she said.

"That is sad and tragic, yes. I'm not saying it's not, but what is right doesn't change by who died. If I die, I will die knowing that I did the right thing. I will be at peace."

Elizabeth slowly climbed to her feet. The fall had awakened her, but she was still tired. She was always tired.

"You look worse than some of us fellows in here."

"Well, that's not too nice to say to a lady, especially one who could accidentally pour cold water on you," Elizabeth said with a smile.

"You wouldn't do that. You're too nice."

"Maybe I'll do it because I fall asleep holding a pitcher."

"Oh."

He obviously believed that it was a possibility. She was going to have to do something to get some sleep.

It wasn't going to be anytime soon, though. Troops and wagons had been moving through the city for the past two days. Most of them had been heading north to the forts there that ringed the city. They were obviously expecting trouble, which meant that there would be more wounded coming to the hospital. It didn't matter which side won, there was always more wounded to be treated.

The hospital staff had started hauling out the cots to set them up to accommodate the additional wounded that were soon expected.

"Elizabeth, could you come over here for a minute?" Mrs. Carlyle called to her.

Elizabeth patted Josh's arm. "Got to go. I'll come by later."

"Take care of yourself, Elizabeth," Josh said. "You can't help anyone if you're jumping at every sound.

She stood up and walked over to the head nurse. Mrs. Carlyle was folding the sheets she had just brought in off the clothes line.

"Yes, Mrs. Carlyle?"

"You look a fright, dear. I'm sending you home to get some sleep."

Elizabeth started to object, but how could she explain that she couldn't sleep? Sometimes she doubted whether she would ever get a good night's sleep again. If she said that, though, Mrs. Carlyle might not let her return to help nurse and Elizabeth had to be able to come back. She had to help.

"You've got to get some rest, dear. We've helped who we could and now we've got to help ourselves."

"I'll work if I'm needed."

Elizabeth looked around for something to do. She didn't want to go home and sleep. She would hear the cannons again.

"What I need you to do is rest and also I need you to identify the patients who you think are healthy enough to be moved to a different location further east outside of the city." There were wounded men lying on blankets on the lawn outside because they had no empty cots inside the hospital. "I've arranged for some ambulances to carry them to another hospital where they can be indoors."

Elizabeth looked around and started naming soldiers whom she dealt with daily and were healthy enough to easily endure an ambulance ride. She included Josh Montgomery and Wilbur Layne in her list. She would miss them and the others, but it was time to move them closer to home. Mrs. Carlyle dutifully wrote all of the names down. When Elizabeth had finished the list, Mrs. Carlyle patted her on the arm.

"Now, go home. I'll send Chess for you if you are needed before tomorrow."

While Elizabeth wanted to return to help, she didn't want Chess to have to fetch her. That would mean there had been fighting and that would mean men were hurt and dying.

Elizabeth turned around and headed out of the church. She walked back to the Sampsons' house. The sun was still out. Had it only been hours since she had come to the hospital or had she been working all night? She couldn't remember.

Elizabeth's stride was actually more of a shuffle and she wondered if she had slept through stretches of it. She would stumble on an uneven brick or raised tree root and suddenly come awake to regain her balance. Then she would wonder how she had gotten to where she was.

She finally made it to the house and let herself into the quiet house. Mr. Sampson was at the Capitol and Grace was still working at the hospital. Elizabeth walked upstairs and lay down on the bed.

She was exhausted, but how could she be expected to sleep with all of the booming in her head.

She jerked awake from a fitful sleep. It was night out. The clock told her that she had only been asleep for four hours.

Chess was knocking on her door.

"Miss Elizabeth, are you awake?" he called from the hallway.

"What is it, Chess? Do they need me at the hospital?"

Please say no.

"No, ma'am," Chess said through the door. "Things are quiet for now, but there's a gentleman downstairs who asked to see you. I told him that you were asleep, but he was quite insistent. He said he knows you and your family."

"What's his name?"

"Michael Armentrout."

Elizabeth jerked upright in bed. Michael? How had he found out where she was living? Her family wouldn't have said anything. They all knew how the Armentrouts had treated her.

And now he was here.

"Tell him that I'll be down shortly, Chess. Thank you."

Elizabeth rushed to her mirror to look at herself. She smoothed out her dress so that it didn't look like she had slept in it, which she had. She poured some cool water from the pitcher into the basin, dampened a cloth and wiped her face. It helped wake her up. Then she pinched her cheeks to bring some color to her cheeks and quickly brushed her hair. It wouldn't lay down properly since she had slept without combing it out. She settled for tying it back with a bow.

Then she stopped and wondered why she was worried about how she looked for Michael. He was the one who had stopped seeing her. Maybe that was why. She wanted him to be jealous. It seemed a petty thought to have in the midst of a war.

She walked out of her room and down to the parlor. Michael was sitting on a stuffed red chair holding a hat in his hands and running his fingers around the edge of the brim as he slowly turned the hat. She was surprised to see him wearing a light cotton shirt and wool pants. The cuffs were frayed on the edge and the shirt was dirty, though not filthy. He used to pay more attention to his appearance, wearing tailored clothing that was always clean.

Elizabeth wondered what his mother would say.

"Michael," she said politely.

He looked up and when he saw her, he jumped to his feet. He stared at her and blushed. Then he looked down at his feet.

"Elizabeth…you look wonderful," he told her.

Despite wanting to be mad at him, she smiled. "You don't need to be polite. I finished a day of work and barely had any sleep. I saw myself in the mirror before I came down. I know how I look."

"It's the truth. I think you look beautiful."

"Thank you." She paused. "You look different."

He chuckled and ran his hand through his hair. "I guess I do. I've been working on the canal."

"For my mother?" she asked with her mouth slightly agape.

Michael shook his head. "No, I'm working on the *Hannah True*. We're waiting in Georgetown until things calm down with all the fighting to the west and they can off load the coal in our holds. Captain Harrison doesn't want to run into Rebels crossing the canal on their way south."

"And your mother let you do this?"

Michael snorted. "She doesn't know. I left home not too long after you left the canal. I couldn't take it any longer. I hated what she was doing to me; what she did to us." He paused. "Can we sit down?"

Elizabeth nodded. She sat down on the sofa. It was soft and inviting and she was *so* tired. As tempted as she was to slip back and relax, she kept her back straight and turned to look at Michael who had sat back down in the chair.

"How did you find me?" Elizabeth asked.

"Your brother and David helped me out in Shanty Town a few weeks back and I wound up on the *Freeman*. I asked about you and they said that you were staying in Georgetown because you wanted to learn how to be a lady."

"They told you where I was living?"

Michael shook his head. "No, that's all they would tell me. They kept your secret."

"It wasn't a secret." She paused. "If they didn't tell you, then how did you find me?"

"I've been asking around for weeks and finally found someone who recognized my description of you and your name."

Elizabeth was touched the Michael had searched so hard for her, but he was also the reason why she was here in the first place. But she had been useful here. She had helped people. Could she be mad at him for that?

"Why bother, Michael? You made your feelings clear the last time we talked. I wasn't good enough for you. I wasn't a society girl. I wasn't a lady."

"The feelings…the feelings that I made clear were all about me not you."

"I know. You made it clear that you were too good for me."

Michael jumped to his feet. "No, I made it clear that I was a fool. Otherwise, I wouldn't have said those things. All anyone has to do is meet you and they'll know it's not me that's too good for you but the other way around."

Elizabeth blushed despite herself. Why hadn't he said these things last year?

She crossed her arms over her chest and tried to look angry. "What do you want from me, Michael?"

"Nothing." He sat back down. "I just wanted to apologize. If what I did is what drove you from your family then you should hate me. I just want you to know the truth. You don't need to learn to be a lady, Elizabeth. You are a lady. Don't let my stupidity keep you from your family." He paused. "Well, that's all I wanted to say. Thanks for not slapping me or throwing me out."

He put his hat on his head, stood up and started walking toward the front door.

"Wait, Michael."

He stopped and turned around.

She wasn't sure why she had asked him to stop. It just didn't seem right for him to leave. She looked at him standing in his worn clothes and wide-brimmed hat. He looked like a canaller, but having known how he used to dress, he seemed comical.

"So you really are working on the canal?" was all that she could think to say.

He nodded. "I guess it's getting close to a year now, though I was a bookkeeper in Williamsport for a while over the winter when the canal was closed."

"Do you like it?"

Michael shrugged. "Honestly, I'm not sure. It's hard to make a living on the canal, but I like the work. It's peaceful. It gives me a lot of time to think."

"About what?"

"Just what I really want to do and what kind of person I want to be."

Elizabeth nodded. "That's why I'm here. I mean I came to learn to be a lady, but I quickly realized that I just needed the change to think about who I am."

"I think if two people like ourselves are giving so much thought to who we want to be then hopefully, we'll both turn out all right."

Elizabeth smiled. "Hopefully." She paused and then added, "Thank you, Michael."

He turned around and walked out the door. Elizabeth walked over the sitting room window and parted the curtain so that she could look out. She watched him walk to the street and then head toward the Georgetown wharves.

Suddenly, she let the curtain fall back against the window. She realized that ever since she had seen Michael she hadn't heard the cannons booming in her ears.

23

CLOSURE

JULY 1864

Tony heard a knock on the door to the room, but he remained still. His job was to remain hidden under the bed. When his mother started entertaining the man at the door, he would drop his pants on the floor. Tony would have to wait until both his mother and the man were on the bed and then he would remove some of the man's money from his wallet. Not all of it. If Tony took too much, it would be noticed.

He watched his mother's feet in her high-heel shoes click on the floor as she walked to the door. Then he saw the door open.

"Hello," he heard his mother say.

The man never said a word. Tony only heard the smack of flesh being hit and his mother's yelp of pain.

"What…no!" his mother cried out.

She started to scream, but the sound was abruptly cut off as the man stepped into the room. The door slammed behind him and Tony saw his mother's feet backing up toward the bed.

He heard a muffled scream and then something sprayed on the floor. He realized that it was blood.

He wanted to crawl forward to see what was happening, but he didn't think that he would like what he saw.

His mother's feet jerked around and at times, they even came completely off the floor. It wasn't like what happened if she was on the bed. When that happened, he could see the mattress sag as it took the weight of her body. This was as if the man was lifting his mother up into the air. More blood hit the floor, making large puddles before it soaked into the wooden boards.

Then his mother's body collapsed on the wooden floor. She lay on her side staring at Tony as he lay hidden under the bed, trying to pull himself into a tight ball. Her eyes didn't blink at all.

He was sure that she was dead, but then she whispered, "Why didn't you help me?"

Tony sat up so quickly in his bunk that he nearly hit his head on Thomas's bunk above him. He was breathing hard and sweating. He inhaled deeply to try and catch his breath. It wasn't the first time he had had that nightmare unfortunately.

Once his heart stopped racing, Tony climbed out of his bunk and walked out of the family cabin onto the race plank. The night air was cool and still.

He walked up to the quarterdeck and looked toward the shore. The *Freeman* was tied up at the Cumberland Basin waiting to take on coal in the morning.

Most of Cumberland was dark, except for some street lights that he could see burning. Even Shanty Town was quiet at this hour. It was so late, or rather, so early in the morning that even the saloons had closed down. Some of the stores would open around the time the sun came up, but most of the saloons wouldn't reopen until noon.

Why didn't you help me?

He had tried. Tony had tried everything he could think of to try and find someone who knew something about his mother's murder. He had been met with ignorance and indifference. He had finally come to realize that his mother's killer might never be caught.

With Sheriff Whittaker and his deputy on the run, the sheriff's department was understaffed, not that the new sheriff cared much who had killed his mother. Dozens of people died every year in Shanty Town and their killers were rarely caught. Hundreds of thousands of people were dying in the war and the specific person who killed them would rarely be killed.

Tony shook his head. It wasn't fair. He had been able to find Mr.

Fitzgerald's killers and he had seen that they had gotten what they had deserved.

But now…

Now Tony felt like a piece of him had died. Maybe not died, but was missing. A part of his past was gone and closed off to him forever.

He crept back into the family cabin, snatched up his shoes that he had left on the deck by his bunk and then crept back out again. He sat down on the hatch covers and put his shoes on and then jumped to shore. He needed to take a walk and tire himself out so he could get back to sleep.

It was weird walking through Cumberland at this time in the morning. It was a ghost town except for a few soldiers. The night was quiet. No train whistles. No voices. No hoofs clopping on the cobblestones.

He had set out without a destination in mind, but within an hour, he found himself at the entrance to the Potter's Field. It was a graveyard surrounded by a worn fence that probably hadn't been whitewashed since it was first erected. It was where the poor and indigent in Cumberland were buried.

The moon was full so he could see well enough to make out the rows of wooden crosses marking the graves of the people who had been too poor to afford a headstone and decent burial. The moonlight wasn't bright enough for him to read by, but it didn't matter. He knew which one was his mother's grave. Seventeenth row, third over.

Tony made his way down the rows of crosses, careful not to knock any over. He didn't want to be the last person to disrespect these people. His mother's cross looked just like any of the others. He stood in front of it just staring at the barely visible outline.

He didn't know why he had come. He could only imagine that it would add to his nightmares.

Now that he could see a bit more as the sun was starting to rise, he could see that the grass had grown over the dirt pile marking his mother's grave. Tony sat down on the grass and stared at the cross. All it had written on it was "Carol Grovenor."

Tony tried to remember if he had ever heard his mother using that name. He wondered if was her real name or just the last one she had been using when she had been killed. She had changed her last name whenever she got so behind in her bills that she needed to make herself harder to find. Of course, since she never left Shanty Town, she wasn't too hard to find if someone was willing to look for her.

That was the problem. No one had cared about her to look for her or to look out for her.

He sat in front of the cross until the sun started peeking above the tree tops. Then he walked down to the river to one of the locations where he used to like to fish when he had lived in Shanty Town with his mother. It was away from Shanty Town along a section of the bank of the Potomac River. An oak tree had a thick branch that hung over the river. He could climb into the tree and rest on the branch while he fished. He also hid his fishing pole in a hollow place in the tree trunk.

He had shown Tony his fishing hole once, but his younger brother had been more interested in a robin's nest that he had found in the tree rather than fishing.

Tony pulled his pocket knife out and dug around in the dirt until his found a few worms. He unfolded his handkerchief and dropped the worms onto it and then stuffed it into his pocket. He shimmied up the tree until he could grab hold of the lowest branch and start climbing.

His fishing pole, which was nothing more than sturdy, fairly straight branch with a long piece of yarn tied to the end, was still where he had left it hidden the last time he had fished here weeks ago. Tony baited the hook with one of the worms and dropped it into the water.

It wasn't that he was anxious to fish. He just wanted to sit some place that was familiar and quiet. He wanted all the jumble of emotions that he was feeling to settle down.

He wasn't sure how long he sat there fishing. The day got hot even with him sitting in the shade of the tree. He wasn't even really paying attention to his fishing. He finally looked down and pulled his pole out of the water only to see that the worm had long ago been snatched away by a fish.

"It's all right. Half the time the hook wasn't even in the water."

Tony looked down and saw Thomas leaning against the trunk of the tree.

"How long have you been there?" Tony asked.

"Since you've been here. I followed you."

Thomas had hold of a black snake that he was letting curl itself around his arm. Tony was surprised his brother had been so quiet. It was so unlike him.

"You followed me when I left the boat?"

Thomas nodded sharply. "Yep. You really weren't as quiet as you think."

"Why did you follow me?"

"You left in the middle of the night."

"Mama will be worried."

"Oh, and she wouldn't be if only you had snuck off?"

"That's not what I meant."

Thomas shrugged. "Doesn't matter. She's not worried. When you started fishing, I went back and told her where you had gone. She'll probably pick us up on her way out of Cumberland if we stay here long enough."

"I think I will."

Thomas nodded.

Tony pulled up his fishing line, baited it and dropped it in the water. Thomas went back to playing with his snake. That was all they said for the rest of the afternoon.

Tony smiled. It felt good knowing that his brother was looking out for him.

David headed out early in the morning to visit Amos at the warehouse. He wanted to get the real news of what was happening in Cumberland from the man who seemed to know just about everything that was going on.

He found Amos standing outside looking out over the basin. It didn't look like he had any new boats under construction, at least nothing that had been started in the warehouse.

"How are things along the canal?" Amos asked as David approached.

"The same. There's minor skirmishes now and then, but you just need to keep your eyes open and things seem to work out," David told him.

"Are you still keeping your pistol with you?" David had been wearing his pistol when the *Freeman* was moving because he didn't want to be caught without a weapon. He didn't remember ever telling Amos that, though."

"When we're on the canal, I wear it. George wears his, too."

"So do my captains." Amos paused and lit a cigar. "And how are you and Alice Fitzgerald getting along?"

David felt himself blush. "Things are…awkward, but at least it is all out in the open. I have hope."

"Life isn't much good without that."

Amos turned and started back to the warehouse. David walked along beside him.

"Have they found Sheriff Whittaker yet?" David asked.

"No, he and his deputy have vanished. Deputy Eyler is the new sheriff, at least until there's another election."

"Is he a good man?"

"Good, yes. Honest, yes. However, that doesn't mean he's cut out to be the sheriff. Time will tell on that."

Amos poured himself a cup of coffee that was brewing on the pot-belly stove in the main room of the warehouse. He poured a second cup and offered it to David. David took a sip of the coffee and winced.

"You made this, didn't you?" he asked.

Amos waved his cigar in the air. "Do you see anyone else around?"

"When are you going to make a good cup of coffee?"

Amos grinned and said, "I tell you what. When you get married, I'll make a delicious pot of coffee for you and your bride."

David laughed and almost spilled his drink, which wouldn't have been a bad thing. Amos's coffee was either too bitter or too watered down.

"You know, David, if you want to make sure that the sheriff and his deputy – or rather, Mr. Whittaker and Mr. McKay – are caught, it would help if you gave me some names I could take to General Kelley."

"You probably know all of them, Amos. You seem to know everything that goes on in Cumberland." David shook his head. "I can't tell you, though. I won't betray the sympathizers I know. Most of them aren't violent. They are just people who don't agree with the federal government. They should be able to do that and not be treated the way that General Hunter treated them. Whittaker crossed the line, though. He endangered other people."

"Nice speech," Amos said as he puffed on his cigar. "It doesn't help, though."

"If Whittaker's on the run, I doubt that he can do much harm."

Amos jabbed his cigar in David's direction to emphasize his words. "You're wrong there. When he was sheriff, he had to at least pretend to be supporting the Union. It helped keep him in check. That's gone now. Who knows what he might try?"

David dumped the remaining coffee in his cup on the ground. He patted Amos on the shoulder.

"It was good to see you, Amos. I'll stop by again sometime. Maybe we can have lunch instead of this God awful coffee."

David walked out of the warehouse and headed back to the wharf where the *Freeman* was tied up. He stopped when he saw a small figure walking hurriedly toward him. It was Ruth Abercrombie.

Her mouth was set in a frown and her eyes burned with fury. David had wondered if he would see her again and what would happen if he did. Now he knew.

Ruth stopping in front of him, barely avoiding running him over.

"You!" Her lips pressed together in a tight line and she shook her head slightly.

"Ruth, I…"

She slapped him. Despite her size, it was still a stinging slap, made even more so because he knew that he deserved it.

"I trusted you and you betrayed me!" she nearly screamed.

"I didn't betray you. I've told no one about you or your friends."

"The sheriff was helping us and now he's being hunted because you told the army that he was a sympathizer."

"He's being hunted because he was going to hurt innocent people who are just trying to make their living on the canal. He nearly killed a young boy who he simply didn't like because the boy had gotten the best of him in the past. He's being hunted because he's evil." David's voice had been rising as he spoke. He hadn't meant to shout, but Whittaker just got under his skin.

David took a deep breath to calm himself down. He reached out to put a hand on Ruth's shoulder, but she stopped back.

"I didn't mean to hurt you, Ruth. You are a kind person and I…"

Ruth covered her ears. "Don't say it! I don't want to hear your lies. You don't care about me. You couldn't. At least my parents are open in their animosity, but you, you pretended to be like me just so you could use me."

Then she suddenly stepped forward and slapped him on the same cheek. She spun on her heels and stormed off.

David rubbed his cheek. He knew that he should feel more guilt about the way he had treated Ruth, but he couldn't. All he had to do was remember how helpless he had felt watching Whittaker beat Tony and how bruised and helpless Tony had looked curled into the ball the way he had been.

He had nothing to feel guilty about. Not that that knowledge stopped his cheek from stinging.

24

ATTACK

AUGUST 1864

David and George wore gunbelts with pistols in the holster whenever they were on the canal. In addition, they kept a rifle in each of the canal boat cabins and near the rudder. As the war continued to turn against the South, the Confederate raiders got more daring, though no one had been hurt yet. David just wanted to make sure that things stayed that way.

David was piloting the boat as it approached Lock 41 south of Williamsport. He picked up the brass horn and blew the first few notes of "Red Rover" to let John Hargrove, the lock tender, know that they were approaching the lock. Besides, night was approaching and Hargrove might be in bed, thinking the boats were tied up for the night.

That was just what David was going to do, too, but first he wanted to be on the other side of the lock. That way, they would be able to start down the canal immediately in the morning.

By the time they reached Lock 41, Hargrove had the west gates open and David guided the *Freeman* toward the narrow opening. It seemed so much smaller when only the lantern hanging on the front of the boat lighted it. He called for Tony to stop the mules. The lock allowed only three inches of clearance on both sides of the boat so getting into the lock without damaging either the lock walls or the boat was the trickiest part of locking through.

David saw three other boats tied up on the other side of the canal so he wasn't the only one with the idea. More and more, he had seen canallers seeking safety in numbers when they tied up for the night. It also allowed for someone to stay awake throughout the night and stand watch over the boats.

Once the *Freeman* had locked through, David let the boat drift to the north side of the canal ahead of the other boats before he tied up for the night and had Thomas picket the mules. He had already eaten supper so once things settled down for the evening, he said goodnight to everyone and headed to the hay house to sleep. He wanted to get an early start in the morning to avoid any back up at the river lock for Big Slackwater.

David woke up around 3 a.m. slightly groggy. He heard shouts outside the hay house and slapped himself lightly on the face to wake up. After a moment of disorientation, he sat up quickly and grabbed his rifle because he didn't recognize the voices. David swung open the window in the hay house.

Men with lanterns were swarming around the canal boats and standing on the hatch covers over the holds. David tried to do a quick count and knew there were more than a dozen men. More may have been in the shadows where he couldn't see them, though.

"Everyone out in the open where we can see you!" one of the men shouted. "If we see a rifle or pistol, we're going to start shooting and some women and children could get hurt!"

"Go to hell!" someone on one of the boats shouted.

One of the masked men fired his rifle. David couldn't tell whether it was into the air or into one of the canal boats.

"Everyone on the shore!"

Canallers started filing slowly out of the cabins and walking across the fall boards to stand on the shore. David could hear many of the women and children sobbing. He saw Alice, Thomas and Tony walk out of the family cabin onto the race plank.

"What do we do?" George asked from beside him.

David had been sleeping so soundly that he hadn't even heard George come to bed.

"I don't see that we have much of a choice. If we start shooting, innocent people will be shot," David said.

Thomas laid the fall board from the race plank to the shore and he walked across to join some of the canallers who were already there.

"We could stay in here," George said.

David's mind raced as he tried to figure out what could be done. This group was obviously made up of Confederate sympathizers, but it wasn't clear what they wanted.

"They're going to burn all of these boats and sink them. If we're still in here, we'll be burned with the boat," David guessed.

"So we leave?"

"I guess so, but I'm taking a little precaution."

He grabbed his pistol, unbuttoned his shirt and slid the pistol into his shirt and tucked it in his waistband. Then he pulled on his coat. As dark as it was outside, he doubted that anyone would notice the bulge under his coat.

David opened the shutters and stepped through and onto the race plank. George followed him after he put on his own coat.

On the shore, the raiders had started a fire and were lighting torches. Once David saw the torches, he knew that the fire wasn't just to see by. One of the men was on the *Blue Mountain*, smashing the lanterns so that the oil would spread over the hatch covers and cabins.

"What about the mules?" Thomas asked loudly to no one in particular.

A couple of the raiders conferred for a moment. When the group broke up, one of the men said, "Go ahead and get your mules, but be quick about it."

So the men weren't really here to kill; they just wanted to destroy things.

People ran back on their boats and started leading the mules out of the mule sheds and onto the towpath.

While David was watching Tony and Thomas bring the mules down the fall board and onto the towpath, one of the raiders walked over and stood in front of him.

"What's your name?" the masked man asked.

"What's yours?" David replied.

The raider punched him in the jaw and David fell to his knees.

"Don't sass me! What's your name?"

Were these raiders soldiers? Had someone recognized him as a Confederate soldier?

"David. David Windover," he said, rubbing his jaw.

"Ha! I knew it. Hey, Whittaker, get over here. I got a present for you," the raider called.

A large man walked along the towpath toward them. He might have had a hood on to cover his face, but David knew who it was from his gait and size. It was none other than former Sheriff Lee Whittaker.

The large man stopped in front of David. David was almost sure that the man was grinning behind the hood.

"I know who you are," David said.

Whittaker punched him in the stomach. "It doesn't matter." He turned to the other raiders. "Burn the boats! Start with this one." He pointed to the *Freeman.*

Torches were flung onto the canal boats and flames jumped as the lamp oil ignited. The smell of burning wood replaced the smell of burning oil. It would take a long time for the boats to burn completely and these men couldn't afford to stay here the entire time. Once they left, then everyone could concentrate on getting the fires out.

All around him, David could hear people crying as they watched their livelihood and their personal possessions start to burn.

With Whittaker as part of the group, David knew that these were the sympathizers from Cumberland that he had been trying to find. Well, he had found them. So what now?

Thomas walked over to Whittaker. He was holding a burlap bag in his hands that looked empty.

"Mister, why are you burning our boats?" he asked. "What did we ever do to you?"

"Go, cry to your mama."

Thomas jumped and dropped his bag. When he bent down to pick it up, he grabbed it by the bottom corners. Then he flicked out the bag as if it were a rug that that he was shaking. Two cottonmouth snakes flew out of the bag and onto Whittaker's stomach.

The man screamed and began dancing around. Then he ran down the towpath. David couldn't tell whether the man had been bit or not, but he had other things to worry about.

One of the raiders raised his rifle butt to hit Thomas with it. David swung as hard as he could and punched the man in his exposed stomach. As he bent forward, David grabbed the rifle and kicked the man between the legs.

"Get the women and children into the trees!" George yelled as he grabbed Thomas by the neck and shoved him off the towpath.

David pulled the rifle free from the raider's grip and smashed him in the back of the head with the stock. The man dropped to the ground and lay still.

"Get the fires out!" David called.

Some of the men from the canal boats were fighting with the raiders. David saw one of the raiders getting ready to throw a torch onto the boat and he shot him. The torch dropped out of the man's hand and caught his coat on fire. The man screamed. He danced around for a few moments. Then dropped to the ground and rolled around trying to beat out the flames.

Amid this chaos, a man galloped up to the boats on his horse. "Soldiers! Heading this way fast! Get out of here!"

The sympathizers ran for their horses. Most of the canallers ignored their departure and turned their attention to their boats and putting out any fires that had started.

A squad of soldiers rode in at a canter a few minutes later.

"What happened here? We heard shots!" a lieutenant asked.

"What do you think happened?" John Harris, captain of the *Larkspur*, shouted. "Confederate raiders tried to sink our boats!"

"Do you need help putting out the fires?"

David looked around. Three of the boats were on fire, but they weren't large fires yet.

"No, we're fine now, but get after those sons of bitches!" Harris shouted.

The Union soldiers galloped off down the canal. They were close enough that they might overtake the raiders, but it would be hard to see if the raiders veered off the canal and hid.

Things started calming down as the fires were put out. David saw Alice beating at the flames of the fire on the *Freeman* with a wet blanket. Throwing buckets of water on the flames would only have spread the lantern oil.

Alice and George paused from their work as they put out the last of the flames and looked around to see if they had missed anything.

Smoke rose from a few of the spots on the hatch covers that had been on fire, but they were out. Luckily, the flames hadn't had enough time to eat through the hatch covers or they could have ignited the coal in the holds. That would have been a much harder fire to put out.

David headed into the family cabin to see if anything had been damaged or set afire inside. Alice followed a few steps behind him.

As David opened the door, it was flung open wider, pulling David off balance.

"David!" Alice shouted.

Suddenly David felt an arm slide around his neck and the barrel of a pistol against his head.

"Drop the rifle," Whittaker ordered David.

David lowered the rifle to the ground. Then Whittaker yanked him back up to a full standing position.

"I guess the snakes didn't get you. Too bad," David said.

Whittaker smacked him on the side of the head with the pistol. David winced, but he didn't say anything else.

"David!"

Alice started to run forward, but David held up his hands to get her to stop.

"Just stay where you are, Alice. Everything will be fine," David told her.

Alice stood on the race plank looking confused. David hoped that she would stay still. He didn't want Whittaker taking a shot at her, given that he hated her more than anyone else here.

"We're leaving. I've got some friends who will want to have words with this traitor," Whittaker said.

"I guess you should know what a traitor looks like," David said. "You see one every time you look in the mirror."

David's smart mouth earned him another smack from Whittaker's pistol. He felt he deserved it for allowing Whittaker to catch him off guard again.

George came up beside his mother and put his arm around her.

"Here's what going to happen now," Whittaker said. "I'm going to keep my gun tucked in Windover's side and you're going to get this boat moving. If you don't, I will kill him and have fun doing it."

"We don't travel at night," George said.

"You may not, but some boats do. So get moving. The mules are already all ashore so hitch them up and get moving."

"Just leave us alone, please," Alice pleaded.

Whittaker shook his head. "The soldiers are looking for mounted riders. They won't be looking for hands on a canal boat. If you do what I say, I just may leave you alone."

"I'll get the boys to hitch up the mules," George said.

"Be careful what you say, boy," Whittaker warned him. "Say the wrong thing and Windover will just be the first person that I shoot."

George stared at him for a few moments. Then he turned and walked across the fall board to shore. He walked over to where Tony and Thomas were standing with the mules.

"Get the mules in their harnesses," George said. "We're leaving."

"All of them?" Tony asked.

George nodded. Then he turned and walked away. The boys seemed confused, but they obeyed their older brother and hitched up the mules.

Harris saw what was happening and walked over to the *Freeman.*

"Are you fixing to leave?" he asked.

Alice glanced at David and Whittaker. "I don't want to be here in case those raiders come back," she told Harris.

"That's not likely to happen with the soldiers chasing them."

"I'd still feel better to be away from here."

Harris shrugged and waved to her. "Well, have a good journey."

The boys lifted the harnesses onto the mules and secured them. Once the mules were hitched, George came aboard to stand at the rudder while both Tony and Thomas decided to stay with the mules.

The four mules leaned into their harnesses to start the boat moving. It wasn't as hard as it usually was since all the mules were pulling.

About a mile down the canal, the boys took the mules over the canal to start walking along the northern side of the canal as the boat moved into the Little Slackwater area of the canal. This was a half-mile stretch where the canal opened into the river and floated downriver before entering the canal again.

George knew exactly when the river took over moving the loaded canal boat. It suddenly felt easier to move the boat since water could flow more freely around and under it. However, with the recent rains, the river was flowing faster than usual. The boys had to run the mules to keep them ahead of the *Freeman*.

"We're moving faster," Whittaker called from the family cabin.

"We're in the river for a stretch," George told him.

George tried to keep the canal boat tight against the shore, but the current kept pushing him away. He leaned on the rudder to hold it in position. However, the boat was loaded so it was slow to respond to the rudder.

George felt a surge and the canal boat moved away from the shore in a quick hop. From the shore, Thomas and Tony started shouting. George looked over toward them. The *Freeman* had drawn even with the mules. The current was too fast. Instead of being slack, the tow lines were rising from the water. George couldn't keep the boat close enough to shore.

If they had waited until daylight, he would have noticed this sooner.

"Mama!" George called. "We've got a problem!"

Alice could see what it was for herself. She ran to the front of the boat where the tow lines were tied to the canal boat behind the mule shed. She grabbed an axe off the wall and began hacking at the thick tow lines. The lines were hard and each swing only took a small chip out of the line. She had to cut them or the mules would be pulled into the river and maybe the boys, too.

A surge from the river pushed the *Freeman* toward the bank for a moment until the current pushed back. It was enough to knock Alice off balance and she dropped the axe into the river.

She ran back to George.

"Are they cut?" he asked.

"No, I lost the axe in the river. I need your knife."

"We don't have time! We're going to lose the mules."

"No, I can cut the lines." She ran into the cabin. "I need help cutting the tow lines. If they aren't cut, we'll lose the mules."

"I don't care about the mules," Whittaker said.

"If we lose the mules, we'll be smashed on the rocks."

"Fine!" He passed her a knife from his belt. "Windover can help, but I'm coming to watch and make sure you don't try anything when you're out of my sight."

David and Alice hurried back to the tow line. David paused long enough to reach into the hay house and pull out another axe he had.

When he got back to the mule shed, Alice was sawing away at one of the lines with her knife. He swung the axe at the other line.

The lines broke after a few moments and fell into the water. Alice reached forward and grabbed onto David.

"Get back into the cabin, Windover," Whittaker said. He turned to Alice. "What happens now?"

"We hope we don't sink."

"What?"

The *Freeman* suddenly shuddered as it hit Dam No. 4, which spanned the river. Alice slipped and fell back onto her backside. David heard something crack and George was yelling from the other end of the boat.

Whittaker looked around frantically, not knowing what was happening.

David rushed forward and tackled Whittaker, knocking the pistol from his hand. The two of them went over the side of the boat into the Potomac River.

Whittaker grabbed for David's throat, but he couldn't maintain his grip and stay afloat. David treaded water with one hand while he punched at Whittaker with his other.

Then he and Whittaker were slammed up against the side of the dam. Lucky for David, Whittaker was in front of him and was the one who hit the rocky dam. He cushioned David's impact.

While the hit hurt Whittaker, it also braced him against the dam so that he could use both of his hands. He choked David and this time, David couldn't break his grip. He struggled for breath.

Finally, David let himself go limp and drop into the water. Whittaker made the mistake of trying to hang onto him. David grabbed Whittaker's wrists and dove deep pulling Whittaker under before he could take a breath.

Whittaker floundered around under the water and David hoped that the man couldn't swim. Whittaker kept trying to punch him, but the water blunted his efforts. David kicked hard trying to reach the surface so that he could get a gulp of air.

His head bobbed to the surface and he gulped in the air. From the boat, David heard both George and Alice yelling from the boat.

He tried to scramble onto the dam, but Whittaker caught hold of his leg and tried to pull him back into the river. His head broke the surface and he yelled in frustration. David spun around and locked his legs around Whittaker's waist and pushed down. Whittaker flailed around as he suddenly went under the water and was held there.

David braced himself against the dam and kept pushing down. After a minute, he felt Whittaker stop fighting him. David released his hold and reached down to grab Whittaker's shirt collar. He pulled him up. Whittaker was unconscious. David pushed him over the top of the dam so that his face was out of the water.

He felt for a heartbeat and heard it. Whittaker was alive.

"Rope!" he called up to George.

George hurried away and returned a few moments later with a coil of rope. He tossed one end into the water beside David. David grabbed the end and used it to tie Whittaker's hands behind him. Then he swam to the boat.

The *Freeman* was listing badly to one side and he could see that it had been damaged by being smashed up against the dam. It was much more than the superficial damage that the fire had caused. David reached up and grabbed the edge of the deck and pulled himself up. George helped pull him onto the race plank.

"Thanks, George," David said as he rolled onto his back.

Alice rushed over to him.

"I told you I would be here…" David said.

He didn't get to finish what he was saying. Alice kneeled down beside him and pulled his head to hers and kissed him.

George whooped, but Alice ignored him.

After a moment, she pulled her head away and just lay her head against David's chest as she held him. David stood up slowly, took her hand and led her toward the *Freeman*'s family cabin.

As he passed George, David said, "Your mother and I need to talk."

George nodded. "We're not going anywhere at the moment, but I think it will be hard to find a place to sit down with the boat leaning like it is." He paused. "I'm glad you're all right."

David grinned and glanced at Alice. "I think I may be better than all right."

The two of them walked down into the family cabin. The floor rose at a sharp angle and the table and chairs had slid across it to rest against the pantry. The lantern hung from a hook and was still lit so he could see easily. The room smelled of smoke more than usual, but that was understandable seeing as how the boat had nearly burned.

David led Alice to her usual chair. She sat on it at an angle. David simply sat on the floor beside her and waited.

"I still love, Hugh," she said softly.

"I know. I'm surprised at what happened out there," David whispered. "Surprised and elated," he quickly amended.

Alice blushed.

"I didn't mean to do that, but when Whittaker took you away and then I heard those shots. Then when you went into the water…" She shook her head. "I felt like what happened to Hugh was happening all over again, but this time with you. But when Hugh died, he had known how I felt and suddenly I realized that you didn't know how I felt. I didn't know how I felt. Then I saw that you were all right, and I was relieved and happy and I just … reacted."

David grinned. "Yes, you did."

Alice slapped him on the arm. "David, stop acting like that. This changes everything."

"I hope so."

"Not like that. I mean…I mean…" Alice buried her face in her hands. "I'm back to being confused again."

David reached out and took her hands in his. "You're not confused. You just don't want to admit how you feel."

"How can I have feelings like that for you when I'm still in love with Hugh?" she asked.

"Hugh's dead. He was a very good man from everything I hear and see, but he's not here anymore."

Tears rolled down her cheeks. "I know, but I can't stop loving him because of that. When I look at our kids, I see him in them."

"And what do you see when you look at Tony?"

"He's my son."

"But he's not," David said.

"I may not have given birth to him, but I love him just as much as mother could love him. I certainly love him more than his birth mother did."

"Does that take away from your feelings for Thomas, George of Elizabeth?"

"No, of course not."

David clenched her hands even tighter. "Then why would loving me take away from your feelings for Hugh? Unless you don't love me."

"But it wouldn't be fair to you."

David snorted. "Fair to me? What wouldn't be fair to me is living like I've lived the past three years. I'm not blind about this. I know you love Hugh and I wouldn't ask you to change that. But I also know you have a heart large enough to include Tony and me."

A silence fell between them. It wasn't uncomfortable, just quiet. Then David leaned forward and kissed Alice's hands. She closed her eyes and took a deep breath.

Could she love David without betraying Hugh? Did she already love him?

"I'm afraid, David," she said finally.

"Afraid of me?"

She shook her head. "No, afraid of me. I don't want to hurt either of you. I don't want to forget Hugh, but I do love you."

Tears crept out of the corners of David's eyes. He stood up, walked around to the other side of the table next to her. Then he bent over and kissed her. She reached up and wrapped her arms around his neck, holding him tight with no intention of ever letting him go.

When they finally parted and walked outside, David asked George, "How is the boat?"

George shrugged. "There's damage. I just don't know how much. A lot of it is under water. I looked into the holds and they are flooding where the dam smashed the sides in."

"We should get to shore and check on the boys," Alice said.

"The *Freeman* is not going anywhere anytime in the near future. We'll have to walk across the top of the dam."

They hopped from the deck onto the top of the dam, which was about two feet wide. It wasn't hard to balance and walk across the top to shore. Water swirled around their feet as it spilled over the top of the dam, but it wasn't fast enough to push them off balance and into the river. They all had plenty of experience walking along the *Freeman's* fall boards.

When they reached the shore, Thomas ran over and hugged his mother. She stroked his hair and then bent down and kissed him on the forehead.

The soldiers who had ridden by earlier approached again from the opposite direction.

"Did you catch the raiders?" David asked.

The lieutenant frowned. "No, they must have crossed the canal at some point."

David pointed to Whittaker's body on the dam. He wasn't too worried about Whittaker running off. His hands were tied behind him and the rope was tied to the boat.

"That's Lee Whittaker. You'll find that he's wanted in Cumberland. He was also one of the raiders."

"What's he doing out there?"

"He hijacked our boat, but he didn't get away."

The lieutenant grinned. "I can see that."

The lieutenant waved to two of his men. They dismounted their horses and started trying to make their way across the dam.

"And what about you?" the lieutenant asked David.

"What about me?"

"Where are you from?"

David hesitated and then answered, "Virginia."

"Well now, that presents a bit of a problem."

Alice stepped between the lieutenant and David. "It shouldn't. This man works for me on my canal boat and he has for years."

"But is he a Confederate sympathizer? He is from Virginia."

"I am not a sympathizer," David said firmly.

"What he is is the man I love," Alice declared.

25

BAD DREAMS

AUGUST 1864

Tony's eyes opened and he felt the rough texture of wood against his cheek. He was lying on the floor, though he had no idea why. He pushed himself up and his back hit something above him. He was under a bed…his mother's bed.

Then he felt the floor moving underneath him and realized that was on a boat not in a room. He was probably under his bunk in the family cabin of the *Freeman*.

He started to crawl out from under the bunk when he heard shouting. Although he wasn't in his mother's room in Shanty Town, it was her voice that he heard. Then he heard someone pounding on the door.

"Everyone get out!" his birth mother shouted. "We're going over the dam."

Tony shook his head. This was wrong. All wrong. Carol didn't live on a canal boat and she certainly wasn't on the *Freeman* when smashed against the dam and nearly went over it. She also wouldn't care about making sure anyone else was all right.

Then the boat hit the dam and he felt as if he was thrown against the floor and the bottom of his bunk at the same time. One end of the

230

floor lifted and he slid across the floor, wincing as splinters went into his legs and belly.

He felt water wash over him. The canal boat must have sprung a leak. The water level rose higher and higher. Tony tried to scramble up the floor, which was now a wall, but it was too steep. He kept sliding backward into the water until finally he went completely under.

Tony's eyes opened and he lay still, taking deep breaths. He wasn't on the floor. He was in a bed. He wasn't even wet unless you counted his sweat.

He sat up and rubbed his eyes. He looked around and tried to get his bearings. He still wasn't used to waking up in this room. It was about the size of the family cabin on the *Freeman*, but he and Thomas had it all to themselves. They also didn't have to sleep on bunks. This was their room in the house that his mother had rented in Sharpsburg.

It had taken more than a week to get the *Freeman* out of the river. The coal had first been removed or at least what hadn't fallen into the river when a portion of the hull had been ripped away. The boat had then been hauled to the shore, which caused even more damage as it dragged along the rocky river bottom.

His mother had cried when she saw what had been left of the canal boat.

Some people suggested that she break up the boat for scrap wood, but his mother couldn't bring herself to do it although it was obvious that the boat was beyond repair.

David insisted on patching the boat enough so that it could be towed back to Amos Lewis's warehouse in Cumberland. Tony doubted even Amos could fix that boat, but David wanted to try.

Even his mother hadn't seen how the boat could be repaired. The hull was mostly missing. David had helped build canal boats, though, and he had wanted Amos to look it over to see what could be done.

Left without a boat, the family had ridden the mules to Sharpsburg where Mrs. Fitzgerald had rented a house with three bedrooms. No one had lived in it for a while. The owners had been scared away because of the battle that had been fought near the town.

Tony was beginning to think Mrs. Fitzgerald was right about how dangerous the canal was. Almost nothing was moving on it right now because General Early had crossed with his troops near Hancock.

They had stirred up a lot of trouble there and shut down the canal among other things. Then up near Oldtown, some Ohioans had been overwhelmed by Confederate troops and forced to surrender.

At least things were quiet here for the time being.

Tony stood up and quietly left the room so as not to wake Thomas. Of course, as heavy a sleeper as Thomas was, Tony could have stomped out of the room and still left Thomas asleep.

He walked down the stairs, pausing when one of the stairs creaked. The front door was cracked open. Tony knew it hadn't been last night. He peeked outside and saw David sitting on a chair on the porch.

"Good morning," David said when he saw Tony.

Tony stepped outside.

"What are you doing?" Tony asked.

"I'm just watching the sun rise. I used to do this in Virginia. I kind of miss it."

"Why?"

David shrugged. "I don't know. I just like it. Watching it rise higher into the sky is like watching a new beginning. The light chases the shadows away. It is warm and inviting. It washes over me like warm water."

Tony raised his face into the sun. It did feel good. He felt like the bad dreams couldn't reach him as long as the sun was shining. Then he walked over and sat down in the chair next to David.

After a few minutes, David asked, "Why are you up so early?"

"Bad dream," Tony mumbled.

"What was it about?"

Tony hesitated. Did he really want to expose himself like that? Maybe David could make sense of the confusing dream. Tony certainly didn't know what it meant. So he started to tell David about what he had seen in his dream.

When he finished, Tony asked, "Am I a coward?"

David's eyebrows rose. "Coward? Why would you think that?"

"Because I was cowering under the bunk and wouldn't come out when Carol warned me."

David shook his head. "I use to worry that I was a coward at times."

"You're not," Tony said quickly.

"No, I'm not. But my dreams taught me something. It's all right to be afraid. It doesn't mean that you're a coward. The war gave me bad dreams and I learned to deal with them."

"What happened?"

"They went away when I left the army and decided to work for your mother."

"That's all?" Tony asked, confused.

"Isn't that enough?"

Tony thought about that. David had made it sound simple, but he had deserted the army and abandoned his life in Virginia to get rid of his dreams. Would Tony have to do something that drastic?

"I think dreams are our minds trying to tell us something is wrong even if you don't realize what is wrong," David explained.

"The bad dreams I used to have were like that. They were about my mother and scared me. When I finally admitted to myself that her killer would never be caught, they ended. Then this one started. What's it mean?"

David shrugged. "I don't know. That's something you'll have to find out for yourself and when you do, the dreams will stop."

They heard a stirring in the kitchen, pots and pans rattling and wood thudding.

David stood up. "Well, I guess everyone's getting up for breakfast."

They walked back into the house and saw Alice getting the morning fire going so that she could cook breakfast. She smiled when she saw Tony and David.

"Good morning," she said. "Tony, can you fetch the eggs for our breakfast?"

"Yes, ma'am."

He turned and hurried to the back of the house where Mrs. Fitzgerald kept a half a dozen chickens in a small coop. He searched the nests and came up with seven eggs. He laid them in a basket and went back inside.

He walked back inside and stopped when he saw David and Mrs. Fitzgerald in the kitchen. David was frying bacon the stove while Mrs. Fitzgerald mixed dough for biscuits. They were talking quietly and laughing. They smiled at each other and shared looks full of emotion. Tony watched Mrs. Fitzgerald lay her hand on David's shoulder. Tony saw his face beam, though he didn't say anything.

Thomas and George came downstairs as the smell of frying bacon wafted upwards.

"Ummm," Thomas said.

"Good, you're awake. Thomas, we're going to need milk. George, can you set the table?" Alice said.

Thomas picked up a pail and headed outside to milk the single dairy cow that the Fitzgeralds had. Mrs. Fitzgerald had had to sell all of the mules to have the money to purchase the farm animals to help feed the family. Thomas missed the mules, but he now had other animals to turn into his pets.

Tony felt a weird feeling in his chest. He looked around at everyone. He had a family. It was an odd family. They were all he had, though, and he was glad that he had them. He loved them and he didn't want to lose them.

That's what his dreams were about. He was afraid of losing the good feeling he had.

David fished out the strips of bacon from the pan and held them over a cup until they weren't dripping any grease. Then he cracked the eggs into the pan to fry them. The biscuits were still baking when the eggs were finished so everyone sat down to get started on their breakfast.

Everyone was enjoying a hearty breakfast when Alice announced, "I am going to buy some property in town."

"Really?" George asked. "Why?"

"Isn't it obvious? The *Freeman* can't be repaired. We have no home and no way to make a living on the canal. I've been talking with Mr. Arnold and he's willing to hold the note for us on a piece of property."

"Don't you at least want to see what Amos can do with the *Freeman*?" David asked.

"There's no reason to," Alice said.

"Can we stay here?" Thomas asked.

Alice rocked her head back and forth. "Maybe if the owners are willing to sell. There are other properties I'll want us all to look at, though. We may find something more suitable. I would like a larger yard for the animals."

"So we're just going to stop canalling?" George asked.

"It looks like fate did that to us." Alice sighed. "This is my hometown. I can find work here. I know the families. It's safer for the children here."

"It wasn't two years ago," George said.

"And it hasn't really been safe for us on the canal since then. Plus, you and your brothers can get a good education for once and not just attend school here and there."

Alice looked over at David. "What do you think?" she asked.

"It is a sound plan," he said. "But will you be happy being a seamstress and keeping a small farm? The canal has been your life."

"Until two years ago, I never spent much time on the canal," Alice said. "It won't be a huge change for me or the boys and George is old enough to get a job on a boat if he chooses."

"So you're saying you'll be happy here?"

"I don't know, but I need to do something."

David looked at his plate and then slowly wiped his mouth with his napkin. He took a deep breath and said, "Speaking of doing something, Amos offered me work in Cumberland. I think I'll take it."

Alice's eyes widened. "David, no!"

David took his hands in hers. "Alice, it good pay. I can save my money and stay in the warehouse like I was doing before. We're going to need every cent we can save to pay off that note."

"We?"

David nodded. "Yes, I'm not leaving you. I'm not running away from you. I'll visit as often as I can, but this is what I need to do until we can get our feet back under us. We're building our lives together now. I want to do it right."

Alice wiped away the tears running down her cheeks and hugged him.

"What's that smell?" George said.

Alice and David looked around.

"What are you talking about, George?" Alice asked.

"Take a deep breath."

They did and David gagged. "Something went bad," he said.

Thomas started backing out of the room. His family stared at him.

"Don't look at me," he said. "Mama made me take a bath yesterday."

George moved closer to his little brother and nodded.

"Empty your pockets, Thomas," George ordered him.

Thomas frowned and pulled out a large wad of cloth from his pocket. George leaned toward it and took a deep breath and pulled back quickly.

"Unwrap that!"

Thomas did. In the center was an egg. It was obviously the source of the smell.

Alice pointed out the door. "Get rid of that now."

"And don't throw it at anybody," David added.

The smell noticeably improved once Thomas left.

"Open the doors and windows, please, Tony," Alice said. "We need to air out this house."

When Thomas came back, Alice said, "What were you doing with a rotten egg, Thomas?"

"I wanted to hatch a chicken. I didn't think it would be hard. All the chickens do is sit on them until they hatch. I thought if I could just keep it warm, I would have a baby chick."

Alice shook her head and started to laugh.

"What's so funny, Mama?" George said. "He made this house smell like skunk sprayed us."

Alice took a deep breath and said, "Well, at least he didn't try sitting on it to hatch it."

26

GOING HOME

AUGUST 1864

Elizabeth closed the carpet bag that sat on the chest at the foot of her bed. She looked at the room that had been her home for the last year. Gone were the little things that had made it her room. Mementos from her time in Washington – sketches she had made, trinkets soldiers at the hospital had given her, books she enjoyed reading and more – had lined the dresser. Now they were wrapped and packed in the trunk. Clothing that she had carefully left draped over the wooden rocking chair was neatly folded and also packed. The vase that she had kept filled with fresh flowers when she could find them now stood empty.

It was just a simple guest room now.

So much for making a lasting impression on anything. She hadn't even left yet and it was as if the house had forgotten her already.

With a sigh, she lifted the carpet bag and walked out of the room. Chess came up the stairs and saw her in the hallway. He straightened his back and puffed out his chest a bit.

"Miss Elizabeth, I told you I would come and get that for you," he said. Though he didn't raise his voice, it still sounded like he was scolding her.

He rushed forward and reached down to take the bag from her hand.

Elizabeth shooed him away. "Chess, I can carry it. I'm not helpless. Remember I grew up working on a canal boat and for the last year I've been lifting soldiers in and out of cots."

He nodded repeatedly. "I know that, ma'am. Just consider this my going away present for you," he told her.

Elizabeth chuckled. She held out the carpet bag and he took it.

"Thank you, Chess. It's a lovely gift. However did you know that it was just what I needed?"

"Because I knew that you wouldn't be able to carry this here bag and hug Mr. and Mrs. Sampson."

With that, he turned and headed for the stairs.

Eli and Grace Sampson were waiting in the parlor for her when she got downstairs. Grace had tears running down her cheeks. She rushed forward and grabbed Elizabeth in a tight hug. That was all it took for Elizabeth to start crying.

"I wish you didn't have to go," Grace said.

"Mama will need me now."

Elizabeth had gotten the letter about the wreck of the *Freeman* and that her family was once again living in Sharpsburg. She knew that she would be able to help her mother. Elizabeth could take in sewing or washing or do any number of things to earn money for the family.

Grace stroked the back of Elizabeth's head. "I know. I know, but I will miss you so much."

"I'll miss you, too."

Grace pulled away. "Wait here a minute. I've got something for you."

Elizabeth shook her head. "You don't need to give me anything, Mrs. Sampson. I'm just so grateful that you took me in for so long. I can never repay that."

"Nonsense. Now wait here."

She walked toward the back of the house, sniffling as she went.

"I guess it's my turn to say goodbye," Eli said as he stepped up in front of her. "I want to thank you, Elizabeth. Your being here helped bring Grace, and me, truth be told, out of our depression after Abel's death."

Elizabeth hugged the congressman. "I'll miss you both so much. You're part of my family now."

Eli blushed a bit. Then he reached into pocket and pulled out a small roll of bills. He pressed them into Elizabeth's hand.

"Here, take this," he said.

Elizabeth shook her head and pulled her hand away. "I couldn't. After all you and Grace have given me, I don't need anything else."

"It's for the trip. You might need it."

Although she didn't know how much was in the small wad, she knew it was far more than she would need.

"Please," Eli said. "Make an old man happy, well, happier. Take this. I feel better knowing you won't have to sleep in a haystack in a barn tonight."

"Mr. Sampson!" Elizabeth said, slightly shocked.

Eli grinned. Then he placed the bills in her hand and closed it around them.

"May God protect you and your family," he said in a low, reverent tone.

Grace walked back into the room carrying a large basket.

"I cooked you a few things to take with you. You and Chess will have plenty to eat whenever you want to stop. When you eat, you can remember us," Grace said.

"I don't see how I could ever forget you two," Elizabeth said. "I will miss you. I already do."

"Did you find what you came here to find?" Grace asked.

Elizabeth nodded. "I learned what I needed, but it wasn't the same thing that I came here to find."

Eli raised one of his bushy eyebrows, but he didn't say anything.

The Sampsons walked Elizabeth outside where Chess was waiting with the small carriage hitched to two horses so that it would be able to maintain a fast rate of speed for the journey to Sharpsburg. Chess was driving her home and then he would return with the carriage.

Chess helped her step into the carriage and then he closed the door. Then he climbed up into the driver's seat. Elizabeth leaned out the window and waved to the Sampsons. Chess snapped the reins and the matched bays started walking.

Elizabeth leaned forward and said, "Chess, before we head out of the city, I would like to stop at the hospital."

"I thought that you might, Miss Elizabeth."

The carriage pulled up in front of the hospital a few minutes later and Elizabeth climbed out of the carriage and went inside. She paused in the entryway and looked over the room. It would be the last time she saw it. True, it had been a place of misery, but it had also been a place of great joy when a soldier was able to go home.

Now it was her turn to leave and return home.

Mrs. Carlyle saw her and hurried over. "I wondered if you were going to stop by."

"I've spent so much time here this past year it's like another home to me," Elizabeth told her.

Mrs. Carlyle nodded. "I know that feeling. I will miss having you here, Elizabeth. You worked hard and were a good nurse. You brought happiness into so many wounded soldiers' lives while they were here. I'm sure they will miss you, as well."

"It feels so odd me being the one to leave this time."

Elizabeth hugged the hospital matron and then began making her rounds for the last time to say goodbye to the soldiers. The cots were only about two-thirds full at the moment, but Elizabeth knew that as long as the fighting continued a time would come when they would be full again.

She stopped at Wilbur Layne's bed and sat down next to him.

"You look dressed to travel," the young soldier said.

Elizabeth nodded. "I'm on my way out of town, but I couldn't leave without saying goodbye to everyone here."

"I'll miss you. I wish you didn't have to go."

"I need to. You met my family." Wilbur nodded. "Well, they ran into some problems and they could use an extra set of hands helping them out, and truth be told, I miss seeing them."

"I understand. I miss my family, too."

Elizabeth patted his hand. "Well, I hear you will be going home soon, too."

"I probably should have been gone a long time before now. My enlistment ended months ago."

"Better late than never."

He nodded. "That's true. For so many of us, it was never. I'm one of the lucky one like your brother."

Yes, George had been lucky and Wilbur was lucky that George had visited here. He had been just what Wilbur needed.

"You take care of yourself. Write to me in Sharpsburg when you get home," the young man said.

Elizabeth smiled. "I will. I'm sure my parents will want to write to you, too, and thank you."

Elizabeth made the rest of her rounds and felt drained from saying goodbye to so many people she had cared for. She waved to them all from the doorway and started to tear up when they waved back.

She hurried outside where Chess was standing beside the carriage. He helped her inside.

"You did good here, Miss Elizabeth," Chess told her.

Elizabeth nodded. "I know, but it's not what I came to Washington for."

Chess scoffed. "Why do you need to learn to be a lady? You did something better. You became an angel for the men who passed through the hospital. What's a lady got that can compare to that?"

Chess closed the door and climbed up into the driver's seat. He started the horses off and pretty soon got them into a nice trot, pulling the carriage through Washington. They headed north on the road to Frederick. They stopped twice at road houses to rest the horses and themselves.

Night was falling by the time they arrived in Frederick, fifty miles to the north of Washington. Chess found a respectable road house with a room available for Elizabeth. He was forced to sleep in the stable with the horses. The room was more expensive than Elizabeth had thought it would be. She was forced to use some of the money from the roll of bills Eli had given here. That's when she found out that he had given her fifty dollars. That was the profit from two trips on the canal that her family made!

The next morning, she and Chess got an early start driving west on the National Road and arrived in Sharpsburg by mid-day. It has been so long since she was in her hometown. She had always considered it a nice-sized town with everything she might need, but after having lived in Washington, she realized how small and quiet it was. It didn't feel like her home anymore. She wondered if it ever would.

Her house – her childhood home – was gone. A new house had been built on the lot and the house her mother had rented was on the opposite side of town. It just wasn't the same. Her family was here, though. That is what mattered and that is what would turn this house into a home.

Elizabeth climbed down from the carriage and hurried inside the house, calling, "Mama!"

Her mother called from the back of the house, "Elizabeth!"

Elizabeth ran down the hallway to the back door. Her mother was coming inside from the back yard where she had been hanging a load of laundry.

"Elizabeth" Alice shouted. Then she ran forward and swept her into a tight hug.

Within moments, Tony and Thomas had come down from their room upstairs and were hugging her.

Yes, everything was different, but not this.

Never this.

David stopped on the porch of the house. He swung his arms back and forth and knocked the dirt off of his boots. Alice wouldn't be happy if he left clods of dirt all over the floor inside the house.

He opened the door and walked inside. He heard laughter from the back and walked back to the kitchen. It was a large room across the back of the house. A large table where the family gathered to eat dominated the space. Tony, Thomas and George were sitting at the table while Alice and Elizabeth stood at the counter kneading bread dough and talking.

"Elizabeth!" David said as he walked into the room.

Elizabeth looked up and smiled. "Hello, David."

"Welcome home."

Elizabeth walked over and hugged him, careful not to touch him with her flour-covered hands.

"It's nice to be back. I didn't realize how much I had missed everyone until I saw them again."

"She was telling us about Michael," George said.

"Did he finally find you?" David asked.

He walked into the kitchen and sat down at the table with the boys.

"Are you thirsty?" Thomas asked. "Mama made some lemonade."

David poured himself a glass from the pitcher on the table.

"He came to visit me in Washington and apologized," Elizabeth said. "He's written me a couple times since then."

"So he is courting you now?" David asked.

Elizabeth blushed and Tony laughed. George nudged him to be quiet.

"I don't know. There's still his mother," Elizabeth said, not wanting to meet anyone's gaze.

David shrugged. "There always will be. If you want to be with Michael, then you're going to have to find a way to deal with her."

"That's what Mama told me."

"Then you should listen to her. She's a smart woman," David said.

"Thank you," Alice said.

They talked through the dinner preparations and dinner. Everyone was together again. David knew he would miss this when he was in Cumberland.

Alice was up early in the morning as she always was. She needed to get the kitchen fire going so she could make breakfast. She was usually the first one up in the mornings, but this morning she heard stirring in one of the other bedrooms.

She dressed and then stepped into the hallway. The noise was coming from the bedroom that George and David shared. She tapped lightly on the door.

The door opened and she saw David. He had his rucksack open on his bed.

"What are you doing?" she whispered.

"I'm packing."

"What?"

David held his finger to his lips. "Shhh. George is still sleeping."

He stepped out of the room and closed the door behind him.

"Let's go downstairs where we can talk," he said. "I was going to talk to you last night about this, but I didn't want to put a damper on things."

They walked downstairs to the kitchen. They sat down across from each other at the kitchen table and David held Alice's hands in his.

"I know that the past few weeks have been hard on you, but I have to say, I have been happier than I've been in a long time," he said.

Alice smiled and David felt his heart swell.

"But it's time for you to go to Cumberland," she said after a few moments.

David nodded.

Alice frowned. "For how long?"

David shook his head. "I don't know. It will be awhile. I'll visit as soon as I can."

"But why couldn't you find work here?"

"I probably could find something, but it wouldn't pay as well. Besides with Elizabeth here, I realize that you have a large family. I'm only doing day work now. That won't be much help to you even with Elizabeth working."

Alice squeezed his hand. "We'll get by. We always do. I don't want to lose you again like I did earlier this year."

"But you didn't lose me. Here I am. I came back. I'll always come back for you," David said. He paused. "I want to be able to give you more, Alice. Amos has the work and he pays well."

"But I don't want to live in Cumberland."

David nodded and patted her hand. "I know. I've got some thoughts that I want to talk over with Amos. If it works out, we can still make a life here."

Alice grinned. "Now you've piqued my curiosity."

"You'll have to wait and find out. I'm going to leave today."

Alice closed her eyes. Then she stood up and came around the table and kissed him. "Make sure you come back as soon as you can."

David nodded vigorously. "Yes, ma'am."

He slung his rucksack over his shoulder and started walking down the road that led to the canal. He caught a ride back to Cumberland on a canal boat, working for his keep as it traveled west. When he arrived in the basin two days later, he went to see Amos at his warehouse.

The remains of the *Freeman* sat in the main warehouse. The hatch covers were missing and a lot of the hull had been torn away so that David could see through the canal boat at points. The roof on the mule shed and hay house were also missing.

Amos saw him and walked over to shake his hand.

"It's a shame," Amos said.

"But can it be repaired?"

Amos shook his head. "No, but it can be rebuilt, which will cost nearly as much as the boat probably cost to build originally."

It was money David didn't have. He walked closer to the boat.

"Then let's talk about how I'm going to pay for it."

27

A NEW LIFE

MARCH 1865

It had been a long winter for David. Not so much because it was unbearably cold or heavy with snowfalls. No, it had been a long winter because he hadn't seen Alice as much as he would have liked. He had been able to borrow a horse from Amos and ride to Sharpsburg three times over the winter. Each time, he had spent a few days with Alice and the children. Each one of those trips had had to carry him through until the next visit.

Alice had suggested that he find a place in Sharpsburg or at least nearer the town than Cumberland. As tempted as David had been, he knew that he needed to be in Cumberland to accomplish what he wanted. It had taken a lot of wheeling and dealing with Amos, but in the end, an arrangement had been reached.

David glanced to his right and saw Alice sitting beside him on the driver's seat of the wagon. She was wearing a bonnet and a light cap. She looked lovely. He just hoped that Alice would agree with the arrangement when he explained it to her.

He had arrived in Sharpsburg yesterday with a rented wagon and told the Fitzgeralds that he was taking them all to Cumberland. Alice, Elizabeth and George had grumbled about it because it would require them to rearrange their work schedules. Tony and Thomas had been thrilled not to have to go to school for a while. David had insisted, even pleaded with them, though, and they had finally all agreed to go to Cumberland with David.

Alice saw him staring at her and said, "It's a beautiful day."

David nodded. "We got word that canal will open on the first."

Alice frowned. "It will be weird to not be part of all the opening madness at Cumberland."

David nodded, though it wasn't noticeable with all of the bouncing that the wagon was doing on the rutted road.

"It might even be a peaceful season of boating," he said. "The talk is that South is on the verge of collapsing."

Alice put her hand on his. "How does that make you feel? I mean, given that you were a soldier."

David didn't answer at first. How did he feel about it? It had been awhile since he considered himself a soldier. He was still a Southerner by heritage, though.

"I don't think it changes things," he said.

"Don't you want to go home?"

"I do miss my room and the rolling hills around the main house. I dream about it sometimes, but always what it was like not what it would be like now. I wouldn't be welcome there anyway."

They followed the National Road out of Sharpsburg and spent the night at an inn near Little Orleans. They made it to Cumberland the next day and David took the Fitzgeralds to a boarding house on Mechanic Street that Amos had recommended. It was a three-story brick building with wooden side porches and a wide one along the front. A war widow owned it, but was only able to keep it because she ran it as a boarding house.

"I still don't know why you insisted we come here. There's nothing here for us now," Alice said, once they had unloaded their luggage at the boarding house. He had arranged for them to have two rooms there; one for Alice and Elizabeth and the other one for the boys.

"You'll find out in the morning," David told her.

"I need to get my garden ready, David. It's going to be a big part in helping us get through the summer."

David patted her hand and kissed her on the cheek. "Trust me.

You'll be happy you came."

Alice laid a hand on David's arm. "I am happy we came. It's been six weeks since your last visit."

David smiled at that and squeezed her hand.

"I would have loved to have stayed closer this winter, but I needed to get some things taken care of here and it took some time."

"David, can we come with you to the warehouse and help work on the canal boats?" Thomas asked.

David ruffled Thomas' hair. "Sorry. Amos would skin me if he saw you climbing around on a half-finished canal boat."

"Come inside, Thomas. We need to unpack," Alice said.

David watched the Fitzgeralds go into the boarding house. Then he turned and hurried off down the street toward the canal basin. It was going to be a long night for him.

David met the Fitzgeralds for breakfast at the boarding house. Alice helped Mrs. McKnight cook the food for not only her children but also the other boarders. The kitchen was filled with the delicious smells of frying eggs and bacon.

David was more interested in the coffee He kept yawning and downing one cup after another.

"We're not boring you, are we?" Alice asked after watching him close his eyes and seemingly doze off at the table.

David jerked himself upright. "I'm fine. I just had to work most of the night to finish things so that we could have the day together."

"Did you get it finished?"

"Oh, yes."

When they finished breakfast, David ushered them all back out to the wagon. He drove it down to the Lewis Boatworks.

"I thought you said you were done work," Alice said.

David nodded. "I am, but there's something here that I want you to see. You'll have to come inside with me."

David helped Alice down from the wagon and led her to the Judas gate in the warehouse doors. He held the door open for her.

Alice stepped inside and gasped. David followed her inside with a big grin on his face.

Though the warehouse doors they had come through were closed, the opposite doors were wide open flooding the warehouse bay with lots of sunlight. A finished canal boat sat in the middle of the bay. The hull had been caulked and it was ready to be launched. On the aft end, David had painted in red, white and blue letters *Freeman II.*

Alice turned to David, "What is this?"

"This is what I've been working on all winter…your new canal boat."

"Mine?"

David shrugged. "It will be eventually. I worked out a deal with Amos. It's his boat for now, but if you are willing to make monthly payments along with some extra work that I'll do for him, it will be yours."

She turned to stare at him with her mouth hanging open. "I can't believe that you did this."

David paused, unsure of whether she was happy or sad.

"You belong on the canal, Alice. You weren't happy in Sharpsburg. How many times did I catch you staring off toward the canal? And I wasn't even there that often. You miss it. It's been a part of your life all of your adult life even when you weren't boating, you still watched for your family to come home and traveled with them on occasion."

Tears ran down her cheeks.

"I can't believe that you did this," she repeated.

"That's not all I did this winter."

David reached into his pocket and pulled out a small diamond ring with a ribbon tied to it.

"I did a lot of thinking about my future and decided that it wouldn't be much of a future if you weren't there to share it with me. I love you, Alice. Marry me."

Alice threw her arms around his neck and began kissing David. It lasted so long that the children began to look at each other.

Finally, Thomas said, "Mama, I think you need to take a breath."

ABOUT THE AUTHOR

James Rada, Jr. is the author of historical fiction and non-fiction history. They include the popular books *Saving Shallmar: Christmas Spirit in a Coal Town, Canawlers* and *Battlefield Angels: The Daughters of Charity Work as Civil War Nurses.*

He lives in Gettysburg, Pa., where he works as a freelance writer. Jim has received numerous awards from the Maryland-Delaware-DC Press Association, Associated Press, Maryland State Teachers Association and Community Newspapers Holdings, Inc. for his newspaper writing.

If you would like to be kept up to date on new books being published by James or ask him questions, he can be reached by e-mail at *jimrada@yahoo.com.*

To see James' other books or to order copies on-line, go to *www.jamesrada.com.*

If you liked
LOCK READY,
you can find more stories at these FREE sites from James Rada, Jr.

JAMES RADA, JR.'S WEB SITE
www.jamesrada.com

The official web site for James Rada, Jr.'s books and news including a complete catalog of all his books (including eBooks) with ordering links. You'll also find free history articles, news and special offers.

TIME WILL TELL
historyarchive.wordpress.com

Read history articles by James Rada, Jr. plus other history news, pictures and trivia.

WHISPERS IN THE WIND
jimrada.wordpress.com

Discover more about the writing life and keep up to date on news about James Rada, Jr.